CHAT SHOW

CHAT SHOW

A Novel

by

TERENCE DE VERE WHITE

LONDON
VICTOR GOLLANCZ LTD
1987

First published in Great Britain 1987
by Victor Gollancz Ltd,
14 Henrietta Street, London WC2E 8QJ

© Terence de Vere White 1987

British Library Cataloguing in Publication Data
White, Terence de Vere
Chat show.
I. Title
823'.914 [F]   PR6073.H53

ISBN 0-575-03910-8

Photoset in Great Britain by
Rowland Phototypesetting Ltd, Bury St Edmunds, Suffolk
and printed by St Edmundsbury Press Ltd
Bury St Edmunds, Suffolk

For my sister
Patricia Wilson

CHAT SHOW

"THEY ARE BEING very good today."

He was talking to himself about the people in the street. Everyone—or nearly everyone—had smiled openly or looked and then politely stopped looking and told his companion to look. It was an enormous improvement on yesterday when no one had seemed to recognize him and a perishing wind blew. But today had been different, from the moment he got up, not only in the matter of the weather. There had been an after breakfast telephone call from that old fox Barney Roche to say that Jerry Dunne wasn't expected to last the night and asking Miles to "say a few words at the funeral". He was really touched by that, and he said "Oh, you must do it yourself, Barney. You are the daddy of us all." Barney denied this and insisted that he, Miles, was recognized by everyone as the archetype of the Irish in the media. Had Barney left it there he was doing splendidly, but vanity got the better of him and he dropped out something about the Edinburgh Festival and his not being able to let down Duncan or Alistair or someone or other. "Maureen was very anxious that you should do it. Poor girl, she has been having a rotten time."

A slightly shop-soiled compliment then, but still it was something, and it would put the rest of them in their places. Since his troubles with the BBC began Miles had noted, with a growing sense of disappointment in his countrymen, that not one of them had even registered as much as a bleat of protest against his treatment at the hands of that corporation.

The cemetery engagement was only a start; after his hour with the *Sporting Life*, he had dressed with more care than usual, pondering over the hair-piece that Rowena had been so much against. "It does nothing for you," she said, but the situation had become much more serious since Rowena made that pronouncement. Two years had passed, for one thing, and since the BBC had astoundingly refused to renew his contract and offered instead quite offensive alternatives he had let his appearance go to seed. There was no other way of describing it. He had always been at a disadvantage with his age, having come into television rather late. He should have listened to Rowena who was forever telling him to "gather ye rose buds while ye may" and so forth, with a rider to

9

the effect that he should save us much of the money flowing in as he could. He hated that sort of rainy day talk; it came from Rowena's being English. In their fifteen years together he had never got used to her down-to-earthness. But he wouldn't argue with her if she were here. Every moment that he spent looking at himself in the glass reinforced the correctness of her judgement. What was special about today was a strong feeling that something could and must be done about it. The hair-piece, for the time being, was put back in its drawer. But he shaved himself with extra care and took trouble choosing what he was going to wear, plumping, after some hesitation, for the floppy bow-tie with the Morris pattern.

Leaving the premises, there was an established procedure. He stood in the foyer of the hotel and called out "Any letters for me? I'm going to the club. If anyone's looking for me, take their number and say I'll call them back." It was a simple ceremony and often performed alone, but he had established his routine and he would feel disorientated if he had to abandon it. When Willie, the porter, was in the vicinity he always came out from wherever he was and listened respectfully. Willie was half-witted, but in his low moments Miles thought of him as his only friend in this horrible establishment.

"There's a letter for you. I was going to bring it up for fear that it was urgent, but then I thought I wouldn't be bothering you with it when you were studying form."

The letter was there, in Miles's pigeon-hole, plain to be seen in its lavender-coloured envelope, outstanding among manilla covers and long unclaimed correspondence. A letter to match the mood of the morning. A cheerful-looking letter. He had to restrain an undignified impulse to rush across the hall and grab it. With admirable composure he let Willie hand it to him.

It was a good envelope to feel, an expensive envelope, and he liked to see "Esq" after his name. That was a hang-over from his Irish childhood's aspirations. Willie, who lived on unsatisfied curiosity, waited to discover as much as he was allowed about this impressive-looking envelope. Miles was the only great man it had been his privilege to know, but he was aware that the world had suddenly given his hero up. That didn't shake his loyalty; in spirit he was like those Irish of old who went into exile with Sarsfield, although Willie had never heard of the "Wild Geese" and if called a wild goose would have defended himself. What everyone did was of importance to Willie; he lived off other people's lives, and anything to do with Miles was of supreme importance.

Miles put on a sceptical expression as he slowly opened the envelope, and then ran his eye over the letter to take in its general tenor before he embarked on a closer perusal. He was aware of Willie, and on the whole preferred his inquisitive presence to having no one to share his triumph with. One would have to be aware of his plight, the height from which he had fallen, the suddenness of the world's neglect and the shortness of its memory, to regard it as a triumph at all; and it had to be seen in the context of the morning, his sudden appetite for life, that telephone call—he remembered it suddenly. Mustn't forget to tell Willie he was expecting this very particular call, not that Willie would need any priming: Jerry Dunne was another of his heroes and it was exciting to be asked to take telephone messages from one celebrity to another.

This lavender letter was also an invitation to speak, but in very different circumstances. Miles had never heard of the Alma-Tadema Society, nor of its President, Samuel Slaughter RA nor of its committee, Count Bosdari, Constantine Zaimis, Simeon Sikinos, Countess Melashoff, Aristides Carlovassi and U. Wright. The letter was from the secretary, Lalage Dubonnet. He was invited to speak at the first of the Society's winter dinners at the Aegean Hotel on the New King's Road, on Wednesday October 16th. The subject was left to himself. The President wanted it mentioned that he was "a fan of yours". Special guests, time, transport—these matters could be settled over the telephone if Miles was willing to accept.

"They want me to make a speech. That's two speeches, and the day has hardly yet begun." Miles said. "And who better fit?" Willie replied.

That was the note on which Miles set off for his "club". It was a harmless euphemism. Miles had never become a member of the only club that he wanted to join, and in the one to which he did belong he found, since his troubles began, that everyone was over-hearty when they saw him coming, and he had inglorious recollections of occasions when he had worn out his audience with his account of the rascally behaviour of the British Broadcasting Corporation. He hadn't put his nose inside the place for nearly a year. Willie knew as well as he did that "the club" in the context of his morning valedictions meant Ladbroke's at the end of the road. There he would make his bets on the day's racing and collect, if there were any, the spoils of yesterday. Quarter of an hour's walk—it helped to keep him alive, and today he was very much alive. He felt it in his step. He was weightless. He met smiling faces with answering smiles. Happy thoughts ran through his mind like water through a colander: orations at gravesides were traditionally watersheds in Irish history. These were the occasions when spoken words were remembered. What could one say in Jerry's favour?

The only way to avoid embarrassment was to start with a conventional statement of regret for the passing of an old friend "millions of viewers would share the sense of loss"; sympathy with his widow and children (were there children? check); then think of some outstanding quality. Make heavy weather about this. His "boundless enthusiasm". That would do very well if nothing better occurred to Miles in the interim. After the corny preliminaries, change gear, drop Jerry, and make a plea to the Irish in the media to use their gifts and their influence for something more than self-advancement. The invention of television opened up interesting possibilities for the Irish. It was already apparent in the number that were enjoying a good living over here. England was still a class-ridden country. Every accent had disagreeable associations for as many people as felt at home with it. The Irish accent was without these class-conscious associations. No one cared about what kind of school an Irish television personality had gone—or not gone—to. Apart from that, and the fact that to English ears Irish voices are soft, a new field of employment opened up to a type in which Ireland has always abounded: the natural entertainer without any talent other than a quick tongue. In the past it led to nothing if one discounted the amount of drink that it caused to be consumed. Miles's own father was such a one. Where the crowd at the bar was thickest "The Smiler" would be found in the middle of it. His presence could be deduced from the loudness of the laughter. This talent caused money to be spent but didn't earn any. Nowadays television entertained millions more than the groups huddled together, not only in the pubs of Ireland, in London, Liverpool, Glasgow and wherever the hope of work had attracted Irish labour. "The Smiler" would have had a huge following on television, with women and men; he had such a glad eye and was obviously a good sport. But this exploitation of a personality, based on nothing more substantial, was a challenge to the gods. In the end there could only be deflation—no big bang, just a steady leak as of gas.

"Of course"—Miles was now addressing a sea of expectant faces—"people hired to entertain would soon be out of jobs if it was apparent that they were using their exposed position for propaganda. Nothing was more certain to alienate possible sympathizers. One could get people all worked up for a short time about anything, but if they detected even the' tail end of a hobby-horse boredom set in at once. Irish troubles should make the English feel guilty, but they only bore them. The idea of a mission was beset with difficulties, but at least the Irish in the media should get together and form a corps."

"Look where you are going."

The old lady was angry. Miles raised his white panama in apology. She was in her rights. He had been so carried away that he had forgotten he was walking on a public foot-path. But he found it hard to break off just when he was coming to the peroration. Here he must drag in dreadful Jerry again. "It would be gratifying to think that our dear friend's death inspired the revival of the Irish evangelizing genius. There was always the golden example of St Columbanus and"—he couldn't think off-hand of another missionary—"his like carrying the Christian message to Europe and elsewhere (check). Think what those intrepid saints could have accomplished had television screens been at their disposal."

That ending touched him. So much so that he found himself quickening his pace, and once again he collided with someone, a man this time, who snarled. In every sense this encounter brought Miles back to earth. He had fallen so much in love with the picture of himself giving a graveside oration that he had overlooked the whole point of his speech. It was to shame his fellow countrymen in the media for their failure to rally to his support when the BBC did the dirty on him. That is what he was really talking about, but it was essential to put it inside a wider context, to let it follow as an obvious consequence and conspicuous example of the way the Irish entertainers pursued English fleshpots and ignored a gross injustice to one of their own.

A pretty woman smiled at him, a happy May morning smile. Did she recognize him? Was she laughing at him? Or were they for that second in eternity sharing the pleasure of being alive? The

13

effect was to take his mind off funeral orations and his standing grievance and direct it towards an attractive woman—Lalage Dubonnet. He had no proof that she was attractive, but he found the stationery she used attractive; he found her invitation attractive; he found her name attractive. Lalage used to suggest furniture-removers to him until he learned how to pronounce it. Then La-la-gee sounded attractive, not to say seductive. And Dubonnet was the *apéritif* Rowena asked for on hot days when bewildered by the range of choice. In conjunction, the names were doubly attractive. Very soon he would discover whether Lalage Dubonnet had an attractive voice.

Keep away from the women was the only instruction he remembered having received from his father. He had never forgotten it, but its force only became apparent when it was too late, when the damage had been done. Would Lalage be his idea of a French woman? It was an academic question. If put to it he might have been at a loss to describe his idea of a French woman other than that she would speak broken English rapidly and probably have dark hair and wear too much make-up and expect sex after lunch. It was equally pure coincidence that he happened to be passing a grubby-looking newsagent at that precise moment who had on display a generous number of girlie magazines with almost identical covers. If he hesitated, it was only for a second, and if he thought of Lalage it was only because there was no competing image of her to restrain his indulgent fancy.

"Naughty", a voice said.

Without looking round he picked up the nearest newspaper to hand—for racing car enthusiasts—and bought it with suitable *empressement*. He had retrieved the situation he felt, but it was a sharp reminder, now that he was on the way back, how cautious he would have to be. That little incident was the sort of carrion that *Private Eye* dished up for its readers' consumption. From this point he increased his walking pace, stopped looking at faces coming towards him, and got the impression that people were not looking at him. He wanted more than anything to talk to Russell. Russell was his friend. He didn't know his christian name, but it began with G. (Miles learnt this, and his address, from glancing at occasional envelopes.)

Habitués of bookmaking establishments are wholly absorbed in their business and do not take kindly to being addressed, putting their hands automatically where their wallet is on receipt of a question. Passing what is called "the time of day" is a convention that is strictly ignored. Total concentration on the task in hand is the hallmark of the dedicated punter. Miles had never set foot in the shop until recently when he had taken up as a therapy one of the several ways by which his father had ruined himself. Occasionally he did get a nod or smile of recognition, but of the most fleeting character. Here there were men at work. Miles and Russell might have gone to this betting shop for the rest of their lives and have never spoken to each other if they hadn't met in the doorway one day on their way out. Miles stepped back; Russell stepped back; Miles indicated spaciously that Russell should take precedence; Russell shook his head in extreme agitation. They might have been left in this static situation indefinitely if a more pragmatic customer had not made a bee line between them. Seeing that the other was really unhappy, Miles gave in. Outside Russell said, "Forgive the presumption, but am I right in thinking that I am addressing Miles—or I should say—'Mister O'Malley?' I thought I recognized you, sir. Goodness knows I have seen you often enough on the screen."

"I enjoy a flutter. It lends a little excitement to the day."

"I'm sure you must find time on your hands since you retired."

"But I haven't retired. Not by a long chalk. I can see how the public has been given this impression—it is the BBC's lousy policy. A war of attrition, is the name for it, I believe. But they haven't done with me yet."

"I see that I spoke out of turn. You must forgive me. I don't know anything about the matters you allude to. My wife, I should say, was—I mean is—a great fan of yours."

"I was going over to the Cock and Candle," Miles said. "Would you care to join me? I usually take a sandwich and a pint at this time of day."

"It would be an honour, but you have your own circle, I'm sure. Don't let me barge in. I couldn't resist the temptation of speaking to you just now. Mrs Russell would never have forgiven me if I told her that I could have and let the opportunity pass."

After that they met regularly. Miles had the advantage of his post-breakfast research, and his mind was usually made up by the time he arrived at the bookmakers; but his friend relied on the newspapers that covered the walls of the office, for which there was a certain amount of competition. Russell arrived an hour earlier than Miles—a change in his routine that suited him very much better, he insisted.

It was from such shreds of confidence that Miles formed the impression that Mrs Russell had something the matter with her. He didn't ask, nor did he ask—although it intrigued him—why Mr Russell had retired from the bank. He might, of course, have been older than he looked. He wore a cap and pale yellow tweeds and gave a most respectable impression, like the father in insurance company advertisements for policies maturing on retirement.

Mr Russell was excessively humble and self-deprecating, apologizing in advance for uninflicted bother. His own doings were of no importance in comparison with any detail of the life of his new and famous friend. That he made clear from the start, and it suited Miles very well. In the hotel his only confidant was half-witted, and today he was itching to talk to a grown-up person about his busy programme. When he was feeling favourably inclined towards the world in general or Russell in particular he offered the latter a glass of whiskey. Although his reference at their first encounter was to beer, Miles had very little time nowadays for any liquor but his native spirit. Sometimes he invited his friend to join him on the second time round. The pattern of his hospitality was an index to changes in his volatile moods: they had no bearing on his friend's behaviour. He was always the same, reverence incarnate.

"What happened afterwards? You told me you were going to have a show-down with Doyle about the stables."

The encouraging events of this morning, which Miles had been looking forward to talking about, had put out of his head his complaints of yesterday. Doyle, the hotel manager, had been strangely secretive about the comings and goings of strangers at the back of the houses that had been knocked together to form the Parnell Hotel. From his penthouse windows Miles had watched men in earnest conferences with Doyle and had confided in Russell that he suspected his manager of IRA sympathies. He kept on raising objections to the proper conversion of the old stables saying that he had to oblige friends with storage space for which they were paying handsomely. To the question "what were they storing?" he could only reply that it was still in transit. These friends, he told Miles, had supported the hotel at a difficult time. The support took the form of getting the hotel on to the list of accommodation hired by the local authority at outrageous rents for the housing of homeless families in the borough.

This morning Miles was in no mood to concentrate on the miserable circumstances in which he was living, due entirely, in his considered view, to the misjudgement of Rowena in the last months of her fatal illness. These Doyles had taken her over, and she left him in their grasping hands. This morning marked the beginning of his renaissance. He told the attentive Russell (to whom whiskey had been supplied) about the oration at the grave.

"I didn't know the man was dead," Russell confessed.

"He isn't. Not yet, but he is expected to be at any moment."

"I'm sorry about that. As one gets older the loss of friends is like a nail in one's own coffin."

"I really couldn't claim that I was a friend of Jerry's, but he is the first of the Irish brigade to go. That's why I think it's so important not to lose this opportunity of making a rallying call to those who remain. I'm glad Barney suggested it because you know what people are—"

Russell gave a quick sympathetic nod and moved a little closer.

"If I had suggested it they'd say that I was making Jerry's death an opportunity for airing my own grievances."

"Would they sink as low as that?"

"Even when we are actually burying the poor sod? I've no doubt they would. Now the way I look at it is like this: my trouble with the BBC has taught me things about life and human nature and my fellow-countrymen that I didn't know before. I want to put my experience to use so that the same thing can never happen to the people who come after me. I will find out beforehand if Jerry ran into troubles of his own. That would strengthen my case. It's hard to believe that he didn't because, strictly between ourselves"—Russell moved in even closer—"in all my long life I can't recall having ever come across anyone with such a brass neck as Jerry. Talk about hints. You might as well hint to an express train to take it easy as to hope to convey to Jerry that you preferred his room to his company. That laugh of his—you would think you were in a bottle bank."

"I didn't want to say so because I assumed that he was a very special friend of yours, but I am myself distinctly allergic to Jerry Dunne—as a television personality I hasten to say. As a private individual, of course, I know nothing about him."

"I saw quite a lot of him at a time when he thought I might be useful to him, but neither sight nor sound of him, I need hardly say, since my own troubles began. However, I am putting all those thoughts on one side. Jerry will give me a chance to do something for others in my own case, and for that I must be grateful."

"I admire the way you are taking it. I had assumed he was a friend of yours."

"Jerry is Jerry's only friend. It was a lifelong romance, but the poor divil is dying and I don't want to speak ill of him. We must make sure the cameras are rolling when we are burying him. Will you come?"

"I'm afraid I'd be rather out of place on such an occasion."

"Nonsense. The more the merrier. I never met such a retiring customer. My old man dearly loved a funeral. Never missed one in the locality, and thought nothing of going as far afield as Cork or up to Dublin, for that matter. There's nowhere the crack is so good, he used to say. Much better than at weddings where the women are weeping and the men are sloshed. I wish you had met the daddy. Anything I've got I owe to him. Finish what's in the glass before you. I'm ordering another for both of us. I want to consult you about a letter I got this morning."

Russell preened himself delightedly and started to deny his competence. All he was required to do was listen, and Miles took no notice of his squirming.

"I got this letter," Miles continued, but he didn't produce it at once. He instinctively worked up even his audience of one, titillating him by his hesitancies. A lesser man would have thrust the letter without any preliminary editing into Russell's nervous fingers.

"The Alma-Tadema Society. Have you ever heard of it?"

"No. I can't say that I have, but that doesn't surprise me. I'm the last person to ask."

"I just thought . . . The president is an RA. Samuel Slaughter. That sounds all right—doesn't it?"

"Indeed."

"The committee, by the looks of it, might be the cast for a Greek tragedy. The only name I miss is Onassis. Let me show you."

Miles had his fingers on the envelope, and it passed at once to Mr Russell, who opened it as if it were a Christmas present. His manner was exactly right, a nice blend of curiosity and old-fashioned respect for a significant document. He ran his eye quickly over the page before concentrating on the names at the top.

"What do you make of it?" Miles said a little impatiently. Russell was going on as if the contents were written in Chinese.

"Alma-Tadema rings a bell certainly, I believe he is a character in a children's story."

"You are thinking of Ali Baba."

"And the Forty Thieves."

"I don't like the sound of that particularly. I've got it. Isn't it the name of some sort of game?"

"You are thinking of Halma. That's a kind of draughts, if I'm not mistaken."

"It shouldn't be too difficult finding out a little more about the gang. Let's take a look at the telephone directory."

Obligingly Russell took the hint and went off at once to borrow a directory, but he returned looking despondent. No Alma-Tadema Society in the book.

"But, dammit, we have this address and telephone number in Clapham on the letter. When you come to think of it, if this is only a dining club, it wouldn't rent an office."

"If you were to ring up this Dubonnet lady, I'm sure she would fill in the picture. Have you a *Who's Who* at home? Look up Samuel Slaughter. He's bound to be in it."

"My copy is ten years old. Rowena bought it when I got in."

"A great day, I'm sure, for both of you. I wonder if your friend Jerry Dunne is in it?"

"Forget Jerry Dunne for a moment. I'm intrigued with this mysterious dining club. Lalage Dubonnet is a fascinating name, don't you agree?"

"Exotic certainly. I'll be very interested to hear the outcome. I might be able to check some of the names on the committee for you. I still have bank contacts. Let's take the letter to the copying shop across the road and have it photostatted."

They parted in the street. Miles would have been pleased to walk as far as Russell's door, but he didn't like to suggest it. There was something almost painfully secretive about his modest friend, and Miles respected his privacy. His own return journey was something of a Roman triumph. Two whiskies and the exhilaration of talking about himself for two hours lent him an effulgence. He was walking downhill, and his tripping step unconsciously rehearsed the way his victims on television used to come prancing down the stairs into the studio to the cheers and excited clapping of the captive audience. In despondent moments he told himself that those Roman circus days were gone for ever. Hope came back this morning, and telling decent Russell about it had made it all seem real.

In the foyer he called out as usual, announcing his return, but there was no one about.

He was safe upstairs. The penthouse had been Rowena's creation when the hotel was purchased as an investment. As a rule, when he came in from his outing to the bookies, he poured himself a whiskey and played one of his video tapes. Whenever he was very down, any of the scenes when he was on back-slapping terms with the great and famous put him on good terms with himself. He insinuated himself with such brio into any gathering. Sometimes, when he had been more lighthanded than usual in replenishing his glass, he felt tears come into his eyes. He was getting glimpses of a lost Paradise.

But today he needed no comforting. The first thing his eyes met when he came into the sitting-room was Rowena's portrait over the fireplace. It had been the subject of acrimonious dispute, Miles having tactlessly described as typical a tightness around the mouth and a suspicious look in the eyes. The hotel had changed beyond imagining in the two years since Rowena died, but the penthouse was still as she had arranged it ten years ago, if considerably shabbier. The carpet that had once been white was now the colour of old sheep in winter. What looked like an incontinent dog's tracks from the sideboard to the chair, permanently fixed in front of the television screen, were whiskey splashes. The prevailing note was Irish. A Jack Yeats landscape —a cavalier chasing a clown across a peat bog—hung over the fireplace, six sugaun chairs (now the straw needed replaiting) surrounded the Connemara marble table in the recess. The curtains and covers were Kilkenny design. The small space for books was given up to Rowena's special interests, food, sex and flower pictures. Every other spare inch in the room was taken up by photographs of Miles in various groups—sporting, artistic, ecclesiastical, royal—always in the very centre and always smiling broadly. The photographs went round the corner into the bedroom where Rowena began to make an appearance. One of her in a silver frame showed her coming out of the sea on a Greek island, naked to the waist. Miles had wanted to take her as Botticelli's Venus, but Rowena had not felt quite sure it was a good idea, and this was a compromise. He liked to look at it when he was dressing.

Today it was Rowena's disapproving portrait that engaged his attention. She seemed to be calling him to heel. He could hear her north English voice—how uncompromising it sounded on these occasions—saying: "I would take a pull at myself if I were you." Lalage Dubonnet was the trouble. That girlie magazine cover had made more impression on him than he thought at the time. He had intended to let a day pass before ringing up, but now he asked himself what was the point of delaying. This would be in the nature of an exploratory call. He need not commit himself to speak at the dinner. Ask for time to consider. Before doing that he looked up "Slaughter, Samuel" in *Who's Who* and was taken aback to discover that he was born in 1897 and had been elected RA on his seventieth birthday, eighteen years ago. He had taught art in the provinces, had married a Miss Grubb and had one son, now deceased. Mrs Slaughter died in 1969. His studio was on the north side of Clapham Common. The chairman's weight of years was a facer. Was this some crank gathering? Potentially a vast bore? Miles fancied himself as an interpreter of voices. If there were the least trace of senility in Lalage Dubonnet's he would turn the invitation down flat.

There wasn't. He was startled by the promptness of the answer, as if his call was being waited for. "This is Lalage Dubonnet," the voice said, without any trace of a foreign accent. When he said who he was she became pleasantly animated. "I am so glad you rang. There has been some confusion. Our chairman, as you probably know, is on the elderly side, and he gets names wrong. Without consulting anyone the old dear rang up that nice Mr Barney Roche, thinking he was you."

"Then you won't be needing me?"

"We need you very much. It is our first dinner. Did I not tell you that in my letter? We want to keep to all our arrangements. Mr Roche will be very welcome on some other occasion. I hate having to tell you about our chairman's little gaffe, but if you were to have heard about it from another source you might have jumped to a wrong conclusion."

"Would you tell me a little more about your society?"

"We are a group of friends with interests in common. We like food, wine, intelligent conversation, and some of us are interested in art and beautiful things."

"And where does Alma-Tadema come in?"

"He is one of Mr Carlovassi's favourite painters. Uncle Sam actually met him. I'm his niece. I should have told you that."

"What did you want me to talk about?"

"Yourself, really. You must have met many interesting people when you were on television. Uncle Sam is under the impression that you are still performing, and I had the greatest trouble in convincing him that you retired some time ago. I'm sure I'm not the first person to tell you television has never been the same for me since."

"But your uncle is dead right. I have by no means retired, although I must admit the BBC has been so bureaucratic about the renewal of my contract a great many people are probably under the same impression. But it is not true, I assure you."

"Well, you can tell them from me to hurry up. That's the best news I've heard for ages."

"Are your proceedings private? Would there be any objection if I let it be known that I was speaking and we got the cameras in?"

"Personally, I'd be delighted, but would you mind not doing anything about that before I've sorted it out with my committee?"

"Of course."

"Is that all settled then?"

"I think so."

"Splendid. Tell me if there are any guests you would like me to invite, people you think might fit in. Will Mrs O'Malley be coming?"

"Mrs O'Malley, I'm sorry to say, is dead."

"Forgive me. I should have known."

There was a tactful tenderness about the way she said those few words that gave Miles a sudden liking for Miss Dubonnet. He had to replace that image of a woman leering over her shoulder, as she bounded upstairs with her knickers in her teeth, with something more domestic. He had done this. He had invested Miss Dubonnet—Lalage—with a human personality. There were emotional possibilities there. He could tell. He would have liked to say that what he would most look forward to would be the prospect of sitting beside her at the dinner, but it might give an inept impression, suggest a person unused to the high table. He

22

promised to consider the problem of his own guests and to ring again.

"Are you always at that number?"

"When I'm at home."

He put down the receiver thoughtfully, considering the implications of that call. Sitting where he was he couldn't avoid meeting Rowena's hostile stare from the portrait that had been a bone of contention between them. Miles had foolishly persisted in canvassing opinions about it after Rowena had made it quite clear that she regarded it as an unkind caricature. At a time when he was indulging in a fantasy about another lady, Rowena's facial expression was discouraging. The idea that he might ever again establish even a sensible friendship with any woman still seemed like high treason. Rowena had absorbed him totally, and her two years' illness gave a special quality to their relationship. He really didn't believe that he could go on living without her. But he did. Men left as he had been, particularly if they are celebrities, do not usually lack for offers of comfort, and these, no doubt, would have come his way if it had not been for the peculiar situation in which he found himself. Rowena thought she had made him as safe as a building taken over by the National Trust. The hotel was to provide him with a substantial income; the penthouse, with a suitable residence; the Doyles, with loyal and efficient servants. All her savings had gone into the venture and, she assumed, Miles's as well. She didn't know that he had no savings. It was one of the matters on which he was less than candid. During her illness she became increasingly dependent on Bridget Doyle, and it gave her peace of mind to think that she had insured Miles's future comfort by hinting to the Doyles that they might expect to inherit the hotel if they took care of him. These arrangements were carried out under the guidance of Tod Morris who had introduced her to the Doyles. Morris was a man for all seasons in the Kilburn area, owned the pub in which the Doyles worked when they first came to England, and ran the Hibernian Friendly Society which he had founded and financed to help, he said, "poor divils of Irishmen trying to make their way in this Godfor-saken city". He lived without domestic attachments, worked round the clock, had a stake in many enterprises and saved his clientele from all the worry and trouble of finding and instructing solicitors, accountants, house agents, bankers, builders, plumbers, surveyors, architects—it was said (by Willie) that Tod

Morris could even arrange for personal protection if you believed someone bore you a grudge; not least he had useful police contacts. Rowena—until she became too ill to be worried with business—dealt with Mr Morris. Miles was too busy to bother. He had had one traumatic interview with that prodigy in which Miles revealed his financial position. He had made a more generous settlement on Jean when he left her than he let Rowena understand, and lost all he had left in a disastrous investment made on the advice of an American bishop. He betted on horses and was always ready to take a hand at poker. That said, how was he to put his hand on £100,000?

"Miles—may I call you Miles? I'm Tod, remember? A man like you—an artist—must not be distracted by this sort of thing. The privilege of poor sods like yours truly is to relieve the élite from these tiresome chores. All I ask you to do is to write—you needn't do it now—just write on the back of an envelope an approximation of your annual income at the moment, and I can get you what you need from that little society I run. If you like, I'll have a word with your accountant and save you the trouble. I hope you find him satisfactory, by the way."

"I never see him. I don't think I'd recognize him if I did."

"I told him not to bother you, just to get along with the job. He's a nice boy, Seamus. His father and I were butties when the going was stickier than it is nowadays. We had to fight our corner in those after-war years. We rebuilt their cities for them. Don't ever forget that."

"How will the loan be managed?"

"That's Tod's headache. I might form a little company. I had been giving this some thought before you did me the honour of confiding in me. And—just in case you're worrying about Rowena—I shan't repeat a word of this conversation to a living soul."

"Can I trust the Doyles?"

"The decentest couple I know. Bridget has the brains, but Dominick is a deep fellow, a tremendous worker, brought up one of twelve on a farm the size of a snot rag, if you will excuse plain speaking. They loved Rowena; and you, of course, are the closest they've got, so far, to God. You may trust your life to the Doyles. Don't stand any nonsense, though. If they were ever to begin to get above themselves, put the boot in at once. You are inclined to be more easy-going than may always be in your own interest."

Recently Miles had found Morris elusive. He was never in his office when Miles was looking for him. The Doyles were reassuring about this. Tod's business had spread over the world. Were they not getting on perfectly well as they were without bothering the poor man?

One consequence of all this was Miles's having no friends. No one would believe him if he were to describe his present situation. If he went into London old cronies would embarrass him about the BBC business. The gossip columnists would write him down. Out of sight he was forgotten, but he couldn't ask anyone to visit him at the hotel so long as it was in its present squalid condition. The rooming-house plan had had Tod's warmest approval. "You can't afford *not* to," he said, giving Miles a quite dirty look.

It had been a late spring this year. Today Miles saw it and breathed it in and, what was more, the sap was rising in his own heart. The world wanted him. Two little shoots this morning—he mustn't lose his sense of proportion—but these might grow. They might be harbingers . . . (What exactly did "harbinger" mean? He had beside him, bought recently for a shilling off a barrow, *The New Universal Dictionary*. "HARBINGER. A forerunner; precursor; a pioneer; orig. a king's officer who arranged lodgings, etc., beforehand for royal progresses. v.t. to precede as a harbinger, to usher in." *Royal progresses*—he liked the sound of that.) Could it be—the idea came into his mind only then—that the two invitations were in some way related, that he was being vetted for something really big? If so, it behoved him to make a suitable impression on Miss Dubonnet. He couldn't let her see him in his present surroundings, not until they had established a working friendship.

"Working friendship"—what did he mean by that? Quick thinking on television called for ready-made expressions, and by now he had a store of them available, like empty milk bottles in the mind. Sexual innuendo, for example, had become so much part and parcel (there he went again) of his patter that he couldn't talk to a woman for five minutes—if she looked anywhere under sixty—without making a reference to copulation. He must watch this with Miss Dubonnet.

Rowena was right. That portrait was a libel. He had defended it because he had paid so much to the conceited artist. Now he would make belated amends to Rowena and take the caricature down. It fitted neatly behind his chest of drawers, leaving space for lots of photographs of himself on the wall. Somehow he couldn't face wading through the archives in his present mood. For the time being the large print of Botticelli's Venus in the bathroom could fill the gap.

"Hackneyed" Rowena had called it, but Miles suspected that she was really thinking about the photograph she had refused to pose for. When she was alive he had to keep the half naked snapshot hidden. What was happening to him? He hadn't thought about that little controversy for years.

Then the telephone rang. He grasped it hungrily, all eager anticipation.

"Miles O'Malley speaking."

"It's only me, Bridget. Dominick and myself were wondering whether you could see us for a minute. I hate to disturb you."

"That's all right, Bridget. You won't mind if I ask you to keep it short. I've a job in hand that I let myself in for and I must get it finished by this evening."

"Now, I hate to disturb you."

"That's all right."

"We'll come up this instant minute."

A visit from the Doyles was always an uncomfortable experience. There was first of all their resolute refusal to say what it was they had come about. Dominick stood in the background, never venturing a remark on his own account, while Bridget took a quick inventory of the room. Any attempt by Miles to get at the reason for a call was treated as an untimely interruption of a tribal rite. Before that could be mentioned, there had to be a short service in Rowena's memory during which Bridget recited the litany of her perfections. Just when Miles was on the point of losing his temper Bridget would anticipate it to a finely calculated second and bring up what it was they were looking for. They never called unless they were looking for something.

Today the prospect was more disagreeable to Miles than usual. When he had at last something—much—to think over of an agreeable nature: an after-dinner speech, Lalage Dubonnet, Jerry Dunne's funeral, the rich feel of a conspiracy in progress to rehabilitate him; it was ironical to have to give time to these grim reminders of his fallen state, apart from the threat they represented to what remained to him.

26

"God, wouldn't you swear she was looking at you?"

Rowena's picture—Bridget always made straight for it on these occasions. She was well aware that Rowena hadn't liked it, and as she once asked him if it were "hand-painted", Miles discounted her opinion of its merits. But she would be even more tiresome when she noticed its absence—he had forgotten that he took it down. Back it must go, if for nothing else to spare Bridget's blushes when she saw what had been put in its place.

He was hanging Rowena on her nail when the Doyles gave their timid knock. It was very characteristic, that knock.

"Anyone at home?"

Bridget's gipsy face under its dyed black hair came playfully round the door. This was her favourite ploy. Dominick, a few inches smaller than his spouse, his face as lined as a tired apple, followed her. He gave a little skip coming in as if there was something guarding the threshold, saluted Miles, and retreated to a corner while his wife's busy eyes, having taken in the room, came to rest on the portrait.

"We've come to ask you a great favour," Bridget said, glancing back nervously as though the picture might disappear if she took her eyes off it.

"I couldn't stop her," her husband put in.

She wriggled, suddenly coy. "Dominick said he didn't know how I could have such cheek." The Doyles in their double act sometimes talked as if the other was not in the room. "Go on, Dominick, You tell Mr O'Malley."

"The wife's expecting."

Miles took a moment to absorb this. The idea of the Doyles taking their minds off business for the time required to put Bridget in this condition required an effort of imagination. "This is great news, really great news. Congratulations." Miles was doing his best. He wanted the Doyles to disappear, not to perpetuate themselves.

"I told him he'd have to tell you himself in the end."

"Tell him the rest, woman."

Now it was coming. Miles gave a quick look round the room. What were they after?

"Oh, I can't. It's too much. Reely."

"Go on, woman. Didn't you hear Mr O'Malley saying that he hadn't all night."

"We were wondering if you would stand for it when the time comes," she blurted out, then put her hand to her mouth, amazed at her temerity.

"Be godfather. With pleasure. But I must warn you I have taken on this job many times, and I'm no good at it."

"Dominick Doyle, will you listen to what the man is saying. Didn't I tell you Mr O'Malley was too much of a gentleman to refuse if you asked him properly. I'm only sorry that herself . . ." —she paused to look at the portrait and Miles relieved her from having to finish her sentence by going to the telephone and asking Willie to bring up a bottle of champagne.

"Is it for the Doyles?" he inquired. Miles pretended not to hear the question.

"Can Willie be let into the secret?"

"I'd leave Willie out of it. He'll learn all about it soon enough," was Dominick's advice.

Waiting for the wine gave Bridget a chance to inspect the room thoroughly. There was more than the child on the agenda. "They want to turn me out," Miles told himself, and he was not surprised when, after crowing over a photograph of Rowena she had picked up to examine, Bridget asked Miles in her softest Kerry voice whether he ever found his rooms "too large and lonely, too full of memories."

"I am well content."

"It could do with a lick of paint," Dominick said.

"No use in half-doing it. Mick would give you an estimate," Bridget said to her husband. "But I suppose painters is the last thing you want to be bothered with." The last remark was for Miles's benefit.

"I am quite happy as I am."

"What we were wondering—Dominick and myself—was how you would take to the notion of moving to our apartment. When baby comes it will be too small for all of us that will be in it and when I'm above in the hospital would be the right time to do a really nice job on it. The great advantage is you will be beside the dining-room and not have to be ringing and waiting when you want something."

The last words gave Miles an idea, he opened the door suddenly and revealed Willie standing there holding a tray.

"God, you were nearly after frightening the life out of me," Willie said.

Miles cleared a place on the Habitat glass sofa-table for the tray.

"I see you's are celebrating."

"You must have a glass yourself," Miles replied. "I daresay you are aware of the occasion."

Willie looked equally sly and embarrassed and avoided the question. "No, thank you kindly. I can't drink any class of fizzy wine. It doesn't agree with my stomach. But thanks all the same, and I'll say God bless to all here."

After Willie left the room Miles checked to see that he was not lurking outside in the passage. "He will be telling everyone I'm giving up the penthouse."

"Who would bother to listen to him?"

"That's not the point, Bridget. The arrangement was that I should live in the penthouse unless I decided to let it; and the way the place is running downhill I'm sorely tempted to do that in the near future. I hope to have my troubles with the BBC settled before long."

Husband and wife exchanged glances. Dominick took over.

"We never thought of turning you out of your apartment, Mr O'Malley. What we had in mind for ourselves was moving into the back premises when they have been converted, which should be by next summer. Then if you were nice and comfortable downstairs this penthouse could be let out. It would accommodate three families, and we would get a great rent for it—so long as the present housing shortage lasts.

"We need all the money we can lay our hands on if we are to do a proper job on the hotel. We don't like having the place cluttered up with such a dicey crowd any more than you do yourself, but it can't last. People are poking their noses into the system. You must have seen the unfair way they've gone on about it on television. In about three years, by my reckoning, the big cash flow will be drying up. By then I hope we will be in a position to renovate the whole place and make the Parnell Hotel second to none in North London. Something Rowena would be proud to see if she were to come back. God rest her."

It was the first time either of the Doyles talking to Miles had referred to Rowena by her christian name. That was not the only reason why he felt that his reserves of amiability were very near the point of exhaustion. The prospects of three more years in this benighted spot and, if the Doyles got their way, most of it in their cramped quarters, with the further prospect of spending the rest of his life in a renovated hotel as virtually their prisoner, released a flood of resentment, the presence of which, until then, he had not been aware. Why had he allowed this dreadful couple to make a cult of Rowena to sabotage his life? He had been sacrificed to this bloody hotel. It was eating him alive. When Rowena died he ought to have sold it at once and found himself a bachelor flat. It had taken only a few months to reduce to nothing his years of achievement.

"Why don't you begin work on the mews at once? Why are we keeping them for storage space when rooms are so valuable?"

"Well, I'm helping a friend, as I told you, but when you see what we are getting in the way of rent no one will be better pleased than yourself."

"But I understand the whole place is empty except for someone who has been sleeping there lately. Why was I not consulted about that? I'd like to know."

"I see who has been making trouble. Willie's been talking to you. That little git loves to be poking his nose into other people's business. What business of his is it who is sleeping in the stables?"

"I saw a man I didn't know coming out and going in. I don't know why you are attacking Willie."

"That was a poor fellow who had been put out of his digs and hadn't a place to rest his head. We lose nothing by his being there. The rent is paid for keeping the accommodation available. It's very hard to get storage space in this area. That's why my friend booked it in advance."

Miles decided not to mention the IRA. He had nothing to go on, and he would be putting Willie into danger.

"If I haven't been troubling yourself I've let Mr Morris know what's going on. He wants to see all the figures at the next meeting. I think you'll be surprised yourself Miles when you see the return we are getting."

"I hope you didn't mind us mentioning the penthouse." Bridget sensed that no concessions were going to be made this evening. "Dominick and myself thought you might like a change, and, to tell you the truth, I was looking forward to getting a really nice job done on our little place to make it snug and homelike for you, the sort of thing Rowena would have liked. She had lovely taste. God be good to her."

"Will you come along out of that, woman, and let Mr O'Malley be getting on with his work. I hoped you were going to tell us it was for those fly-by-nights in the BBC."

"It might be."

"Well, that's splendid. You must get on with it. Dominick and myself have a lot to do before we are off duty."

Miles poured himself out a celebratory glass of whiskey after the Doyles had retreated in good order, Bridget keeping up her monologue until the lift door shut on their smiling faces. Slowly and exactly he replayed the last half-hour. It was foolish, he decided, to over-dramatize the situation; the Doyles' strategy, once he had accepted them for what they were, was not necessarily hostile to him personally. Their ambition stretched no further than to own a flashy hotel. They were prepared to endure the rooming-house for years to achieve this, nor did it hurt their sensibilities all that much: the rustle of notes was the rustle of spring to this practical couple. He still had a card to play. To them he was a great man, a celebrity; that was why they persuaded him to appear for dinner in the only part of the hotel that had not been turned into a human kennels.

The Doyles were sincere when they inquired about his BBC troubles. To be on television was to them the closest to God mere mortals were permitted to attain. They did not grudge him fame. That was not what they were after. There was no conflict of interest. They used his name when they tried to advertise the hotel, not their own. Lying low was a great part of their strategy. It had worked so well that Bridget wondered how much they owed to her devotion to the Blessed Virgin. They were surprised to find Miles so perfectly in agreement with being left out of the running of the business. They knew from Tod Morris that they could lose the half share of the hotel that Rowena intended for them if they quarrelled seriously with Miles. If they played their cards properly they would get it and Miles's share eventually. They knew that Tod Morris owned a mortgage on the premises. For that reason, and because he was formidable, they kept in with Mr Morris.

Miles had tried to forget his own position, but this evening's invasion left him depressed and anxious. On a visit to the bathroom he took a look at himself in the mirror and felt despair at the picture. He couldn't present that image on the screen, and television had become the whole reason for existence. Without it he was only waiting for the grave. Without it he would never have known what power felt like. Inside, he had seen its power in action—Cabinet Ministers pushing public business aside to hurry down to be questioned in the studio like suspects helping the police. Royalty, the churches—none of them could function now if refused access to the cameras. Newscasters, ever since Richard Dimbleby, aimed at the mien of major prophets and there had been a remarkable change in the respective demeanours of the questioners and the questioned, even in Miles's own experience. Gone was the time when one apologized to the great for taking up their time. If you didn't think much of their answers to your questions nowadays, you told them so; and he had learnt from his own experience that public figures would put up with the grossest familiarity if accompanied by a winning smile. Miles was practising those, at two months, in his pram.

Off the screen he wasn't fully alive. No wonder if after this long sabbatical he looked like a case of delayed burial. In front of the cameras again—the place for which nature intended him—his pulse would resume its normal beat. It would be as if some hand unseen had switched him on.

He had had this knowledge of himself in a relevation which he liked to compare with St Paul's, but the circumstances in Miles's case were different. He was in the club house of a Dublin golf course at the time. He had been playing in a competition with Michael O'Reilly, a presenter in the very recently established Radio Telefis Eireann. Miles had an engaging golf-playing manner. Had he taken the game seriously he might have been a first-class player, but he took nothing very seriously, and himself only so far as he liked his comforts and amusements; he was prepared to work as much as it was necessary to ensure a regular flow of each. He was quick and witty, and his malice usually amused its victims so that it hardly deserved the harsh label. He was brighter than most of the people he met, but his tastes were those of the man in the street. He trusted to a friendly manner to persuade where others, less favoured by nature, insisted and argued. He had a good memory; this made him seem cleverer than in fact he was, by providing a hidden fund on which he could draw on a whim or when he wanted to impress. He could surprise people with whom he had been intimate for years by quoting a line of serious poetry or dropping the name of a Greek philosopher. He had always been an enthusiast about television and highly critical of the recently-opened Irish station. It was providential that he had a hang-over that morning and was inclined in consequence to slice his long shots. On his usual game he would never have allowed such an indifferent golfer to beat him. When they came in after the match there was an urgent message for his opponent to ring a certain number. He joined Miles at the bar a few minutes later, excusing his absence. It was "a damn nuisance", one of the panel for a quiz show tonight had gone to bed with laryngitis. Miles, when he told the story, used to say that he knew what was coming.

"You wouldn't like to try your hand, I suppose?"

"You are wrong there. I'd like nothing better."

"Have you ever done this sort of thing before?"

"Never, but I'd like to have a shot at it."

"You might be just what the doctor ordered. We have a rather serious team: a geology professor, a Welsh language enthusiast and, of course, Rory O'Hagen. You would be more entertaining than any of that bunch, I feel certain."

"I'd like to take a stab at it."

That became a catch phrase of Miles's ever after. He went home babbling to himself, and when he told Jean the news she gave him a hug, which was generous because she had been angry with him at breakfast on several counts. But now as a good wife she put her complaints aside and began a long afternoon of telephone calls to relations and friends to prime them.

The next few hours took on for Miles in retrospect the character of a dream. He arrived at the television centre too early, and spent a time that seemed endless watching other people being sent up to some holy of holies or being greeted by officials who came down for the purpose and ushered them to their destined studio. The porter began to look suspiciously at Miles, whose earlier confidence was oozing out through every pore.

"Are you Mr O'Malley, by any chance?"

Miles leaped to his feet, vindicated at last.

"Mr O'Reilly will be with you in a minute." The receptionist was obviously happier now that Miles had been accounted for. His own confidence began to return and flooded back when a smiling Michael O'Reilly came in and looked happy to see him before handing him over to a solemn young man who took him in charge. There was a spartan refreshment session before the programme at which Miles met his co-panellists, a worthy pair who spoke in low tones. The fourth member, Rory O'Hagen, arrived late, having had a row, he told everyone, with his taxi-driver. Rory had become a local celebrity because of his truculence on television. He was establishing himself as the Brian Boru of the medium.

The make-up room was where Miles felt that he had come into his own; the brilliant light, the attentive girls, were all he needed. He had the room in a roar as soon as he entered. Much exhilarated, he followed his solemn chaperone into the studio. There the heat and glare and expectant faces in the audience gave him a sensation of being born again, this time in the right place.

Miles's triumph on his first television appearance became a local legend. The competition was, admittedly, lacklustre. O'Hagen was one of the first personalities Irish television had thrown up. His line was simply to be sullenly rude, and the steady call on his services could be likened to the widespread practice of spilling tomato ketchup over every dish. Miles felt at once that the audience, like the girls in the make-up room, were on his side. He had determined to give the bully as good as he got, and he sensed in the studio an innocent desire for "a bit of gas". With that he felt confident he could supply them. The geology professor was suitably serious, the Welsh language enthusiast almost impossible to stop. Rory was rude to them both, and for a moment looked as if he was going to indulge in a bout of fisticuffs with someone to whom he had taken an objection in the front row of the audience.

Had Miles any claim to celebrity Rory would have concentrated his attack on him. As it was he saw someone who constituted no threat at present and might even be an ally. It was Miles's good fortune to be let off any special assault; he had, of course, to put up with Rory's sarcasm which was his natural manner. Rory disliked women on the panel, and the audience was pleased enough to see him tear the Welsh enthusiast to pieces. Even an addict tires of blood sports after a time, and when the lady had been effectively silenced Miles was given an opportunity to provide light relief.

A slightly dotty woman with a penetrating northern accent, sitting at the back of the studio, embarked on an exchange of repartee about what was the right time to tell children the facts of life. The contest drew loud applause. Miles found it a stimulus to have one person out there who could return the ball when he threw it to her. After the dullness of the early part of the programme and the trauma of Rory's lady-killing performance, everyone was grateful for high spirits. The presenter, who might well have resented the way in which Miles was gradually taking over the show, seemed satisfied to let matters take their course, and when the programme closed Miles was leading the audience in a rapturous rendering of *Daisy, Daisy.*

Afterwards there were some sour faces, and as the panel filed into the refreshment room Miles could hear Rory complaining about him. It reminded Miles of the atmosphere of school where, if you were not the accepted hero, there was always this tendency to make sure that you didn't lose your head over some better than routine performance. A little coolness in the air was a tribute of a kind, but the critical note was hardly perceptible. Gush flowed in on all sides. A wizened lady clasped his arm. He was asked for his autograph. That had never happened to him before. He had never heard his praises sung in public. It was slightly intoxicating. He thought of Jean and asked if he might use a telephone.

"You were wonderful. I feel so proud of you. The phone has never stopped ringing. When am I going to see you?"

"We are having refreshments. I will slip away as soon as I possibly can. Everyone is being very nice except—you will be surprised to hear—our great man. He was calling me by a four-letter word to someone just now. I heard him as I was passing by."

"Jealous as Hell, I expect. Don't you go taking any notice of him. Hurry home. I'll be waiting for you, my darling."

Back then to the lugubrious room where the refreshments were being served, much the better for that support from his encouraging wife. It was a rather cowed gathering he returned to, but he felt wonderfully benevolent towards them all. He had been a little disappointed by Michael O'Reilly's manner after the show. He hadn't said how grateful he was.

"I'm glad you enjoyed yourself. You got me out of a hole."

A perfectly civil speech, but not the way one talks to the lion of the evening. After that set-back Miles was relieved to see himself being appraised by the only good-looking woman in the room. Her eyes were amber, his favourite colour. He liked their intelligent amused expression. She was at the age when only in Ireland would she still be described as a girl. Jean's age, round about forty, Miles decided (people's ages were the first thing he noticed).

She wore her chestnut-coloured hair in a fringe. Rory, who had been hectoring her, paused to retain control over an elusive bottle of wine. Her eyes sent out a plea for rescue which Miles answered at once. A murmur was all he had to give to move out of his own conversational cul-de-sac. Rory, having got his hands on the bottle, had forgotten for the moment the identity of his victim. By mutual accord Miles and the lady moved towards each other. They met at the door.

"Do you think we could slip away without giving offence?" she said.

"I was about to. I don't know about you."

"I have had all I can take from that pugnacious young man. I don't know anybody. I shouldn't have come. But I'm glad I did. You made me laugh a lot, and that takes some doing."

"Have you a car?"

"No, but I expect they will get one a taxi."

"I can give you a lift. Where are you staying?"

"At the Shamrock Towers. It seemed only round the corner when I was coming out. This is very kind of you."

"My pleasure," Miles said.

When Miles said things like "my pleasure" it meant he was nervous. An Irishwoman in the same situation would have gushed over him at once, and he was piqued when his new friend began the conversation by telling him about a very funny lunch she had been at earlier in the day. She had come over, she explained, to advise on interior decoration for some firm who were opening a boutique.

"Everyone is opening boutiques, it seems to me. We got on perfectly well before we ever heard of them."

That was rude, but he was feeling uncomfortable. He knew that he would be invited in for a drink when they reached the hotel and equally well that if he accepted "just a quick one" time would go by the board. There was something so magically appropriate about this end to the evening that it seemed like monstrous ingratitude to refuse it. His workaday self had been looking forward to Jean's welcome and the reassurance of his best pyjamas on the pillow beside her. It was cruel to have to decide between them. One way out was to suggest lunch tomorrow to this woman and a swift return to the other. That had the great attraction that it did not involve the labour of lying; but it needed decision, a power that Miles never possessed in his dealings with women. He was too anxious to please. He could have described in advance what would happen, that pause with the engine running and her "Come in and let me give you a drink. You have saved my life". He had words of refusal in readiness, but she was out of the car before he could use them, and making for the entrance. It was he who muttered something about "a quick one" to her determined-looking back, and he knew that it would not prevent her from suggesting a drink in her room if she was in that way inclined. She saved him a scramble with his conscience when she walked over to a table in the corner of the lounge. She had an air of authority about her which impressed him, but it was not what he usually liked in women. In the present instance it would have been delightful to have some sort of real conversation about the evening and he was anxious to hear anything she had to say about his performance. This was a woman of experience, an intelligent, critical woman. In his own entourage he would hear only songs of praise. If only he could relax, but conscience kept nibbling away, and they had hardly sat down when he remembered a telephone call he had to make.

"I'm afraid I'm going to be a little late. I'm stuck here. I can't explain over the telephone. I'm surrounded. I'll get away just as quickly as I can. You go to bed."

"I'm already in bed."

"I thought you might be. I'm awfully sorry about this. Keep a place for me beside you. Love you." "Love you" was one of the things he said to Jean when he was thinking about something else.

He returned to his new friend as uneasy as he had left her. He should have given more thought to that telephone call before he made it. If Jean was missing him he had said nothing to comfort her or to put her mind at ease. It was bad enough to tell her lies, but not to take the trouble to make them up properly, to offer her the uncooked ingredients, was insulting. Between them these women were ruining his perfect evening. Why did one have to account for one's movements as though one were a prisoner on parole? If he had thought of it he could have stuck very close to the truth by saying he was being interviewed for *Vogue*. That would have been a fool-proof alibi and would fit in very well with the lady's appearance. She did not so much look rich and grand herself as someone who made their living off the rich and grand.

"I have ordered us brandies," she said when Miles came back. "I hope that is all right with you."

Jean would never have had the social confidence to do that. He felt suddenly protective on her behalf. It would frighten him to be married to anyone so worldly-wise as this. She must have read the signals, she smiled at him so warmly and encouragingly as she lifted up her glass. "You were so funny this evening. I can't tell you. Do you do a lot of this sort of thing? I expect you do. If what we saw was anything to go by, talent over here doesn't seem to be very thick on the ground."

One side of him, the one that clung to Jean, was put on the defensive by an air of condescension that she had about her, but it made her compliments more valuable, and after the recent confusion the peace of this place made him call the waiter to bring more brandies before she had more than sipped her first. The odds being even then he was suddenly and irreversibly tempted to tell her more about this evening, how he had felt, as he entered the studio, like St Paul on the road to Damascus. This is what he should be doing. This is what he was made for, not touting women's clothes. "I have this theory that television opens up an opportunity for entertainers that never existed in the world before. Until television came along they had strictly amateur status and were known only to their acquaintances. In this country they usually died of drink. It was really from frustration. I ought to know. That's what happened to my father. He was the best company in the world. Here I go, dammit, and I haven't even asked you your name."

"Rowena. Rowena Atkinson."

"I once knew a girl called Rowena. She was the best friend of the first girl I ever kissed. To be strictly accurate, she kissed me, but it sounds more chivalrous the other way. Daphne was her name."

"That makes us sound like old friends. Tell me more about yourself. What happened to Daphne? I'm longing to hear."

"She married someone in the north of England with a large farm. I don't know where I picked up that information. Our love was doomed from the start. Her father was the Dean in the Protestant Cathedral in the High Street and mine owned the pub at the corner."

"Did the Dean drop in on your father? Or did your father drop in on the Dean? Your father had more to offer."

"It didn't seem so at the time. And when the Dean was made a bishop, and the Dawsons (that was their name) moved to the north, I lost touch with the family."

"Have you ever thought of making a career on television?"

"It never occurred to me. There wasn't a local station until a few months ago. Forty is rather long in the tooth to start." (That was his first lie to Rowena. She thought of herself thenceforth as two years older than Miles. In fact there was a month in her favour.)

He had told her about Shannonwear. Now he insisted that she visit their showrooms in Grafton Street. He would call for her on his way to work. "I will see you get a cut as a walking advertisement for our clothes."

She was enjoying herself. Her business in Dublin had been satisfactory. She was to do up the boutique "regardless". She was intrigued by this man's company. She couldn't place him. That, she thought, could be a great help to him on television, now that Reith standards had gone. Over the second brandy, which he insisted on paying for as well as the first, she told him that she was very good friends with someone in the programme-planning catacombs of the BBC. Would Miles like her to sound him? She was in the strong position of having seen her protégé in operation in discouraging circumstances.

"You really were awfully good," she said. "So spontaneous. So many of our funny men give the impression that they buy their jokes in tins."

"Of course there is nothing in the world I would like better. I haven't really had time to take it in. A few hours ago all this would have sounded like an invitation to fly to the moon."

"The thing is, if I were to pull that particular string, it wouldn't do for you then to say you had had second thoughts. Be absolutely sure that it is what you really want to do. Are you married?"

"I am, as a matter of fact."

"Why do you say 'as a matter of fact'? I knew you were. When we came in and you rushed away so quickly, I wondered if you had gone to the loo or to ring your wife up. When you came back I judged by your expression that it was your wife. Any kids?"

"No, unfortunately."

"Neither have I. On the whole, I prefer it that way."

"Are *you* married?"

"I was once, and as good as another time. I decided long since

39

that a man in the house is more trouble than he is worth. Does your wife have a job?"

"Part time, she works in the afternoon for a doctor."

"How do you suppose she will like the idea of your changing careers at this stage of the game?"

"So long as I had a serious offer I think she would be pleased for my sake. I would have to do a lot of commuting, I suppose. I don't know how she would take that. But Jean is a good sport."

"How long have you been married?"

"Gosh. I shall have to do sums. Over twenty years."

Then Rowena wondered if he had been truthful about his age, and he felt uneasy suddenly and glanced at his watch and said "My God, I must be on my way. I'll call for you at nine fifteen, if that's not too early."

"It will suit me splendidly. I have a mid-day plane to catch."

She insisted on coming out to see him off. When it came to the moment of parting he, who was addicted to kissing women, felt suddenly shy. She was smiling up at him in a quizzical fashion. His inclination was to kiss her hand, and it might have saved him a lot of trouble in the future if he had done so, but he had already lied to her and that put her in a special category; and he was auto-intoxicated as well as having drunk a mixture of wines and spirits. He felt in love with the world, and she, at that moment, represented his Fairy Godmother—a handsome, smiling, encouraging Fairy Godmother. He kissed her full on the lips, and she kissed him in return. As he moved away he saw two people whom he recognized smiling at him through the windscreen of their car. Dublin was the wrong size for romantic gestures.

The lights were out at home. The curtains of the bedroom window were not fully drawn and he could see the vague outline of Jean's face on the pillow. Her mouth, he saw when he bent over her, was slightly open. She looked absurdly young and vulnerable. She woke up suddenly, stared hard at Miles, then dug her head resentfully into the pillow.

"I'm terribly sorry," he said, seeing a bottle of champagne and two glasses on her table. He sat on the bed. "Don't be cross, darling. I want so terribly to talk to you."

"It will keep until the morning."

"It's important. I've got to tell you."

"Then why didn't you come home? I thought something bad

40

had happened to you. I rang up the television centre and whoever I was talking to said that you left immediately after the show. That was at eleven o'clock. What time is it now?"

"My watch has stopped. Will you be patient and let me tell you what actually happened—the whole story?"

"How do I know that it isn't a whole pack of lies?"

"If you are going to go on like that . . ."

"You have lied yourself out of trouble ever since I've known you."

"I don't know what has got into you. I came home at the first opportunity."

"Why did you fob me off with all that nonsense about having to stay to supper and being so much afraid of giving offence? There was no supper. There never is on these occasions. You went out somewhere and you didn't have the decency to tell me. Who were you with?"

"That's what I want to tell you now. I couldn't talk about it on the telephone with people listening to every word I said. This woman—"

"Ah."

"There's no use in my trying to explain if you go on like that. This woman—"

"Go on. I'm listening."

"She came up to me after the show and said she wanted to talk to me about my prospects of getting into television in England. She is very close—that's how she put it—to some high-up in the BBC."

"She uses nice scent."

"Oh God. Can't you see how crucial it is to make the right decision. This woman happened to be in Dublin advising on some new boutique. She was invited to come out to Montrose to watch the show. At least, that's what she said, but I got the impression that part of her reason for coming to Dublin was to do some talent-spotting. She was very cool and businesslike about the whole affair. She thinks I have what it takes, but she was emphatic that I wasn't to waste anyone's time talking about the possibility if I hadn't made up my mind to accept an offer if one was made to me. Naturally she doesn't want to fix up an appointment for me with some of the BBC top brass and then be told I had chickened out. She put me through the third degree examination when I said I liked the idea, but she quite understood that I could do nothing until I had talked to you about it, and of course I would have to know what the prospects were before I threw up my job and pension. Darling, I know it's an awful lot to take in at this time of night, but can't you see why I am longing to hear what you think about the idea?"

"I think you ought to see what the proposition is before you even discuss it. You are not in your first youth, and there must be thousands of people over there trying to get into television. You are not wanted nowadays if you're not young."

"You are very encouraging, I must say."

"You didn't ask me for encouragement. I told you how good you were this evening—I mean yesterday evening—but while I was watching the show I was praying that the applause wouldn't go to your head. Who is this woman anyhow? She might have been taking you for a ride. I bet you invited her to come to the shop tomorrow and get a cut off the marked price on anything she fancied."

"If you are in this mood, there's no point in discussing the problem with you."

"You haven't answered my question."

"What question?"

"Did you ask your lady friend to come to Shannonwear to-morrow?"

"I did as a matter of fact. She asked me what I did, and when I told her it seemed only polite to make the gesture."

"There you are, you see."

"I don't see what you see. You haven't met her. She is a serious sort of person. Nothing flighty about her. I would have suggested bringing her here to meet you but at this time of night it didn't seem to make sense. And she is off tomorrow morning. She can't go too quickly from my point of view."

"What's her name?"

"Rowena Atkinson. Middle-aged, very English and down-to-earth. You will make it very difficult for all of us if you insist on regarding her as a *femme fatale*."

"Is she married?"

"I don't know. I suppose she is. I didn't ask her."

"Did she ask you if you were married?"

"It came up when we were discussing the job prospect. I said I'd have to talk it over with you."

"Well you know what I think. Of course you will be told by

42

everyone who wants to flatter you that you are as good as in Hollywood already. I shouldn't talk about it to anyone in the shop if I were you."

"I hadn't the least intention of doing so."

"Now, if you don't mind, I would like to try to go to sleep again for what's left of the night, and if you want to fascinate your lady tomorrow, I'd advise you to do likewise."

With that, Jean pulled the bed-clothes round her and hid her face in the pillow. Her husband shrugged his shoulders. Ever since he could remember it had always been the same; whatever was worth having was for someone else. Be ordinary; take no chances; above all, do nothing that attracts attention to yourself. Don't look, don't touch, don't taste, don't talk, don't listen, except to the voices telling you to toe the line. *Keep away from the women*—his father's advice came back to him now. Look at this evening: if he had been dealing with men there would have been none of this trouble. Having shattered his peace of mind Jean could now go to sleep. What age was Rowena, he wondered? Had he sown the seeds of more trouble for himself by describing her as serious and middle-aged? Jean was bound to meet her sooner or later. Why had he always to varnish the truth, behave as if there were no future, no presentation of accounts? "Middle-aged" was the most unthreatening description he could have thought of as well as being technically correct; it applied to most of the great lovers of the cinema, but no one would use the word to describe them.

Jean was, notionally at least, asleep. There was nothing for him to do but go to bed himself. He made his undressing into a tragic ritual, it needed only a passing beggar to whom he could have given his clothes away. He should have been rejoicing; it was most unfortunate and unfair. He couldn't categorize his grievance against Jean: it would almost seem that it was her being there at all, having to be coped with. Rowena, for all her friendliness, had expressed no wish at all to meet his wife, and made him feel that it was provincial to have such an encumbrance. Or was he imagining this? He was always writing other people's scripts for them. He arranged himself with elaborate care in the bed so that no part of him should touch his wife; as she had been tossing about in her efforts to go to sleep this meant lying along the very edge with his head at a most uncomfortable angle to the pillow. There he lay, and would lie in acute discomfort staring at the ceiling until morning, like a knight carved on a tomb.

"Success means nothing to me if I can't share it with you."

He brought that out at last, as he reached for her hand. Jean had been hurt, disappointed and angry, but not surprised. This was Miles being Miles. At social gatherings she was accustomed to being made feel like a police guard when Miles made his way across the room as if it were a minefield. He would ask her eventually to rescue him from his own folly and the complications of his conflicting lies. He liked to put all the responsibility on to his genes; he saw all this undignified and unnecessary trouble he got into as his heritage from the marriage between pleasure and duty.

It was as though the arranger of these matters, having provided Father Kevin, Rev. Mother Dympna and Sister Teresa for the Church, left Miles's father to his own devices in the matter of a fourth child. Miles was his father's son. Men of their nature, however much their eyes wander, often marry women who would have had a successful career in the police. An instinct of self-preservation is working for them.

Jean, looking into the dark, was not thinking unkindly about her husband; she was sad because she did not have what he needed in a wife. She was incapable of riding with a tight rein. She had held back criticism at the beginning and learned to watch the inevitable catastrophes happen and not say a word. When he found this out he reproached her, but she had heard him complain so much about houses run by women, she had kept her mouth shut in the face of folly and hoped he would learn at last. She looked forward to old age and a safe harbour.

In this television crisis she saw their greatest problem to date: if she held out against it, he would nurse resentment; he was coming to the age when men start to measure their achievement and can go sour. If she encouraged him to throw up his job it might be the end of their marriage; she would find herself part of the dull world from which he was escaping. She mightn't be able to keep up with him. If she encouraged him and he came to nothing, he would blame her. "Don't you know me? Why didn't you stop me? Couldn't you see that woman went to my head?"

She would like to meet this woman to see into whose hands he had fallen. That inspired "middle-aged" had put her off the track. She saw someone with a spreading figure in tweeds, the sort of

44

decent woman associated with talks on gardening or pet care, horsey women, women in sou'-westers, women with mud on their wellingtons, women whistling for dogs—every sort of woman except the type for which her husband inevitably fell. If Rowena were to answer to that description Jean was going to be generous and remind herself constantly that this was her good angel too. Miles would, of course, play up to her. He would play up to a bicycle or a clothes basket if anything was to be gained from it. Not from fraudulence, but because he saw himself pitted in life against men who used offensive weapons. He could only beguile.

Jean decided to watch and pray, on no account to become a virago, and having thus decided returned the gentle pressure of his hand. That was what his anxious soul required, and he acknowledged it at once in the only way he knew when words failed him. It was not what she wanted at the moment, but it was what invariably gave him a good opinion of himself. When he was finished they would fall asleep having sewn up the tattered fringes of the day.

They slept late. Usually Jean leapt out of bed; this morning she was unusually luxurious as if she was continuing where they left off the night before. This was more than he could have hoped for, and he would have been well content to arrive late in the office, in an uxorious glow, if he hadn't remembered that he was calling for his new friend at a quarter past nine and it was now after half past eight.

As he held Jean's face against his breast he tried to remember what had been said last night about this morning call. Jean had teased him, but had he admitted that he had made an appointment or had he dodged the question (which amounted to the same thing)? Should he invite Jean to come along—she was always welcome at the shop—and let the English woman lump it? Start off as he intended to go on, nip in the bud any idea that a romance was developing? He would cut such an undashing figure. She might well be influenced by the small-town atmosphere and decide he would be out of his depth in London. A devil seemed to be prompting Jean; apart from behaving as if she was rehearsing for the part of the Queen of Sheba, literally holding him when he tried to get up, she suggested that they should meet for lunch. There was nothing unusual about this, but why today? She said she wanted to cash a cheque. He had plenty of money in his wallet. She was welcome to whatever she wanted. No. She had various little matters to attend to; she had better come into town. She would drop in and see him when she was passing Shannonwear. Having sown these depth charges without any reference to the cause of it all, she allowed him to get up. Breakfast was torture, and his relief when he escaped was short-lived.

"Rush hour," he said aloud and bitterly as he joined the caterpillar crawl of office-going cars. He would be late for his appointment. Miles fussed. He was very conscientious in small matters, and disliked being late because it meant beginning on a note of apology. A wrong curtain raiser.

Rowena was waiting for him, her overnight bag beside her. Her suit would be a challenge to Shannonwear. A lot of money had been spent with discretion on her appearance. She would upstage Jean in every situation. The thought saddened him. Keeping them apart at this stage had been a wise decision after all. He had nothing to reproach himself with. He felt less protective of Jean since last night. She was not without resources. With Jean in her present mood he was frankly not up to dealing with both women. It was not the moment to bring them together. For the moment none of this mattered. He was the only member of the Shannonwear executive with anything approaching what he had been told sometimes, late in the evening, was star quality. This morning he was making his entrance having been watched by most of the staff in his triumphant hour. There was a flutter when he came in, and he was not unaware that Rowena's sophisticated appearance was dangerously appropriate in the circumstances.

"You gave that Rory a proper dig. I was delighted." That was a sample of the remarks that were thrown like confetti on his progress with Rowena across the shop.

To his "Is Catherine in?" three voices answered "She is, Miles" in chorus. Catherine, he explained to Rowena, when at last they were alone in his office, was the Home Secretary. He was in charge of Foreign Affairs. "I look after sales; she has to liaise between different branches of our organization. I think at this stage I should hand you over to her. I can join you for coffee when the serious business is over."

He was trying to appear relaxed. Someone told him he had a look of Rex Harrison, and ever since the success of *My Fair Lady* he had practised some of that actor's mannerisms, including a stylish manner of handling cigarettes. He offered Rowena one although she had told him already that she had given them up. It was only one symptom of his unease. He was worrying about Jean. He had already inquired if Mrs O'Malley had telephoned and been told she hadn't. He was secretly afraid that she might look in at any moment. In the ordinary course the least intrusive of wives—Jean was on excellent terms with the staff—at the moment she was unpredictable, and had plainly refused to file Rowena in her mind under the heading of business.

"I'll ring Catherine now. She will want to give you a proper look at our best things, and we mustn't miss your plane. The mid-morning traffic is terrible."

"This may help to explain me." Rowena handed Miles a business card.

"I'm in partnership with Sandro. He's an Italian. We are interior decorators, and recently we have been trying our hands at stage design and costumes. I put my home address and telephone number at the back. Excuse the biro, but I couldn't find my invisible ink." That was a dig at him. This woman saw him as a hen-pecked husband. He couldn't refuse to treat it as a joke without looking a fool. That was the knack this sort of female had. She would eat Jean up for her breakfast, he decided, and felt quite sorry for his wife at the thought of the encounter. In Catherine (with whom he had never had sentimental relations) Rowena would meet a battle-scarred new woman. They might get on very well.

They did, and when Miles joined them for coffee Rowena had acquired an outfit ("for practically nothing", she assured Miles later). Catherine wanted only to talk about the television sensation of the previous evening.

"I might have missed you if Jean hadn't rung up to tell me you were going to be in the programme. I rang up the moment it was over to talk to her about it but there was a queue the length of today and tomorrow waiting to congratulate her on her husband's performance. I rang a few times but the line was always engaged. I'd say you would be asked again, but you may have done too well for your own good. Michael O'Reilly must have been seeing himself out of a job by the end of the evening, and as for that O'Hagen horror—if looks could kill . . . I'd like to hear what Jean thought of it. Your stock with the young ladies downstairs has gone through the roof. But I daresay they told you that themselves already."

The idea of Catherine talking to Jean didn't appeal to Miles. What a noisy little nest he lived in. But his chief concern was to get Rowena away before Jean looked in. He was dreading the mischief Catherine might do from sheer good nature.

"I'm worried about your plane," he said to Rowena, taking care not to use her christian name. She clearly was not, but her extraction was accomplished at last. She was in high spirits on the journey to the airport, quizzing him about Catherine, praising Dublin, rhapsodizing over her tweed suit bargain. Only when they were at the last barrier in the airport did she become suddenly serious.

"You are quite sure you want me to go on with this?"

"Never was surer of anything. God bless you."

"I'll shoot you if you change your mind, remember."

"My mind is made up."

"Very well. I'll go into action first thing. I have your office number."

"I shall be longing to hear your news."

"You have my number?"

"I have your number."

He kissed her then, a swift kiss (observed, as it happened, by his dentist) and Rowena was through the barrier.

The telephone interrupted Miles's retrospection. He realized that it had been ringing for some time when he picked it up and heard a familiar meek voice. "Russell this end."

The idea of his friend in any other context than the betting office and the snug corner took Miles a moment to adjust to. He had to drag himself from a long distance to say "Miles O'Malley speaking." He couldn't have sworn to that.

"I hope this is not an inconvenient moment to call you."

"By no means. I didn't recognize the voice at first. You sound different on the telephone. I know I do myself."

"I've been checking up on those names." (What was the man talking about?)

"Oh yes."

"They are all mixed up in some way or other with importing business, mostly tea and sugar, tobacco also."

"That's what Alma-Tadema is all about, then."

"No. I looked him up in my encyclopaedia. (I don't know where I should be without it.) He was a very well-known

Victorian painter, Greek gods and that sort of thing. He was knighted. Sir Lawrence Alma-Tadema was his full name."

"Yes, of course. Well, what do you make of it all?"

"Rich people without a social background who want to create one for themselves. They like the idea of having a celebrity like yourself as their guest at their dinner. Something to talk to their hairdresser about. What has occurred to me since is that there was no reference to a fee in that letter you showed me. I think the sort of person you seem to be dealing with would think all the more of you if you were to put a high price on your services."

Miles didn't like to admit that he had already talked to Miss Dubonnet. "I am very grateful to you. It was more than kind to go to such trouble. I'll sleep on what you have told me and we can have another word tomorrow."

Having reported his findings, Russell became suddenly shy, and the disconnecting of himself seemed to call for an heroic effort.

It would be really ungrateful not to include him in the invitation list. He probably never got about in the ordinary course of events. But that would involve inviting Mrs Russell. That made Miles hesitate. His friend was unusually reticent about his wife and his home. Miles wasn't curious about them, never really thinking about his friend outside the frame in which they met. This afternoon's research put Russell in a new light—the bank official. Why had he retired? It was remarkable how one could see so much of anyone and know really nothing about them at all. He had no doubt that his friend was perfectly right, if these were rich people using him to inject life into one of their expensive entertainments they jolly well ought to pay for the treatment. Perhaps that was meant to go without saying, and came after the event in a magnificent cheque or a piece of rare ivory or Georgian silver, or even a pencil sketch by this artist with the silly name, a lubricious drawing, perhaps, of a lady with some title like "Leda and the Swan" to license it for hanging in the drawing room. Russell's experience wouldn't have prepared him for such subtleties. Miles was sure his own instinct had been correct. If he had mentioned money to Miss Dubonnet their relationship might have taken on a business matter-of-factness. Besides, if he got his way and could get the media involved, it was exactly the sort of publicity he needed at the moment. A devious plan occurred to him. Why not

49

give the name of one of the leading gossip column characters to Miss Dubonnet for the invitation list, then write to him saying that the affair was very private and he, Miles, would be grateful to the good fellow if he would be mindful of the susceptibilities of his hosts and be sure not to let a word get out? But he couldn't think of a working journalist who wouldn't see through that strategy.

What a kind chap this Russell was—to have gone to so much trouble (and how efficiently). How funny not even to know his christian name. It began with a G. This modest, retired man of business, absolutely disinterested, proud of such a friendship, was exactly the confidant he needed. Russell would be flattered. It might take him a little time to get used to the idea that anyone famous who talked to him in such a lordly way could be in need of help. (Did he have his own troubles?) Miles was under the impression that there was something worrying to her husband about Mrs Russell. Perhaps he had made an unfortunate match. But Miles had never been a one to linger long over possibilities of misfortune in other lives. He found his thoughts turning to the pictures of Alma-Tadema. Greek gods, goddesses too, presumably. This led his wandering fancy to Miss Dubonnet, Miss Dubonnet as Venus, Miss Dubonnet being chased by a satyr. Miles was in a rather goat-footed state of mind. Perhaps he needed the restraining influence of a cautious friend more than he knew. Tomorrow he would talk in absolute confidence to him and, of course, ask him straight out would he like to come to the dinner and take Mrs Russell along. He could rely on the decent man's good sense to refuse for his lady if she were a social liability.

Miles felt deep relief after having come to this decision. He could put his domestic troubles out of his mind and concentrate on pleasanter topics. He had had a brainwave about Jerry's funeral: take a leaf out of Barney's book and invite Terry Wogan, Frank Delaney, Eamonn Andrews and Henry Kelly to act as pall-bearers, say it was at the widow's earnest request. There was an even money chance some, if not all of them, would not have an excuse ready. With that added attraction he could act as his own press agent, ring up all the papers, and give them full details. If the prospect looked more impressive than the resulting reality, that was someone else's problem. He would ring Mrs Dunne later on and enquire for her husband, then keep in touch thereafter, and be prepared. He had the *Oxford Book of Quotations* at hand. He owed a great deal to that compilation. There was sure to be something in it that would lend a touch of old world culture to his address—how long should he go on for? If he could be sure of a fine day it would be worth trying a short sermon length, but he had dismal recollections of funerals where even the priest's few necessary prayers at the grave—and he would have to allow for these at Jerry's funeral—were as hard to endure in a cold wind as a whipping. The best compromise was to send the full-length oration to the press beforehand and decide on the ground how much of it to give. He would put a red line under the most telling paragraphs.

Should he put that idea about the pall-bearers up to Maureen Dunne now? It would ease his mind to know that he really had her authority to invite that famous four to carry the coffin. In her present state of mind, poor woman, she might turn the whole idea down or raise an objection to one or more of them (Jerry had fought with everyone in his time). There was nothing to be lost by trying. He was taken aback when he rang up Maureen Dunne, sounding suitably solemn, and was met by a rather combative response. "The doctor was very pleased with Jerry," she said, as if challenging Miles to produce any diagnosis to the contrary. Miles struck a lighter note at once. That sepulchral voice had been a mistake. "Tell Jerry not to be giving us these frights. Barney spoilt my day with his gloomy report. I'll ask him to get his facts right in future."

"I may have been upset at the time I was talking to Barney. Are you listening to me? Don't say a word to him. At least he has a heart."

Was that a dig at himself? What was Barney up to? Miles spent the rest of the evening trying to get him on the telephone and ran him to earth well past midnight, destroying any chance of future friendship with Mrs Barney in the process.

"Maureen Dunne gave me the impression that I was inventing Jerry's illness. What possessed you to tell me that he was as good as gone?"

"I wanted to make sure that if Jerry were to kick the bucket when I was away someone would help the widow. I thought of you because everyone else is so busy it didn't seem fair to put it on to them."

Barney did not intend to be offensive; he was only defending himself. Miles had put on a reading-the-riot-act voice. It was gall to have to listen to that explanation, but it would do nothing to salve his wounded vanity to say that things were looking up; it would be an admission they had been down.

"You do think Jerry is really ill, then?"

"The poor bugger has terminal cancer. It is only a question of time. If I were you I wouldn't be bothering Maureen at this stage of the game. She knows about the arrangements, and as you have never been a special friend of Jerry's she might put a wrong construction on your anxiety to be kept in the picture."

"I had this idea of Terry Wogan and a few others of that ilk as pall-bearers, but I didn't want to send out the invitations without having first sounded out the ground."

"You didn't say anything like that to his wife in your excitement, I hope."

"I don't know what precisely you mean by that last remark."

"You sound as if you can't get poor Jerry into his coffin fast enough. I mean to say—ringing a man up at this time of night to talk about funerals . . ."

Miles could hear a voice giving instructions in the background. "Tell him to get to Hell", he distinctly heard it say.

"I'm sorry for waking you up, but I was terribly upset by Maureen's hostile attitude."

Barney, probably on a signal from the neighbouring pillow, put down the receiver. It took Miles a long time to go to sleep after that. In his lowest moments he wouldn't have conceived the idea of himself in a position to be snubbed by Barney Roche. He had better watch his step henceforth or he might lose all the ground he had been making up lately.

Willie brought no comfort with breakfast. It always required a certain amount of pressure to get him to leave the room when he had put down the tray, but today there was a look in his eyes which Miles recognized. It meant that Willie found himself in a position of divided loyalties between Miles and the Doyles. The Doyles had taken him on, and he owed his livelihood to them. He would find it almost impossible to get another job. Miles could do nothing for him. He was simply there, a great man; hero-worship was his due. The tradition of the tribe came into it. Miles was the natural chieftain. Willie nourished no hope of ever impressing the Doyles. They knew his worth exactly, but he longed for Miles's good opinion. He would stop at nothing to impress him.

"One of those fellows in the yard has started sending me on

messages," he said. Miles recognized the whine and had learnt to ignore it, but he paid more attention when Willie said, "He has something to do with the people who are renting the sheds. Mr Doyle has allowed one of them to fix himself a bed in one of the lofts."

"Well Doyle damn well shouldn't have let anyone into the yard without first asking me about it."

"Don't let on it was me who was after telling you, sure you won't?"

"I'm going to take a proper look at the whole of this set-up one of these days. I'm too busy at the moment. I've been asked to make some important speeches in the near future. I can't do myself justice if I hear about nothing from dawn to dusk except that bloody yard."

"He was offering the same fellow the use of the car."

"The car? What car? You don't mean the BMW?"

"What other car is there in the place?"

"Willie, are you quite certain about this? You know the way you let your imagination run away with you sometimes."

"I was never more certain of anything. Your man gave me a few parcels and asked me to deliver them and give me all particulars and said I was to ask for the person written on the parcel in each case and make delivery only to them. When Mr Doyle came along he said 'I have been asking Willie here to do a couple of important messages for me. Can you spare him?' Mr Doyle then said, 'Why not take a lend of the BMW? It's standing there in the garage with nothing to do. I don't seem to get time even on a Sunday to give the missus a run in it.'

"'I don't think the car is a good idea,' says your man. 'It's a bit conspicuous. Thanks all the same for the offer. Besides you are doing Willie out of a few quid. He will be reporting you to his union if you don't mind yourself.'"

Miles was really angry now. It was a luxury to have someone on whom to vent it.

"Well that is the damnedest cheek. You know that car belongs to me and to nobody else. I paid a king's ransom for it at the time on Doyle's advice. The idea was that he would act as driver, and I'd let him have the use of the car the odd time, when he wanted to give his missus a run or impress some of his shady friends."

"Didn't you tell me that yourself the night he wouldn't drive you somewhere you wanted to go."

"I get a cab nowadays if I want to go anywhere. I am quite used to that, but I'm damned if I am going to sit here and say nothing when the BMW is being used as a staff car for the IRA."

Willie, having made enough trouble to make his visit memorable, retreated in high spirits. When he had gone Miles took only a cursory glance at the *Sporting Life*. He couldn't give his mind to racing today. How much should he tell Russell? It was humiliating after the show he put on to have to admit that his wife had left him in this position. He had at least let her die in the belief that he was comfortably off whatever happened in the future. It was his last successful attempt to hoodwink her. He hadn't succeeded in persuading her that she was not going to die. She was far better prepared to face the truth about that than he was. What, he asked himself, was going to happen to him? He had let himself go gradually to seed lately, but that, very largely, was due to her not being there. He had put himself completely into her hands; it was one way of assuaging his guilt over Jean. By becoming a man under authority he was not entirely responsible for his actions. Jean would recognize the technique. In her time it was his father's genes that were put forward as an excuse when he let her down.

It was a relief that Rowena died before he had had to tell her that he had had to borrow all the money he put into the hotel. She had been given only a wild approximation. He hadn't told her how much he had given Jean to salve his conscience. (He left Rowena under the impression that Jean was quite well-to-do in her own right.) Nor had he mentioned an investment in a gold mine in Australia that had been a fraud from the start, or how much he lost at cards.

But she would have seen him through it all. She was very tough. How tough he learned at an early stage. There was a call for him as soon as he arrived in the office on the day after she went back to London.

"It's too marvellous. I told Chris about you and he said the news came at a wonderful time for him because there is a mobile quiz programme which goes to places where there are concentrations of various ethnic groups (including the Irish). Whoever was going to present it went sick and won't be well enough in time to do the amount of travelling the programme demands. Chris says that if you are as good as I say you are he will give you a chance. The question is, how soon can you come over? Chris can't wait. Could you manage this evening and be available tomorrow when he is free and there is a studio available?"

He could, of course he could. Had he anywhere to stay? When he went to London on business he always stayed at—

"I have a spare room. You are more than welcome to that."

"I mustn't be a nuisance. You've done so much for me already."

"The room is there for you. I think you are silly not to take it."

"Well, that would be wonderful."

"You have the address. I'll expect you this evening when I see you."

Keep away from the women. It was a pity that now when he was hugging himself, pinching himself, wanting to sing, that he should have his ecstasy spoilt at the outset by this eternal nuisance of women. A toughie would tell Jean where he was staying and let her like it or lump it; the good husband would have gently but firmly refused the invitation; he, as much ashamed of appearing the country cousin to one woman as he was to arouse the never-sleeping suspicions of the other, had worked himself into a position that made lying to Jean inevitable. Women apart, Miles was more candid than most people; it was part of his charm. The trouble was that he had long ceased, except at rare moments, to bother to exercise his charm for Jean's benefit; so that when it came to a choice the newcomer who could be impressed was preferred.

When he rang up with the news, Jean was really as nice as he could have asked. What could she do to help? She knew that his secretary looked after reservations, but she could be useful in other ways—packing clothes, fetching them from the cleaners, ironing shirts. He felt warm towards her, on her side really. For all her kindness, Rowena was exacting a price. Why had she to come up with that offer of a room? She knew perfectly well what sort of terms he was on with his wife and she would not be peculiar if she looked askance at the idea of her husband spending the night in the flat of some woman she had never seen. It was something he had to settle without consulting Jean. He hoped the night would be innocent; if it rested with him it would. But in his code it was unchivalrous to resist any approach by the lady. He prided himself on his romantic attitude towards the opposite sex. The idea of humiliating a woman—and she was in a vulnerable position if she took the initiative—was repugnant to him. That he

55

had let women down quite often was a fact of which he was innocently unaware and would have been abashed had anyone suggested the possibility. He had been wildly complimentary to Rowena at supper and made her laugh; for that she said she would forgive him anything. But he made no move, kept his hands to himself, and was safe and alone in his room when Rowena knocked and said, "I wanted to say 'good night'."

Her mind was made up; if he made the first overtures it was only as if he were taking his partner for a dance. She made love efficiently, as she did everything, and with the concentration of one who has read the instructions on the label. There was nothing of abandon about the exercise, and her concentration did not suggest any great expectation of roses and raptures. The coupling was not so much clinical as compartmentalized and hardly completed before she had cut herself off and was eager to return to earth.

"You *are* the funniest man," she said when Miles broke into exaggerated compliments. She seemed well satisfied, a woman who had got no less nor more than she expected. Miles felt lonely afterwards. So far from the act bringing them closer it seemed to illustrate a radical difference between them. The passion for peace which led him into lies was outside her comprehension. She gave him a warm, final kiss and announced her departure for her own bed, there being too much of a squash in this one. She was friendly and satisfied and without a suspicion that he had not got what he wanted. If pressed, she would have described exactly what they had done and urged him to have some sense of proportion. "Did you expect me to sing?"

Jean had fallen in love with him all over again, she assured him; and for all Rowena's clinical approach to their rites, she gave no indication of slackening in her punctual performance of them. Miles was looking tired—both his women noticed it and urged him to rest more. As he was absent from Jean all the week he could not plead a retreat from uxoriousness to her, and on the other side of the channel Rowena confined their embracement to arrivals and departures. It was extraordinary how she could get her way in this as in everything. If only he was allowed to spread the load, but she always anticipated his objections. Neither woman ever referred to the other.

He had arrears of leave due to him, which he was also exhausting. The time had arrived when he must show his hand at the office. He had postponed it for as long as possible knowing that there was someone available and anxious to succeed him. To Miles's delight an arrangement was come to whereby he would gradually withdraw, letting his successor slip by degrees into his position. By then, his boss informed him, "We expect to see your name up in lights."

Everyone was conspiring to help him—he was entitled to a small pension—and he should have been the happiest man alive. His first television programme was a rather earnest exercise, but it proved that Miles had the light touch even under difficulties. There were professionals working on scripts for him, but that was where he ran into difficulties; he had never been much good at acting. Spontaneity was of his essence. He must be allowed to improvise. He had looked harassed when he tried to repeat lines written for him by other people. Residence raised questions—the first idea was that the O'Malleys should keep their Dublin home and Miles commute. He had not yet told Jean that the room Rowena found him was in her own apartment. She was out all day, and he made a point of ringing Jean up every morning and evening. Whatever Jean's suspicions were, she was keeping them to herself. She never asked him questions. He needed no encouragement to talk about his experiences. They were very happy, but with a shadow on their happiness. The situation was tolerable only for so long as Jean was satisfied to keep away from London. One of her friends had asked her how the present arrangement could work if Miles became so much in demand that commuting by air became impracticable. She mentioned this to him, and noticed the hunted look she knew so well return to his forehead. ("Let's deal with that when the time arrives.")

Jean mentioned a step-aunt, well-placed in the Civil Service, a career woman, unmarried—she had let it be known that she would like the interesting pair to share her house in Hammersmith. "You'd be mad not to jump at the offer", Jean was advised. Miles looked more hunted than ever.

"I hate that awful dead men's shoes mentality."

"No one ever suggested she would leave us the house. Anyhow, Aunt Lily is only what you would call 'middle-aged'."

Jean looked at him so blandly that Miles accepted the possibility that no barb was concealed in that remark. With what he had seen of London with Rowena, a future house-sharing with Jean's step-aunt was too grey even to contemplate.

"I've more than I can cope with on my plate. Let's leave this residence question alone for the moment. We are doing very well as we are."

"It's all very well for you."

"The week-ends are worth waiting for. We have found the way to keep marriage on the boil. We ought to patent it."

"I don't think 'boil' is the word I would have used."

Miles was having recourse to inexplicable illnesses when he was at home for week-ends: tiredness won him respites. He was acutely conscious of the politics at work in the triangle. Jean was able to sustain the fiction that Miles led a chaste life in London; Rowena could not indulge in a similar fantasy. They were both playing for time. When Miles decided that he could not commute any longer, then he must either leave Jean or take her to London. The present arrangement suited both women so long as neither decided to force Miles to show his hand. Each judged the situation by the light of observation. Neither paid the least attention to anything Miles said on the subject. Each saw herself as fighting without an ally. With this difference, Rowena would have preferred a fight limited to the objective. Like boxers, out of the ring she would rather have been on friendly terms with Jean than otherwise. Jean wanted to hear that Rowena was dead.

The moment of truth was unavoidable when Miles made the first of his own programmes, a day-trip to Brighton. He refused the assistance of script-writers and attempted an impromptu hour, commenting on the scene, talking to anyone who looked as if he might be able to contribute to the fun. There was a memorable exchange with a retired prison warder in a bar. He was in favour of repatriating all the Irish who had been in England for less than two generations as a first step towards solving the Irish problem.

"What about me?"

"You'd be the first to go if I had anything to do with it. You've wrecked my lunch."

Students of Miles's work were to say that he was never quite so effective and spontaneous as in that first film. Someone in the Irish Embassy in London got wind of it, and an invitation was waiting for Mr and Mrs O'Malley, on one of Miles's return trips, to an informal reception to celebrate the occasion. Jean made no reference to the envelope, and Miles, who was delighted at the compliment, held his peace until he had had time to think the matter over. What had made him blush with gratification at first became an acute embarrassment. If he mentioned the invitation to Jean she would most certainly buy a new dress and come to London for the party. Rowena would expect him to ask for an invitation for her. He couldn't trust himself to handle the situation. To substitute Rowena for Jean was out of the question. News would get back. He began to curse the desirable invitation, and thought of his father's neglected injunction.

He could not make up his mind what to do. It added to his troubles that he lived on the principle that he interpreted both his women's attitudes towards him and each other correctly. Everything between the trio was tacit and based on assumptions. This invitation could be the occasion for a showing of cards after months of playing them close to the chest. Anything might happen. As he was guest of honour an early reply to the Embassy was essential, but two days passed and he hadn't mentioned the invitation to anyone, much less answered it.

Acceptance for himself, a refusal for Jean and not a word on the subject to Rowena was the formula on which he had settled when Rowena announced her intention of giving a supper that evening in his honour. Which would he prefer—if she were to invite a few couples to a restaurant or have it in her apartment? She rather prided herself on her cooking. He expressed delight and asked for a day to decide between the delicious possibilities. He was desperate, entertaining and rejecting simultaneously the wildest excuses, such as a personal invitation to a bachelor supper with the Ambassador that it would be highly impolitic to refuse. Rowena wouldn't believe in that for a moment. It was what Rowena was soon to recognize as an archetypal Miles situation. His first object was not to annoy anyone, and if this could only be accomplished by deceiving some of them, that could be put down to the smallness of the world. He would have liked to take Rowena into his confidence, but he had already discovered in the course of long talks with her that she had no patience with his unsleeping diplomacy. People were sturdier than he seemed to think, she told him, and less concerned with what he did than he imagined. The Irish Ambassador was unlikely to throw a fit because Miles (with whom he had only a nodding acquaintance) had a girlfriend in London. She would brush aside his difficulties, and he couldn't hope to explain some of them. One was that whatever he decided to do he had no way of ensuring that Jean in

Dublin might not hear about the party. It was a feather in Miles's cap, and her absence would be noticed by anyone at the reception who came from Dublin.

His final plan kept him right with the Ambassador, and with Jean, and with Rowena, if his luck was in and he carried it off with aplomb. He would tell Rowena he had voted for supper at home; she was such a superb cook. Then, at the last moment, he would say the Ambassador had asked urgently to see him if he would call in for a drink during the evening. A very significant gesture which it would be impolitic not to respond to. He would tell the same story to Jean, and report next day that he was amazed to discover that an entertainment had been organized in his honour. Had he only known he would have tried to persuade her to come over for the evening. He would tell the Ambassador he had to leave early because of a recording. That could only impress. Situations like this and his efforts to cope with them won Miles a reputation for making false boasts, for being vain and swollen-headed, when in fact he only invented Arabian Night adventures to get himself out of domestic difficulties.

The morning of Miles's first appearance in his own programme on BBC television, the most important event in his life so far—he was in no doubt at all about that—the telephone rang beside Rowena's bed. She picked up the receiver, then put her hand over the mouthpiece and said, "Your wife". He took the receiver from her, trying to appear in charge of the situation.

"Jean—what a lovely surprise."

He looked round behind him at Rowena who was wearing the neutral expression generally adopted by people when listening to other people's conversations. It was expecting rather a lot, but he thought she should have got up and left the room. He couldn't very well say he would switch the call to another room. It raised a question. He was sweating a little.

"You will kill me, but I've been longing to see you before the rest of the world does, and only yesterday I met Maeve's brother who is working in the London Embassy. He said there was a party specially laid on for you and why wasn't I coming to it? I couldn't resist the temptation and I've booked myself in on a flight that gets me to Heathrow at two. Tell me where I should go. Don't be cross with me. I'm so excited."

"Well, that's a lovely surprise. How long do you think you will be staying? I'll book us a room at the Goya."

"I thought I might stay over and come back with you on Friday if that sounds all right to you?"

"Perfect. Go straight to the hotel. I'll get us a room now. If you arrive before me ask for the key of the room. This is a lovely surprise."

"You said that three times," was Rowena's first remark.

"Said what three times?"

"This is a lovely surprise."

"You shouldn't have been listening."

"What was I to do? Get out of my bed? I'm very accommodating as a rule. Ask any of my friends and they'll tell you, but that is asking rather much."

"I don't think so, but then we don't see eye to eye on some matters."

"I am being reproved, I see. It's not my fault if your wife has decided to come over and find out what her minstrel boy has been up to. Are you going to bring her along with you to dinner this evening?"

"You heard what she said. We have been invited to the Irish Embassy. Jean heard about it in Dublin. I can't very well turn that down."

"I can't believe that even the Irish would arrange a party at a moment's notice and send the invitation to Dublin. Were you holding out on me about it? You are an amazing man."

"As a matter of fact, I did know about it. What I had planned to do was to look in during the evening."

"And I was not going to be told. How were you going to manage that?"

"I would have told you, of course; but I didn't want to seem to be complicating the evening for you."

"That was very nice and thoughtful of you. Are you going to stick to your plan?"

"I don't think I can. Jean says the party is in my honour. If I give the impression I'm only looking in, it would be very ungracious, don't you think?"

"You'll look in on us, then, when the main festivities are over?"

"I don't think I can. Try to look at it from Jean's point of view."

"Why should I, dammit? I don't suppose you will be asking her to look at it from my point of view."

"Now you are being deliberately obtuse. She probably suspects that there is something going on between us, but she has been wonderfully tactful about it. She is only over here for inside three days. Do you think it would serve any useful purpose to bring on a crisis at the moment?"

"You conjure up a picture of a dog which has picked up something rather disgusting on the road. Jean knows exactly what brings us together. If you were to try to pretend that you never see me socially, she is not likely to believe you. As it is she must think it highly suspicious if you never mention my name. I'd be surprised if by this time Jean hadn't got your number, my lad."

"Don't 'my lad' me."

"I could say something much ruder if you would prefer it."

"I don't know why you are making life more difficult for me. It's difficult enough as it is. I am Jean's husband, after all. She has always been as straight as a die so far as I am concerned."

"Whenever you talk about her you become wonderfully old-fashioned. I don't think I have ever heard anyone say 'as straight as a die' before. It makes you sound like the hero of a John Buchan novel. Try to catch up. It's 1963. Has anyone told you that before? I am perfectly certain your wife, knowing you, is fairly sure we have had it off together, and if I'm kept in purdah while she's here she will be certain. Anyway, she has probably come over to get the lie of the land for herself. She can't be blamed if she doesn't rely entirely on her husband's reports. If you come along with her this evening and behave naturally she is much more likely to think her boy is as straight as a die than if you go on as if I belonged to an extinct species. For my part, I promise not to dance on the table or do anything to suggest I'm not a suitable playmate for her white knight."

"I don't think I could carry it off. I'd be watching every word I said. It's all too fresh."

"You must do what you want. If you don't look in, am I to tell our guests the reason?"

"Don't make it harder for me."

"I won't. Can we lunch together?"

"By all means. The Ritz? It isn't an ordinary day."

"I'd much rather see what it's like where you will be staying. That would give me a real turn on."

"The Goya is a boring place. I am only going there because we had an arrangement with them in my office."

"Shannonwear. That name must be full of nostalgia. I'll be there at a quarter to one. I expect you'll be on time."

It was the last remark that frightened Miles; he couldn't have said why. The whole plan was so exactly calculated to ruin his day.

Rowena dressed herself and went out. Miles walked about the flat biting his nails, and took his first whiskey at five minutes to eleven. It was all so unnecessary. If the show were live he would have had ample reason to worry, but it was on film, and he was perfectly satisfied with the result. So was everyone in the studio. "This kind of high-minded programme can be such a bind, but you managed to extract fun from it. I must see that you are on the guest list at my funeral." That was what the producer said to him afterwards over a glass of champagne.

Miles should have been looking forward to this evening. Who was it who said he woke up one morning to find himself famous? That was the way he should have been feeling if only he could have kept away from the women. Between them they were making sure that he wouldn't enjoy a minute of it. One spoilt him for the other. This couldn't go on. But if he were to take a decisive step now he might live to regret it. There was native caution as well as romance behind the uncertain course he was pursuing. So long as he made sure that Rowena was out of the hotel before half past two, there was nothing to fear. All the same, he would take lunch with the sword of whoever the fellow was hanging over him. Rowena was more than likely to bring up the party business again. It was bad luck certainly to have gone to all that trouble if he—the reason for it—stayed away. Was there any excuse he could give to Jean and leave the embassy party for about an hour? That would please Rowena. He couldn't bear to be on bad terms with her. In London, without her, he was lost. At his age it was hard to adapt. He felt old. He had never imagined that the day would come when he would have to take a second whiskey before lunch to steady his nerves. The only person he could have wanted to talk to now was his father. Had he ever been through such trouble as this? And when one wished well to the whole creation? The bitter irony of it. How could anyone square it with the existence of God? He hurriedly packed a suitcase (something Jean always did for him) and only succeeded in arriving at the Goya on the Brompton Road at five to one.

"I was beginning to wonder," Rowena said.

He sensed suppressed excitement, but the bickering at break-fast was left behind. She said something apologetic. All their talk was about the programme and Miles's plans. His bruised ego began to heal. He decided, at parting, to tell her that however he managed it she might count on his appearance at some stage of the evening. Jean might make things easy for him by asking about Rowena and when she was going to meet her. So much of the conflict was in Miles's mind that it was perfectly possible she would do the obvious thing. She had been hailed as a blessing and an interesting and attractive personality—it would have been odd if Jean didn't want to meet her. Perhaps there would be no trouble. Everything that was driving him nearly mad was the product of his guilty mind. How much he would have liked a man-to-man chat with his father.

At two o'clock Rowena got up and said she would like to see his room. He said he didn't have it yet. She told him he had had it since twelve o'clock. She could have taken the key. Why did she want to drag herself upstairs to see a hotel bedroom as predictably dull as the lunch they had just got through? "Indulge me," she said. "A woman's fancy. Don't keep on looking at your watch. There's heaps of time." He complied without grace. Her point won, she didn't seem to notice. In the brown bedroom she said "You are terrified of your wife. Own up."

"I'm nothing of the kind. I think a lot of her. There's no harm in that!"

"You are afraid of her."

"I am not."

"Then prove it. Come to bed with me. I dare you to."

"We haven't time."

"She won't be here for more than an hour, unless she comes by helicopter."

"The bed will be in a shambles."

"Let her find you in it, taking forty winks. Very sensible when you think of the day you have before you. Afraid?"

"I'm not afraid."

"Come on then."

It was exciting. Rowena had never been like this before. If it went on, she would certainly kill him. He was amazed when he gave a furtive glance at his watch to see it was a quarter to three.

"Do you know what the time is?"

"Are you still going on about the time? What does time matter? Haven't we proved we are outside time?"

"Jean might come in at any minute."

"So far as I am concerned, she is very welcome."

"We have just had a marvellous experience. Why spoil it?"

"I'm not spoiling it, delicious man. I wish it could go on for ever."

"Please, Rowena. Rowena, please, please."

"Oh, very well. I don't want my hero to get into trouble. You stay where you are. I'll use the bathroom, if I may. I won't be a second."

She picked her clothes up from off the floor where they were lying about and left him on what was now a bed of nails. As if intent on torturing him the bell of the Brompton Oratory tolled out three o'clock with such excruciating slowness that he dug his nails (what was left of them) into his palms. He could stand the strain no longer. He must get down to the hall and meet Jean there.

He was about to pull on his trousers when Rowena came out of the bathroom. Smiling mysteriously, she put her finger to her lips. He said nothing for fear she might start to talk. When the door closed behind her he fell back on the bed breathing heavily. He was not in training for the Byronic life. It seemed as if there was no time between Rowena's going and the sound of Jean's gentle knock and Jean standing there looking shyer than he had ever seen her before and dressed to kill. She had always been more sensible than smart in her choice of clothes. The suit she was wearing looked hideously expensive. Her hair, her face—everything about her that was on view had had more attention lavished on it than ever before in her existence. They looked at each other. She so dressed up, he with nothing on, but with a sheet round his plumping waist. There was something utterly vulnerable about her whole appearance. He felt tears coming. They did not belong in this play.

"I didn't expect to find you in bed."

"I came in at lunchtime and it looked so comfortable as well as being a very suitable place to meet you, I slipped between the sheets and fell fast asleep. I was fagged-out and I didn't want to meet you in that condition."

She stood looking irresolute, a gift-wrapped parcel in her hand, a new bag in the other.

"Aren't you going to kiss me," he said.

She moved then for the first time and did that, shyly. He put his arms around her and hugged her. He could see his own anxious face in the mirror. Jean's was hidden by her long red hair. It had fallen over her face. He saw streaks of grey in it, and closed his eyes.

"I feel better already," she said, nestling up to him.

"Let's stay like this forever," he murmured into her hair, and meant it at the moment. She was Jean, his dark-eyed pussy cat. Here, with her, was certain safety and deep comfort. But sooner or later, he knew full well, the Lord of Misrule would begin his tricks.

"These garments will be so crushed they won't be fit to wear." Jean sat up suddenly and was out of the bed in the next second, peeling off her skirt. She had still her boylike figure; her movements and gestures were quick and decisive. Still in her slip, she went into the bathroom without a word. Rowena would have announced her intention robustly. It was extraordinary how long women managed to stay in bathrooms. His hand, roving idly under the pillow, came across a crunched-up piece of damp kleenex. He pushed it over the top of the mattress and was about to search for more when Jean came in.

"That's more like it," she said, climbing back with very little on. This time she came under the clothes, but lay very still. He would have to make the first move. He remembered the priest at home praying for rain. He wondered about it at the time. Not now. What a ruthless woman Rowena was. Why had he been such a fool? Much troubled, he made the statutory move. She sighed.

"I'm out of action at the moment, I'm afraid. It's very stupid of me."

Miles clucked commiseration. He recognized her embarrassment. She must be impressed by his magnanimity. He had been known to sulk on these occasions, seeing God's hand raised against him. He should leave himself more in the hands of God. He worried too much. Perhaps everything else that was troubling him would be disposed of with the same benignity. If his smile was fatuous, Jean wasn't in a position to see. But she knew when her husband was in good humour.

"When am I going to be allowed to see her?"

The question was in the air for some time before Miles reached out for it.

"Do you mean Rowena?"

"Is that her name? You treat her as if she was a boil on your bottom."

"If you feel like it after the Embassy party, she is having some people to supper and she said she would be delighted if we came. I don't know whether you would feel up to it."

"I'm dying with curiosity. Catherine gave such a glowing report when you took her to Shannonwear."

"Catherine goes on like that about everyone."

"Now I'll be able to see for myself which is the true picture —your middle-aged dog-fancier bursting out of her tweeds or Catherine's *Vogue* cover."

"I never said Rowena was a dog-fancier."

"I'm sketching in the general picture."

"To be quite frank—"

"Oh, that would be lovely."

"I was in a dilemma. Here was I putting our whole future in the hands of a woman I had known only for a few hours. She became enormously important at once. I was so afraid that you would get the wrong impression."

"And lump her together with all the other ladies you have taken a fancy to—"

"Please."

"I'm not complaining, just getting the record straight. You were making such a mystery of your Rowena, I wouldn't have been natural if I hadn't wanted to see what I was up against."

"You are both very different. I wonder if you will like her. You and I are romantics. She is so terribly down-to-earth."

"I don't object to that. It might be restful after years of pretending that everything is anything but what it seems."

"Come out with me and let us get you a dress for this evening. Then I will take you to tea at the Ritz. This is too good a day to be spent in a hotel bedroom when we can't do anything about it."

"How lovely. But aren't you being recklessly extravagant?"

"Not if what my agent tells me is true. He said I'm a hit. Can you believe it? We must make sure we enjoy every moment of it while it lasts."

He got up first and went to the bathroom. The first thing that

67

met his eye was Rowena's make-up bag. He put it on top of a cabinet and pushed it well back.

How had Jean failed to see it? She might have, of course, and thought it belonged to the last occupant. Certainly there was nothing but welcome on her face when he came back into the bedroom. She threw back the bedclothes and made a gesture to him to come beside her.

They saw the ring lying on the sheet at the same moment, and Jean instinctively felt her fourth right hand finger to see if it had lost the Claddagh ring he had given her. She hadn't. This was identical. He had purchased it at the airport coming to London as a present for Rowena. It had no sentimental significance so far as he was concerned. He was in a hurry, and he wanted to bring her something as a token of appreciation. He hadn't felt treacherous to Jean at the time.

"Let me explain—"

She beat down his outstretched arm as if he was a dog jumping up at her, and began to dress herself with a concentration he recognized when she had quarrelled with him in the past.

"If you will only listen to me—"

Once again she made a slapping-down gesture with a busy hand, not turning her head.

"If you had a shred of self-respect left you would hold your tongue," she said over her shoulder. He sat on the bed, beside the ring, feeling as if they were in a sinking ship with no room for him in the lifeboats.

When Jean was dressed she looked about her with exaggerated calm to make sure that she had left nothing behind her. He restrained himself with difficulty from calling out as she opened the bathroom door to give a last look there. Hiding the vanity bag was the most unimaginative thing he could have done in the circumstances. Now she could hang him on that without any other evidence. Her face betrayed nothing when she came back. After one final look around, her mouth slightly open, tongue resting on the upper lip—that familiar leaving-a-hotel-room look—she picked up her suitcase and went out, closing the door gently behind her, as if making certain that on her departure there would be no reflection of the loutishness that led to it.

"Slept it out this morning." Russell had laid his bets for the first few races when Miles arrived at Ladbroke's, then, noticing that

Miles was looking more worried than usual, his crony hastily altered his tone which for him bordered on the jocose.

"Nothing wrong at headquarters, I hope?"

"There is. Very much. I'd like to talk to you about it if you can spare the time."

"My time is my own, and it is at your disposal. I'll wait until you have done your business here."

"I can't be bothered betting today. The pub isn't open, but we might go to that lorry drivers' café across the road if' it isn't beneath your dignity."

"Tea is better than coffee in a place like this," Miles told him, as they sat down at a formica-topped table. Russell ordered a pot of tea as the one now in charge of the proceedings.

"What's the trouble?"

"I don't know where to begin. You know how I'm situated as regards the hotel. It must have struck you sometimes as odd that I put up with such a régime."

"It was no business of mine. But certainly—"

"Exactly. I'll tell you now. My wife thought she had provided for me. She had a poor opinion of my business sense. What she never knew—and you are the first person I've ever told this to—is that the half stake I put into the place was borrowed."

"From whom, may I ask?"

"Tod Morris. Who else?"

At mention of that name, Russell looked around apprehensively.

"Could we call him Fido? You never know who is listening."

"Certainly, or Bastard, or any other name you fancy. You always closed up, I noticed, when I brought his name into the conversation."

"You were obviously deeply involved with the man, and I was in an awkward position. I know a good deal about him through my bank contacts. He is certainly very influential. How wealthy, I could never discover exactly. He ran some kind of co-operative society. I was never quite sure how it worked."

"Is he dishonest?"

"Certainly, but that is not unusual. What is more to the point, is he mad? I can't make up my mind on the question. I am waiting for the police to catch up with him. I've been longing for an opportunity to bring up the subject. I couldn't very well until you gave a lead. May I say that Morris never did me any harm

69

personally, but I know he has connections with people who are in a very nasty line of business. They ruined my career, apart from other troubles I have had to bear and which, if you don't mind, I would prefer not to discuss. I've come to terms with them."

"Tod's a crook. Is that what you have been trying to tell me?"

"He has had business dealings with crooks, worse than crooks. That is too respectable a description for the people I have in mind. Tell me, if you will, the extent of your involvement with Morris."

"To put it in a nutshell, when it came to paying for the bloody hotel, I just hadn't the money. Tod said he could raise it for me if I gave him the deeds."

"How could you if your wife owned a half share?"

"She signed what she thought was a trust deed. She was thinking only of making me safe—she knew she was a bad life at the time. I stuck my head in the sand. Then we found ourselves in the hands of the Doyles. I've told you about them often enough."

"What happened this morning to upset you?"

"You know about these unauthorized people in the yard. I thought I saw someone there I hadn't seen before when I was coming out this morning. I can see what's going on from the windows of the penthouse; it's like living in a balloon. This fellow was smoking a cigarette and lounging about as if he owned the place, and it suddenly got on my nerves. I decided to alter my usual practice, and instead of coming out through the front door I went round by the back. The chap saw me coming. I just gave him a nod and began to look into the sheds. There was nothing there, which amazes me because, according to Doyle, someone is paying us a colossal rent for them. I saw signs of life upstairs —some washing on a line to be exact—and I was making my way up the steps when my friend in the yard came over and asked me who I was looking for. 'Nobody in particular,' I replied. 'I was just curious to see who is using my premises as a residence without my permission.'

" 'You will have to see Mr Doyle about that,' he said. 'I do my business with him.'

" 'How many people are living here at the moment, may I ask?'

" 'You can ask Mr Doyle about that. It's no business of mine.'

" 'I certainly will talk to Mr Doyle,' I said. It was a humiliating position to find myself in.

"What should I do? If I talk to Doyle about it he will try to palm me off with his usual rigmarole about people to whom we are in debt for past favours. I'm afraid to ask what these were. I could see this morning that I was dealing with a really tough type. I don't know what to do. For years we have been going to Tod Morris with our troubles. He landed the Doyles on us. He landed the hotel on us. He gradually took over everything. I'm lazy, and it suited me. Lately he has changed in his manner. The gush has gone. I hardly ever see him, and when I do he goes on as if he was tired of helping me. The man took me over. I suppose there is nothing to be got out of me now. I wouldn't have bothered you with all this—you have your own troubles—but I am frightened about this yard business. If Doyle has involved me with the IRA—and that's what I believe—what can I do about it? I wish you had met that fellow this morning; you'd have seen what I mean. I got the feeling that he would put a bullet in my back without thinking twice about it."

Miles came to a halt. What could this timid creature who, seemingly, couldn't stand the pace in the bank, do for him? He must not go round showing his sores. Russell was thinking. He waved a hand for silence. Then, in the best bank manner, he said, "Don't ask me for my reasons, but I don't believe your Mr Morris has anything to do with the IRA. He is interested only in money. He has some doubtful business connections, and that might explain the demand for store space. I will follow this clue for you. Don't you do anything. If you see things happening in the yard, you can just let me know."

"But why would you do this for me?"

"Because you are my friend, and because I have an old score to settle with certain people. You haven't told me about your sick friend. I hope the news is better."

"I haven't the least idea. I don't know who you are talking about."

"Your television colleague."

"Oh, Jerry Dunne."

"Exactly. You were telling me about the funeral preparations. Perhaps you would prefer not to discuss the subject. I wouldn't have opened such a painful topic if you hadn't been so full of it on the last occasion. No doubt the melancholy of the circumstances has preyed upon you."

"Now that you have mentioned Jerry Dunne, I don't mind telling you that I'm feeling rather sore about that whole business. I told you, didn't I, that I got a telephone call from Barney Roche at an unearthly hour asking me to speak at the funeral. It was the widow's wish. She wasn't a widow technically, but the way Barney spoke about her I had her clothed in black from head to heel.

"I really gave myself to the subject, planned something that would do the old bastard proud, and had the idea of roping in all the top brass—Terry Wogan, etc., as pall-bearers—a royal send-off for Jerry who, between ourselves, if the positions were reversed would have thrown me into the nearest skip—and I rang up to tell his missus. She bit the nose off me. Jerry, she as good as told me, was fighting fit, and when I rang Barney up to ask him what he thought he was doing telling me that Jerry was as good as dead, he read the riot act to me for doing precisely what he told me to do. I wonder what's behind it?"

"At times like this people's nerves are strained. They say things that they wouldn't in ordinary circumstances. Afterwards it is all forgotten."

"You are a true Christian. All the same I feel I would like to know precisely what Barney Roche is up to. I saw behind it all a plan to get me into the limelight—the BBC might have dropped a hint. But it could well be that there is jealousy at work somewhere. Anyway I agree with you; it is better to drop the topic."

"You great men—I don't think I could have survived in such a competitive atmosphere."

"What is the cruellest part, when all is going well everyone seems to love you. Run into a bald patch and you find that you haven't a friend in the world. Which reminds me of something: since I have reason to regard you as a true and—I have no need to assure you—valued friend, would you mind very much telling me what the 'G' in your name stands for?"

"Gideon."

"How do you spell it?"

"G-I-D-E-O-N. My father was a Bible-reader. I should be honoured if you would call me by it."

"I'm not very well clued-up on the Bible. It may sound strange coming from the brother of a curate and two strapping nuns, but Irish Catholics were never encouraged to read the Bible."

"I didn't know that. It seems strange. In case they might start thinking for themselves?"

"I suppose so. Good trades union principles."

"How is Miss Dubonnet, if I may touch on such a delicate subject?"

"I meant to raise the topic. I am allowed to ask a few private guests to the dinner. Would you, and your missus, needless to say, like to come? It's all on the house, so don't hesitate on that account."

As Miles went on about the invitation he noticed that his friend became gloomier.

"Thank you for thinking of us, but we never' go out in the evening."

Miles was left with the impression that he had made a gaffe.

"I will be interested to hear what happens," Russell said, after a pause, and then, in the manner of shy men when they get a conversational bone between their teeth, he rattled on about the Alma-Tadema Society. So far as his researches went this would be its first meeting. And then, as if to make up for his momentary ungraciousness, he invited Miles to stroll home in his direction; it was only a little out of Miles's way.

"There's a wonderful buddleia in a garden near my place; I'd like you to see it."

He seemed pleased when Miles said he would be delighted to, and even chaffed him about Miss Dubonnet. "With a name like that she might go to your head." It was his first joke to date, and Miles slapped him on the back.

They were walking on the footpath along the main thoroughfare. Russell took a road off it which ran up a steep hill bordered by small terraced houses with bays and a uniform appearance of depressed gentility. There was no one about until a woman appeared on the crest of the hill. She walked towards the swaying about in the middle of the road. Her long white hair floated behind her and she was waving her arms as if in time to music. When she drew nearer Miles could hear her singing. His companion had come to a halt and stood, arms folded, to block her way. His eyes never left her. Out of the corner of his mouth he said, "Leave me to manage this."

Miles stayed away from the betting shop for a few days. Then he decided that it was gratuitous to deny himself one of the few pleasures left in life. He had been indulging in an orgy of video tapes, washed down with whiskey. The result was euphoric, nostalgic, unfocussed, and induced a tendency to tearfulness. He was neglecting to shave.

When Miss Dubonnet, full of apologies, told Miles that her committee thought that the idea of a television crew at the dinner might give an intimidating character to the evening, he had picked the names of eight other journalists with whom he had appeared on television programmes and sent the list to Miss Dubonnet. It was a bold stroke; she would be put on her toes; if even one of them came it would justify the ploy. He had nothing to lose and an outside chance of a press paragraph. Were they all to come . . .

After that, there was nothing to do. He had already begun to prepare the talk; it would start on a homely note—his father made excellent copy—then he would have fun with his first appearance on television—a story he had honed and polished and kept ready for conversational emergencies. Names would be let fall, but like feathers. There was plenty of time to do his home-work over the pictures of Alma-Tadema and, of course, Samuel Slaughter, the Methuselah in the chair. Old, deaf (probably) and wandering, he seemed to be an extraordinary choice to preside over a new and fashionable dining club.

Miles had decided to shut his eyes to his own circumstances until he had had another talk with Gideon Russell. He thought of him a lot. There was something heroic in his stance in that nightmare scene. This was the shadow under which his friend lived and about which he never complained nor looked for sympathy. Their next meeting would be painfully embarrassing.

It was not. When Miles went into Hill's betting shop at the other end of the street he saw Gideon filling in his betting slips. He nodded when Miles patted him on the shoulder, asking not to be interrupted, then, looking up, as if they had broken off in the middle of a conversation, "I'm going for a treble today on Willie Carson."

There was a pub at the corner, very like the Cock and Candle, to which they repaired. It was as if the other day had been a dream.

"I haven't been neglecting your problem," Gideon said, sipping the most expensive claret the pub provided. They had never drunk wine together before. Miles could not have explained his whim to order it, perhaps an atavistic instinct to celebrate the first hurdle crossed in their friendship. "Have I your permission to discuss your case with the solicitor who saw me through my troubles? We meet occasionally, and we have been very good friends since that ordeal. I won't involve you in anything, I promise you, so long as I may give him to understand that if it does seem advisable to take legal steps you would entrust your case to him. It is all a matter of timing. Timing is the art of life. If you move at the wrong moment Tod Morris may strip you bare, but there might be a time when it would suit him very well to buy you off. From what I can gather he is now in a much bigger way than he was when you took him on. I am quite sure that if you looked into them you would find the hotel books are cooked. It suits him very well to have his creature in charge. He would not like any publicity about a side-show just at a time when he was trying to star in the big league.

"From what I hear he is very possibly slightly touched. He was prepared to do anything for you when he could boast about your friendship. At the time it was probably all he asked in reward. Now you are just another of his complications. I'd love to look at those books. The Lord only knows what a mess they are in. He hates anyone else but himself to do anything, I understand, and the amount of unfinished business he has on his tray would frighten you. He will end up in prison if he doesn't do himself in before that. We must get you out of his clutches."

"I give you *carte blanche*," Miles said impressively and felt the better for it and as safe as if he was on an Alpine road in a car with no brakes. All he had to hang on to was this diffident friend.

There was some question Russell was obviously longing to ask. He edged towards it but then lost his nerve, time and again, and changed the subject. Miles recognized the signals, but was not sufficiently curious to ask what was on his friend's mind. Feeling emboldened today, Russell came straight to the point. Miles expected a request for information about a celebrity and was surprised when he was asked for information about Willie. He was inclined to forget Willie's surname. Willie was supremely of no importance. What a strange man this Russell was.

"He is almost a dwarf with a twisted shoulder and a hunched back. He might be a very old-looking child or a very juvenile old man. I wouldn't like to think of his beginnings. He is a curious mixture of cheerfulness and surliness. He loves a little notice. He is very like a magpie, intensely curious and an inveterate gossip.

"His world has always been a tiny one, and what is happening in it is of infinite importance to him. I believe he is fond of me and is jealous of my attention. I wouldn't trust him across the width of the street with any gossip about me, not because he is malicious. He is much more like an infant who must show the first person around a shell he has picked up on the beach. I give him money from time to time and I blush when I hear what we pay him. He knows very well that no one else would employ him. He has no qualifications whatever. He ought to be in parliament. We give him a bed, the run of his teeth, and something to talk about. He thinks I am the greatest man in the world."

"Does he run messages for people?"

"Loves to. Makes him feel important. That matters more than the tip."

"I'd very much like to lay eyes on Willie. I'd like to see for myself what he looks like. You must forgive this nosiness. He is a piece that is missing from my jigsaw."

"Come to my terrible hotel and have a drink with me. He is almost certain to be hanging about. Anyhow it is about time you saw the sort of kip I live in."

"I only wanted to get a glimpse."

There was no sign of Willie in the cramped hall, and when Miles rang the bell on the desk a girl's face came round the door. Willie had gone out on a message, she said.

"You might as well come upstairs and see the whole catastrophe."

"Another day. I must be on my way," Russell had suddenly become his closed-up self again.

When the two friends came out on the street, Willie came towards them on a bicycle grinning with delight and furiously ringing the bell. He blushed as always after his little exhibition, but Miles saw no sign of his recognizing Russell. The latter, however, bristled, and muttering something unintelligible about meeting Miles tomorrow, bustled off.

Miles was sufficiently curious to ask Willie if he had seen Mr Russell before.

"He looks very like your betting friend."

Who, Miles asked himself, was he keeping up appearances for? His every move was known. Why did Gideon want to see Willie and take so little pleasure in the sight? Miles was curious about it until everything was put out of his head by another vision.

*

76

He had been inspecting his wardrobe to make sure that he would do himself credit at the Alma-Tadema dinner. His bottle-green dinner-jacket had come back from the cleaner's looking pristine; Bridget had let out his black evening trousers the necessary inch. (If she wasn't one of a pair, he sometimes told himself, he could put up with Bridget. She could turn her hand to anything.) Socks were no problem, and his patent leather evening shoes only showed signs of wear if one stuck one's face into them. The floral waistcoat, a collector's item, Rowena's gift when she was showering presents on him, had been attacked by moth, but not on the salient part.

A shirt—that was the only unavoidable purchase. His best ones were a size too small. He might as well do it properly and buy a couple as he was about it. He spent nothing on his wardrobe nowadays. There was no one to dress up for. Would he, or wouldn't he, wear the hair-piece? That wasn't a question he could ask Gideon Russell and there was no one in his entourage for whose opinion he gave a tinker's curse. This was one of the occasions when he felt the need of a woman friend.

At every milestone in his life there had been a woman—sometimes two. Why should fate alter that pattern now? And who more likely than Miss Dubonnet for the last lap. He had nothing to tell him what she looked like. As Miss Dubonnet, a telephone acquaintance, she sounded eminently sensible and as refreshing as the spirit she was called after when mixed with lemonade. As Lalage she appealed to what was left of the old Adam in him. Because he had not as yet looked up Alma-Tadema's work it had begun to take on an increasingly bacchic character in his imagination, and in the course of his fantasies Lalage was invariably undressed. Her connection with the Alma-Tadema Society would be discovered in due course. Meanwhile he had a fixed image of Lalage to dress and undress as it pleased his fancy.

Miles was feeling buoyant. He had forgotten his funeral disappointment. It was Jerry's good luck, he was magnanimous enough to tell himself. Although his financial position was volcanic, its eruption was something that other people were probably no less anxious than he to avoid.

Time was on his side. So was Gideon Russell. God was good who had sent him this friend. His thoroughness was reassuring and Miles had always operated on the basis that when troubles could be handed on they ceased to be troubles. To find someone prepared to take them on and still to worry was as wasteful as it was ungrateful. A trip into the West End, that was the tonic he needed at the moment. The shirts provided an eligible excuse. He had not been in this part of London for an age. He felt enlarged by his surroundings. This was his proper setting, not the Kentish Town Road where drunken Irish formed an alfresco club. He strolled past the Ritz and made for the club-land, where he had never belonged, but there was still time for that. He must show that he had *gravitas*, what the Latin teacher at school told the class was the mark of great men. He hadn't paid much attention at the time and was probably exchanging rude notes with some other occupant of the back benches, but now he saw the point. A red face staring through the window of White's discouraged further speculation, but Jermyn Street was in sight—all those windows full of shirts for sale. Here was distraction, here was the tangible. He felt nervously for his wallet as he gloated over a salmon pink and a dove grey—the Impressionist school. His own reflection in the glass at that moment discouraged adventure. Perhaps the black and white stripes would be safer. In any event, there was God's plenty to choose from. He went in.

There was no one in the shop except two assistants who made it clear to Miles that they were not impressed by his patronage until one of them recognized him—he always knew when he had hooked a fish—and asked if he could be of any assistance. Miles only needed this encouragement. He put on his Miles-buying-a-shirt turn for the benefit of the shop, its employees and customers (should any happen to come in). Bales of cloth piled up on the counter while Miles jested. It looked like being an expensive as well as an absorbing game.

Miles was testing the salmon pink against his complexion for colour clashes in a looking-glass when a man came into the shop. He signalled at once that he needed no attention. So far as he was concerned, his nod seemed to say, the other customer could monopolize the staff's attention while he took a look round. He was a spare, soldierly-looking man, much older at close view than his walk and carriage suggested. He did not look like a man who needed help in clothes shops. There was something authoritative about him, as if he was much practised in presenting medals. His arrival successfully brought the curtain down on Miles's perform-ance. He settled without further parley for the pink with a dove-grey stripe and, defiantly, ordered six. He thought he saw the other customer taking a quick glance at him as he left the shop, but that was something he used to be accustomed to. He felt resentful, as if he had been put down. It was quite absurd. He could not expect to have shops to himself; and the military-looking man had behaved faultlessly. Since as long as he could remember that self-sufficient manner had made him feel uncomfortable. He associated it with the days at the Deanery when he used to play tennis with Dicky Dawson.

He hadn't thought about Dicky Dawson for years. He would look like that if he were alive. Miles stopped, turned back, halted—would he go back and make sure? The Dawson household had been the great influence on his youth. He wondered what had happened to Daphne? She had kissed him and mocked him at the same time, an allegory for his whole experience of the family. Why did he hesitate? He, after all, had become a celebrity. Even though Dick might look like a Field Marshal in mufti, he had never become anyone.

As an undergraduate he had that appearance, even when he was alone, of a patrician among the plebs. He would always look not so much like someone who had had an honour conferred on him as of someone who had recently turned one down. Whatever Miles achieved in life there would be no point in bringing it to Dicky's notice; he had graded his cheerful cheeky friend as second-rate. Nothing could alter that decree. To impress Dicky Dawson would be to succeed in life.

A sudden attack of acute nostalgia made Miles turn back. It might be the last chance to see Dicky again this side of the grave. Not to take advantage of it was a deed of treachery to the past. He hurried to the shirt shop. That customer had gone.

"A very nice gentleman. Comes in here occasionally. Might not see him for months. Probably lives somewhere in the country."

"I haven't seen him for half a century. We used to play together as children."

"I'll tell the gentleman next time he comes."

"Would you? That is very kind of you. I'll give you my telephone number."

"We have it."

"Of course." Miles had forgotten. He was to be rung up when the shirts were ready.

There was no more to be extracted from the coincidence. He

79

went away feeling that he had, through his carelessness, let a large slice of the past slip through his fingers. He had never liked Dicky Dawson much or thought of him as a real friend, but the Dawsons had played an historic part in his life. So much so he was amazed that he hadn't thought of bringing them into the talk he was preparing. He had never been inside a Protestant household until Dicky invited him to the Deanery to play tennis; not from any friendly motive, but because he wanted someone to practise against in the holidays. Daphne, the daughter of the house, who had an impudently pretty face, found him useful. When she had girls from school staying with her the local shortage of young men presented a problem. Her eye lit on Miles, who had been until then a boy in the village, and he found himself more often with the Dawsons than at home during the holidays. The Dean smiled on him absently and seemed quite happy to see him at his table. The Dean's wife, a grim and rather stupid lady who ran her husband and the parish, took a liking to Miles from the first. Formidable to her family and all the world beside—she was English and had private means—she never frightened Miles after he looked through family photographs and noticed that, as a girl, she looked very like Daphne did now. Mrs Dawson offered one water at table with a righteous and defiant air. She was well-supplied with gossip, and any young man with a reputation for drinking was not allowed inside the Deanery. Gambling was also on her proscribed list. She did not know that Daphne, away from home, was already, at seventeen, taking "Gin and It" as to the manner born. The children were able to fit in with their mother's iron rule because of her grand assumption that because they never argued with her they agreed with what she said and acted upon it. Compared with his own genteel and pious sisters Daphne was a revelation to Miles. Religion in the Deanery was much more committee work and a social affair than in his own house where rosaries were recited and red lamps before statues of the Sacred Heart burned perpetually and the Parish Priest came for Sunday dinner after last mass. Then the table groaned and there were lashings to drink.

Miles and Dicky were never close. There was much of his mother's complacency about the son, and although Miles who was a year younger could beat him at everything, he had an inimitable way of conveying that he could have reversed the result if he had thought the effort worth while. As Miles was always trying to impress him it was a subtle technique and kept Miles effectively in his place. Daphne fascinated him. The tomboy side of her was in such contrast to the primness of his own sisters. She was avidly curious to know about what happened in his house. He was the first Roman Catholic to come to the Deanery as a friend, she told him. She had grown up believing certain things about Catholics that she thought she would never quite succeed in casting off: that they didn't wash as often or as thoroughly as Protestants, that they didn't tell the truth, that they would do anything a priest told them, that priests could do pretty well what they pleased, no one would have the guts to stand up to them. Roman Catholicism was a religion for peasants.

This depressed him to hear because he had romantic feelings about Daphne. He wanted to have a best girl, but he could see no hope of her ever looking at him in any other light than the village boy. She had the power to make him miserable, and he was in love with her—hopelessly. There was still (in the thirties) a chasm between a Catholic home like the O'Malleys' where God seemed to be sitting on the roof all night and all day and the detached attitude at the Deanery where He was treated more like a distant connection of the family.

Daphne would never leave Miles alone. She was forever asking him why Catholics didn't come into the church at the weddings and funerals of their Protestant friends. It was so un-Christian. When he said they were forbidden to—they couldn't help it—she said she couldn't understand how grown men were not ashamed to be so priest-ridden. The playing of games provided a nice point in theology: it was plebeian to play football on Sundays in public—only Catholics did. However, there was nothing wrong with playing tennis, provided it was on one's private court. To object to that would be nonconformist and therefore lower class.

There was much more snobbery than theology in these differences, he thought, even at the time, but he couldn't say so. Sometimes Mrs Dawson forgot he was there and said outrageously bigoted things. That amused him because Daphne saw the joke. At home he made no effort to conceal his dejection, and its cause was generally known. He hated his parents for having handicapped him from the start. With his background Daphne would never even consider him as a possible mate. She made this all too plain when she told him she would be surprised if he got married before he was thirty-five, and not with a catch in her throat, but as if she were filing vital statistics. She didn't mind how miserable she made him whenever he became intense, because she enjoyed his company while he was amusing her, something he was always able to do so long as he kept off the subject of love. He was romantically chaste. It was all words with him. Had he been closer to earth it would have been less confusing for both of them. "I am tired of boys", he heard her tell her friend, and he blanched at the thought of what would happen when she encountered men.

Keep away from the women. That was all his father had to say when he diagnosed his son's condition. How coarse it sounded at the time. With a father like that and sisters forever lighting candles in church for their intentions, what hope had he of escaping from his prison? He was confused about sex and full of inhibitions. On one occasion, when he put an arm around Daphne's waist, she shook him off with what he thought was contempt. She was inconsistent; sometimes talking to him as though he was her friend, sometimes ignoring his feelings; then she sounded like an echo of her mother.

She was trying to get a place next year at Oxford or Cambridge. When that happened he felt sure he would lose her to marauding English boys. He was amazed by her frankness. "You will have to do something about that bum of yours." She said that to a friend. It wasn't the way he thought girls talked. Once at a picnic he found himself alone with Daphne. She had something she wanted to tell him, so they sat down on a bank covered—he never forgot—with primroses.

"You'd be all right," she said, "if only you could get away." Compliment mixed with condescension as usual.

"I'm not going to stay in Ardrath all my life, if that's what you mean."

"We shall probably be moving. There's a bishopric coming up—you mustn't mention this to anyone—and it looks as if Daddy may get it. Mummy says he is bound to because there is hardly a gentleman left on the bench in the Church of Ireland. Daddy was quite funny about it. 'I would not like my elevation to depend on any anxiety to protect a threatened species.' 'You know perfectly well what I mean.' You can hear Mummy can't you?"

"Does it ever worry your mother that Christ and the apostles were working class?"

"She would say that was a red herring when it is a question of finding bishops for the Church of Ireland. I shall hate leaving the Deanery."

Miles reached out an uncertain hand.

"Has anyone ever told you you were rather nice to look at?" she said.

"They have not. Have I ever told you you are the prettiest girl I've ever met in all my life?"

"What are you going to do about it then?"

He knew all about close-ups in the cinema, but he was vague about what led up to them. He made a grab at Daphne and kissed her but it was done awkwardly, and she was clearly disappointed.

"Come on," she said, getting up. "They'll be wondering where we are. On the way back she walked a pace ahead and neither of them said a word. Later he heard the two girls laughing together and Daphne saying, "You owe me a shilling."

Thoughts of Daphne had distracted him. He had to stop and ask himself where he was. A covered passage-way, rather elegant, not familiar, windows full of things it would be fun to buy if only he knew what he could afford. He went to the end and saw that he was in the Royal Opera Arcade with Pall Mall facing him. He was undecided what to do. Across the street were clubs. He could only recognize one—the Athenaeum. An Oxford don had taken him to lunch there and the food disappointed him. It would suit him very well at the moment to go into any of them and flop into an armchair with a copy of *The Economist* or some other paper that he would never dream of buying for himself and ring for a waiter and order something more recherché than the inevitable "large Irish". He would be safe in there. Out in the street he was not safe nor in the foyer of a hotel. It was what he needed at the moment more than anything, a sense of belonging somewhere, of being in the right place.

He had achieved the widest celebrity, but at the end of it had not acquired the social confidence Dicky Dawson had at eighteen, and still retained. What Dicky had no one could take away from him; it was innate even though he had never been seen on television with world celebrities, quizzing them, laughing at them, scoring off them, delighting millions of viewers, whose champion he was, when he made someone look silly. Occasionally he came across modest people who were reluctant to appear in public, but they were rare, and bishops were often more eager to exhibit themselves than boxers.

He strolled in the direction of Trafalgar Square; ever since he came to London he had intended to go to the Gallery and look at the pictures, but today that seemed to demand an act of concentration of which he knew himself incapable. He glanced idly at the pigeons, then at the lions round Nelson. That was fame: to be stuck up like that on a pillar, and bombarded with pigeon-droppings ever after.

A 29 bus disturbed his meditations; it would leave him near his horrid hotel, and he was pleased to find a front seat vacant when he climbed upstairs. He came into central London so seldom that this was in the nature of a treat, and he looked around and about him like a child on holiday. A taxi stopped in front of the bus to take in a fare, holding up the traffic outside Foyles. Miles, staring at all those books, reflected that he read perhaps one a year. It was extraordinary how well one could manage to get along without them. There was something familiar about the back view of the man getting into the taxi. Miles leaned forward so precipitately that he bumped his nose against the window. He had seen Dicky Dawson again. It was becoming ridiculous. Miles made an involuntary move to get up, but checked himself. He would never get downstairs in time. Already the taxi had spurted ahead, and in a second was lost in the traffic.

After so many years Dicky Dawson twice within the hour, it was extraordinary. If it did nothing else it made Miles discontented with the gallimaufry of anecdotes and old jokes he had been getting together to entertain the Alma-Tadema Society. He could do better than that. The revenant had set his mind alight with recollections of his youth that he had pushed into the back of it but had never forgotten. They would have undermined his confidence. If he had been simply on the make, the Dawsons gave him opportunities to pick up useful tips. He did, but he could not overcome an innate sense of inferiority. The cause was not Dicky's aloofness but Daphne's allure and contempt.

That whole Dawson experience at an impressionable age in his life made useful copy. He would, of course, draw on imagination to colour the picture. It was worth taking trouble in a vein which could form the basis of radio talks and might even make a play on television (how would he feel when he saw some fledgling disporting himself as the young Miles?). The end of the Raj in Ireland had been done by Mollie Keane and others, but always from the angle of the Raj, written with a downward look. He knew what it was like to be regarded as native. So much of it was about private language, unfamiliar references, quirky pronunciations—one could, of course, be oneself, exploit one's Paddy quality, not give a damn (the Ascendency were down and out), but he had minded. He was someone special. He knew it always, but television had to tell him where he could demonstrate his quality. And now he could look back at Dawson days and his clumsiness and un-certainty with amused affection.

There was no point in getting in touch with that agent until after the dinner. Then, with any luck, word would have got round that he was ready to break new ground. The old Miles who had depended for his effects on the exploitation of his own personality and other people's was exploiting his charm in a serious field. He was leaving the entertainers to join the artists. If you were Irish it wasn't difficult to get a literary reputation. You had only to get people to argue about you, you had to become a talking point; not being read didn't matter. In his own time he had seen reputations made overnight by the censor, and to get one's novel seized by customs officers was better for one's reputation than a full-page review, and even sold a few copies of the book.

His appearance needn't worry him any more. All that brooding over his jowls and the hair-piece was over. He would be judged over here by his work, not by his smile. Respect from the discriminating few—that was what he was after now. He thought about the Dicky Dawson apparition. It might seem superstitious —sober, he would never confide in anyone about it—but old habit dies hard; did he still long for Dawson approval? Did he want Dicky to acknowledge his achievement, to admit that he was impressed?

He was so deep in meditation that only the unfamiliar appear-ance of the Seven Sisters Road recalled him to the world. His bus stop was a mile behind him.

"Preoccupied" might best describe Miles's manner in the days that followed. He found it more difficult than he had expected to put nostalgia into words and to recreate a child's world. Inno-cence was hard to distinguish in the mist. Words died on the page; it didn't suit him to be serious. Dicky told him once that he would be laughing on the Last Day. After innumerable drafts in a poetic vein he started to poke fun. His pen ran away with him then.

Between the O'Malley Montagues and the Dawson Capulets he was the go-between, the precocious observer. He contrasted Father Murphy PP surrounded by ministering angels in the O'Malley house with the Dean looking wistfully at the water jug on the dinner table at the Deanery; the turf fires blazing in June in one house and the Siberian winds that whistled round bare knees in every passage in the other. Thrift was a Protestant virtue, he discovered; his people were ashamed of anything that even looked like meanness.

Sometimes he lost faith in the undertaking. Every peasant who had worked as a servant in a big house had seen the same things. There was nothing new in all this. It would sound like an Irish variation on the *Upstairs Downstairs* theme. When he became thoroughly discouraged he pushed the paper away, put on a video of the great days, and put away half a bottle of whiskey.

Miles went very seldom to the betting shop these days, and then only as a civility to Gideon Russell who was pursuing his enquiries. He reported a most encouraging chat with his solicitor friend, and when the Alma-Tadema evening was behind them he would outline a plan of campaign against the strangers on the premises and, if needs be, the Doyles. Clearly Russell was on to something. There was an impressive air of suppressed excitement in his manner. He advised Miles to keep away from the Doyles and concentrate on his speech. Everyone knew about the speech by this time. Whenever Miles, inadvertently, ran into one of the Doyles a polite enquiry was made into the state of its health. Willie was incapable of framing an articulate question upon such a matter, but he, too, had caught the excitement in the air. He could not meet Miles's eye.

Miss Dubonnet rang up to confirm arrangements. A car was being sent to take Miles to the dinner. The greatest interest was being shown and there were many enquiries. All Miles's guests had accepted.

"You mean Peter Haddock, John Pulveriser, Mackenzie Thwaite, Letty Lorne and all that lot are coming!"

"I can't remember the names, but you certainly put them on your list and we have had no refusals. You are a great draw, you know."

The voluptuous image of Lalage had receded recently, but Miles felt a rush of tenderness towards her. His eye wandered moistly in the direction of the mantelpiece and the lavender-coloured envelope that had started all this. A note of cajolery came into his voice. At such moments his accent became unmistakably Irish. The pipes were calling. He was fascinated by the idea of a dual identity. Lalage was luxury, Miss Dubonnet that something else, protective of him, he always longed for in a woman. He might need her support when he had to cope with all those flash journalists and their womenfolk. Why were they coming? Why was everyone acting in such a self-conscious manner? After-dinner speeches were being made at golf club dinners every night of the week somewhere in the country. Why the air of mysterious excitement about his? A few years ago he would have demanded not less than a thousand quid for having his health drunk. Now he was going on spec to an hotel he had never heard of, invited by people he had never heard of, to talk to people he had never met. There was some large piece of the puzzle missing. Could it be a "This is your Life" programme? That would have to be got up under some sort of smoke-screen and everyone would be sworn to secrecy. But would Eamonn ever give him a boost like that? And would his lot agree to it? At the moment it would have the atmosphere of a service in a crematorium. If he was back in his old slot or—as he would hope—in a new and more prestigious one, then it would be a very timely gesture. Should he ring E.A. and explain this situation? Better not. If he had read the signals wrong he would look very foolish indeed, and the news would be flashed round making him a laughing stock. Better leave that one to sort itself out.

He gave himself a research course in the art of Alma-Tadema, and pondered over it for a telling description if the subject came up. The old boy had given his public exactly what it wanted. Like many of his generation he showed that he was an artist when he was painting for his own pleasure. At other times he seemed to be catering for rich people who wanted pictures that went with rich dinners. Samuel Slaughter presented no problem. So far as the evidence available went, he was painting the same cows in the same field under the same rain cloud before the first World War. There were rude ways of describing them and kind ones. "Old friends" might do at a pinch.

A week before the dinner Miles had twenty copies made of his talk and spent a busy afternoon posting them with an explanatory note to the editors of every reputable newspaper and magazine he could think of. After that, Gideon Russell agreed, there was nothing more a man could do.

Dominick Doyle offered to drive Miles to the dinner—an extraordinary precedent. Miles took a malicious pleasure in telling him that he was being sent for. He had his hair cut at Trumper's and consulted the barber about his hair-piece. "Decided against", he noted in his diary. He had taken to the diary again recently. There had been nothing to record for so long. There needed only to complete the picture the first letter he had ever received from Tod Morris that was not about business wishing him the best of luck with his address to such a distinguished gathering.

Miles was to be called for at half-past seven. Coming up to the time he was ruffled to discover that there was no one about, not even Willie, when he rang, not so much for assistance as support. Jane, who helped in the kitchen, said Willie had gone out and told her to keep an eye on the place. That was not what he needed. He had pictured himself being seen off by the entire staff. He prized little attentions of that sort, and everyone at the Parnell Hotel was aware that this was a great occasion.

In his fussing he had spoilt two of the new shirts, and he was regretting that he had economized on footwear. The old patent leathers pinched like tweezers. His confidence was being slowly eroded. What would he not have given for the sound of a woman's voice begging him to take it easy? He was having last-minute misgivings about his script. All that nostalgic stuff about the village boy might be meaningless to Middle-East millionaires. Making desperate last minute changes, he knocked over a glass of whiskey and saturated several pages. "God damn it," he shouted aloud.

He called off the revising operation then. Last-minute changes tended to be counter-productive. He put down the manuscript and returned to the adornment of his person. Should he wear the sombrero? With his red-lined evening cloak it looked dashing. The Laughing Cavalier. The appearance of a rebel of an earlier generation—a no-longer-angry-old-man—was exactly the note he would like to strike, not so much before the Alma-Tadema crowd (he didn't give a damn about them) but Peter Haddock and that lot must be given the right impression. They were being offered vintage fare. Wine matured in the cask. He was sorry now that he hadn't put his pride in his pocket and accepted Doyle's offer of a lift. The Parnell Hotel was an inauspicious address to be collected at. Even though the block in which he was living had the superficial appearance of what is called a private hotel, through the walls came an incessant hum from the human bee-hives next door. He did not want the driver to be greeted by a slattern from the kitchen. He must station himself in the hall. No sooner had he done so than a white limousine drew up at the entrance. Its sleek appearance was exactly what his agitated spirits required. He was on the pavement when the huge black-liveried chauffeur stepped out. He said "Mr O'Malley, sir?" Not emphasizing the question mark. And Miles said "You are very punctual." The chauffeur held the door as Miles stepped in, reminding himself at that moment of Douglas Fairbanks in one of the Saturday night pictures in the village hall long ago. A small boy cheered. Miles heard him, but did not see him bend down, pick up a broken tile, and hurl it at the back of the car as it drew away from the pavement. It missed.

Miles was one who talked to taxi-drivers. Their two professions had many circumstances in common, he found. Before the end of the journey—if they didn't know it already—they had discovered who he was, and if they were Irish refused to accept the fare. But this driver was all impersonal back. His impassive concentration made Miles feel like a parcel. Stepping out he pressed a fiver into his hand. The deep bow with which it was received reflected credit on both parties.

Miles was faced by the Aegean Hotel. It was brand new. There was glass everywhere, giving the general impression of a fish tank. The commissionaires looked as if they were wearing their uniforms for the first time. One speck of dust would have been grossly conspicuous on them. Baroque arrangements of artificial flowers, in elaborate urns and exotic vases, covered every flat surface. In whatever direction he turned Miles was met by his own reflection. There was no comfort in it. He had taken—God knows—trouble with his appearance, but the effect, every mirror proclaimed, was of some old sport dressed up for theatricals in a village hall. All his garments pinched him somewhere. When he was about to make a retreat a notice caught his eye:

Alma-Tadema Society
Dinner 8 o'clock in the Tower Room
Tickets (wine not included) £10

A voice at his elbow. "Mr O'Malley, will you come with me, sir." One of the Aegean commissionaires was at his side and a step ahead. The evening had begun.

"May I take your hat and cloak?" Perfect service, but disrobing even to that extent made Miles feel like a patient in a casualty ward. Thank God he had invested in the shirts. He was tempted to point out to the cloakroom attendant that one of his garments was as new as anything in this aquarium. He heard his name being announced as he went into a large room that might have been designed for women's fashion displays. The pale pink walls were decorated with panels in which satyrs were pursuing nymphs with different degrees of success. This room was also liberally supplied with mirrors, and it had a glass ceiling. The furnishings were neo-Georgian, but the marble chimney-piece looked like the real thing. Leaning against it, dominating the room, was an old man, a genuine antique, with a mane of white hair brushed back. He was surveying the gathering with a reproving stare, not unlike Michelangelo's Moses. Something in his stance, the arrangement of his shoulders and knees, cried out for a plinth. He was magnificently out of place. This was the man who for three quarters of a century had been painting the same cows in the same field under the same threatening cloud—Samuel Slaughter. Someone unchanging in an increasingly evanescent world; Miles walked across acres of frightening floor to one whom he needed as an ally in whatever was to come. The old man was waiting for him; Miles saw that Moses stare was fixed on him; then, just as he was about to receive his accolade, Slaughter turned away.

"That's the other fellow."

There was a short stampede in the neighbourhood of the fireplace: then someone took charge, a man of the world, authoritative, with expensive teeth and smelling like a garden of herbs. He descended on Miles. "You haven't been given a drink. This will never do. Let me get hold of a waiter. Do you dislike champagne? I hope you had no trouble finding your way." Then, sotto voce, "Old gentleman slightly confused."

A tray was held under Miles's nose. It was loaded with glasses of champagne but he asked for whiskey for comfort. While Miles was engaged a little lady on tiptoe was calling into the chairman's more distant ear, "*Miles O'Malley*".

"No. He's the other fellow, I tell you."

The little lady looked round to see how Miles was getting on, and seeing that he was fully occupied she gave such signals of distress to the chairman that, still grunting and not convinced, he inclined his great head in Miles's direction as if promising not to bite. When he was not staring his eyes disappeared into folds of flesh.

"My sight is terrible," he said to Miles, who was frantically anxious to know for whom precisely he had been mistaken. "Can't make out anyone's phiz. As for my memory—sometimes can't remember my own name. Do you know any of these people? I never laid eyes on one of them before in my life. Lalage could tell us. Where the hell has she got to? Lalage has a lot of friends —meets them at her work. Clever girl. Not my type, most of them. Know what I mean. Eh? One or two of them have bought my pictures, I believe. No objection to that. Would you do me a favour like a good chap and write your name distinctly—you can't write it *too* distinctly—on a piece of paper so that I won't make an ass of myself when I have to introduce you later on. I'll have forgotten. My niece's friends—remember. I can't tell you how long it is since I last spoke in public. Munnings was there. He congratulated me afterwards. I hit out. I don't mind telling you. I was always hitting out in those days, thought the world was going mad. I wasn't far wrong. You won't mind if I only say a very few words when I'm introducing you. I'm usually in bed by this time."

"I hope Uncle Sam is not trying to subvert you, Mr O'Malley." The little lady on tiptoe was smiling up at him. "How nice to meet you in the flesh at last. A face on the screen, then a voice on the telephone; now the great man himself."

"Miss Dubonnet."

"Lalage, please, here."

"You are the first Lalage I have ever met and it's my favourite name."

"That's flattering, but then—or so I've always heard—the Irish are shameless flatterers. I'm so glad you were able to make it. The car must have been on time and the driver was able to find you. All most satisfactory."

Miss Dubonnet—Lalage. At last. The serpent of old Nile, the houri of his luxurious fantasies was one of nature's bird women, bird-eyed, bird-beaked, fluttering, chattering—bird-brained. Impossible to tell her age. Her plumage a gold lace coat over a black and white spotted blouse. Miles didn't know enough about birds—Miles didn't know enough about anything—to tell what sort of bird she was. Her speckled hair was drawn up and bound with a ribbon, making a crest. Now chattering, now making little darting rushes at people as if they might have scattered crumbs and introducing them to each other, she was never still. Some of their names were as familiar as the names of litanies of the saints he used to hear in childhood; these were the names at the head of that first letter: Count Bosdari, Constantine Zaimis, Simeon Sikinos, Countess Melashoff, Aristides Carlovassi. They had wives with them this evening—the men, that is. The Countess was unchaperoned.

"I must fill you in about the Countess," Lalage twittered. "I put her beside you, and I took the liberty of placing myself on the other side."

"Exactly what I had hoped might happen. Now I know I shall enjoy myself."

"I have to keep an eye on Uncle. He really isn't up to this sort of thing. But Mr Carlovassi wouldn't hear of a refusal. The old dear will need me if he gets confused."

"He asked me to write my name on something. Perhaps you would be good enough to put the card on my place at table in front of him when he is introducing me."

"How thoughtful of you. I hope he will see the connection."

There were not more than twenty people in the room. Most of them looked as if they had been conscripted for a coroner's jury, others as if they were waiting to go on to some other entertainment.

"We meet at last." The Countess fixed Miles in a tragic gaze when they were introduced. Its intensity belied her cleavage. Neither was telling the truth, he felt, but he forgot the Countess when his eye lighted on a fancy clock which told him that it was dinner time, and not one of his special guests had arrived.

"Miss Dubonnet tells me that you are wonderfully witty and very dangerous to females." Miles could not even force a smile. This evening should have witnessed his comeback. What had happened? Why did those swine accept in the first place? Ruthless ruffians. Someone had sabotaged the recovery plan. But who? The BBC seemed the obvious suspect. That lot were quite unscrupulous enough to stage this evening in his honour and then use it for cutting his throat.

Ignoring the Countess who had begun another little speech, he sent up distress signals to Lalage. She was interpreting for her uncle, but she came at once.

"My guests—I can't see any of them. Did you get cancellations?"

"Oh, this *is* a pity. Such interesting people. We may find them upstairs when we gather in the dining-room."

But he knew they wouldn't. His triumph was turning into a bad joke. He was nearly forgetting that his hosts were not responsible for the rude behaviour of his chosen guests.

"They may have mistaken the evening," Miss Dubonnet said.

"I can only apologize for their bad manners. They are not friends of mine, you understand, but I thought they might, between them, have given a puff to your society."

"Mr O'Malley is a kind man, thinking always of other people." The Countess was hovering round him, and Miles had to fight an impulse to make some excuse and go home.

"All those empty chairs," said Lalage on a long-drawn-out note, then, in a warble, "They may turn up at the last moment."

"This *is* the last moment," the Countess said, as a Swiss admiral, at least, took up his position at the door to announce that dinner was served in the Tower Room, and would members kindly take their partners upstairs.

"Not everyone has a partner," said the Countess, squeezing Miles's arm encouragingly. She pointed at a little man who had been sitting all alone reading the evening paper.

"Mr Wright," the Countess explained. "He doesn't like my sex."

"Not *U. Wright*, by any chance?"

"U for Ulick. How clever you are."

"His name was on the list of your committee. It caught my fancy. I never thought I would have the privilege of seeing him in the flesh."

"In the flesh is an exaggeration," the Countess said, but Miles did not give her any encouragement to explain why she thought so.

They had decided to walk up the few steps to the dining-room instead of taking to the lifts. Another Swiss admiral threw open a door to let them into the Tower Room. All the walls were windows, and London lit up stretched out in every direction. There was one long table. The rest of the room was given up to

93

separate tables which were nearly all occupied. Miles remembered the advertisement in the foyer. These were people who had actually paid to hear him, old fans to whom his endearing ways must have been as familiar as breakfast cereal. Bless them. He saw Lalage picking up the place cards of the absentees on the high table; and the sight reminded him that, in a restaurant as wildly pretentious as this, one would expect to pay more than ten pounds for dinner. This was some cut-price entertainment, an attraction for hotel guests who must be puzzled by the name of the Alma-Tadema Society and fascinated by the prospect of finding out about it. Whatever his misgivings, Miles was on stage and an old professional. He must play to this gallery, a homely-looking lot without the Orient Express appearance of the members of the society. Miles could not make out faces at first in detail; he could dimly see three people at a table, one with his back turned, the other two waving. Old faithfuls. Bless them. Bless them. The discreet lighting arrangements—shaded candles on each table—gave him no help, but someone coming into the room let in light from the lobby by which Miles was able to recognize Bridget and Dominick Doyle and, when he turned round, Tod Morris, together at a table. If he was appalled to see them, they greeted him like children getting their first sight of the sea. Bridget waved her napkin; Dominick's face was fixed in a grin; it remained for Tod to give the V sign, and Miles seized on this as the most appropriate way to return all the signals at once.

He was now prepared for anything. *This Is Your Life.* Was old Eamonn going to turn up trumps after all? It would put a decent face on a farce and explain the madness of everyone's behaviour. It would even explain the presence of that discreet couple in the furthest corner of the room, obscured, until he had moved into his place, by a rubber plant. The man was Dicky Dawson, the woman, the sort of wife Dicky would have certainly married —the general's daughter, not the pretty one, the good sport. The couple were taking no notice of their surroundings. He was wearing a suit that had been expensive when it was new and was well looked after. She was determinedly dowdy. A diamond regimental brooch was a word to the wise. Large feet, Miles noticed, and wondered that in his panic he could observe such details; but people waiting to hear the fate of loved ones in danger will count the number of bricks in a wall. The Dawsons were not returning his gaze. All their attention was being given to the business of buttering rolls. Miles could imagine their conversation—ellipsis for the most part; very few words required when so many subjects were kept in a joint account.

"So elegant, I find all this."

Miles had forgotten the Countess.

"Deep in your own thoughts. You Irish are dreamers."

They had taken their places. This woman would be on one side of him all evening and the bird Lalage on the other. It wasn't possible. What devil could have devised such a plan? With Dicky out there—the Doyles and Morris didn't matter, but he could have done very well without them—the evening which was to mark his return to the world of entertainment was taking on the appearance of a bad dream. It wouldn't surprise him at all if Jean and Rowena were to come in and take their seats in some of those empty places. But, first of all, there was Dicky to be dealt with.

The manuscript of the talk was making one of Miles's side pockets bulge—he had worked on it so assiduously and revised it so often, he knew it by heart; but now when it was all important to remember what was in it his mind was in a flux. After so many drafts, what had slipped in? What had slipped out? It was essential to know. He couldn't trust himself to edit the script as he went along. At the beginning he would be in control (if he was careful about the wine) but as he saw DAWSON and DICKY staring at him from the middle of every paragraph how could he carry on? It would be like stepping into a boiling bath. Points had been scored off all the Dawsons. Dicky would resent that. And there were stories that Dicky would recognize as untrue. Miles had let fantasy run way with him—deliberately. That "Cider with Rosie" scene, for example, in the bluebell wood, when Daphne let him take down her knickers. Dicky hadn't been a witness to the embarrassing true version of the scene—not that Miles would put it past Daphne to tell him all about it—but there were other references to life in his house which he would recognize as distortions, the purpose of all of them to establish Miles in the character of the Playboy of the Western World.

Had Miles even considered the possibility of anything like this happening he would have brought along his first draft; in that, he was established in his media character: the shrewd commentator; nobody's fool; unimpressed by titles or trappings; always seeing the funny side; a match for the best. Could he remember it? How did it begin? When he was composing he had given more thought to the project than it deserved, as if he were making his public apologia. Here, with the Doyles and the awful Tod in one corner, and Dicky and wife in another, he couldn't discipline his agitated brain. He was like a man in compromising circumstances who is being questioned by the police.

On one side Lalage was busy attending to her uncle who needed as much attention as an infant in a high chair. On the other, the Countess, having abandoned her efforts to engage Miles's attention, had been reduced to striking a picturesque pose for the room. Miles between this Martha and Mary struggled in vain. Anything distracted him. He couldn't keep his eyes off the Dawsons who might have been alone at home, judging by their demeanour. U. Wright on the Countess's other side was eating his soup in resounding slurps. She appealed with her huge eyes for a respite. Before it came, a waiter at Miles's elbow was telling him in broken English that there was a man outside whose name he couldn't catch who had an urgent message and insisted on seeing him.

Miles asked Lalage and the Countess to excuse him. He was not optimistic about the interruption, and ready to add it to his vexations. There was always, of course, the possibility that help had arrived. He was desperately in need of some.

Outside the door, peering at him round a pillar, he saw Willie looking very like a dog waiting for his master. He came forward at once and performed the human equivalent of wagging his tail. Miles's short "What *do* you want, Willie? I'm in the middle of dinner" was met appropriately by a put-down dog expression.

"I tried to get you on the telephone, but it was no use. I was told you were to be given the message wherever you were. I came in the tube."

"What message, Willie? Don't be too long about it, like a good chap."

"Jerry Dunne is dead."

"You went to all this trouble to tell me *that*?"

"I heard it on the radio. When I told John Joe he said I was to let you know at once."

"What has John Joe, as you call him, have to do with it? I'd like to know."

"You told me often enough to take the message if anyone rang up when you was out. Many and many's the time."

"I'm very grateful, Willie. That is sad news, but I have to make

96

a speech in about an hour to a lot of important people, and I find I left my notes at home. Would you be an angel and fetch them for me? I'll give you money for a taxi. You'll find what I'm looking for in a child's exercise book in a puce cover in the table drawer beside my bed. 'Speech' or 'Talk' will be written on it. If you are in any doubt bring any exercise book you find lying about. Here's a tenner. That ought to be enough. Bring the speech up here and give it to the head waiter and tell him to give it to me without a moment's delay. Off you go. Don't lose it whatever you do."

"He won't let me."

"Who won't let you?"

"John Joe. He's in charge tonight."

"Do you mean that ruffian in the yard?"

"He gave me a tenner when I was coming out and told me not to show my nose in the hotel until after the pubs shut."

"You can say I sent you. You needn't go into details. Tell him I want to see him in the morning in any case. What's this nonsense about his being in charge?"

"The Doyles is out. Mr Morris called for them in his car soon after you went out."

"You run along now, and if you want to hear me talking I'm sure we can find a quiet corner for you. I really must go back to the table."

Willie went then, but with extreme reluctance, leaving Miles as anxious as ever. It was only when he met inquiring faces when he returned to the dining-room that he saw an escape route. Looking preternaturally solemn, and as if in answer to the general question, he said "Jerry Dunne is dead". Then he rejoined the company at the top table.

"Don't let Uncle Samuel hear you," Miss Dubonnet fluted anxiously. "News of deaths raises his spirits as a rule; but he has already confused you with Barney Roche, and this will only perplex him even further. He isn't up to efforts like this evening, really. Mr Carlovassi was so insistent. The fact that Uncle is the only living artist who actually met Alma-Tadema counts for so much with him. He talks about them as friends, but that is a slight exaggeration. Uncle met the great man once at a prize-giving. But you know how everything gets exaggerated with time. Do you know the sad story about the Roman villa Alma-Tadema built for himself on the Regent's Park Canal?"

Miles did not, nor had he heard the question. His mind was far away from Alma-Tadema. Too much was threatening. Would Willie get back in time? What was going on at the hotel? Since when had the trespasser in the yard started to give orders? What was Tod Morris up to, taking the Doyles away from their work and without a word to him? Why did that ruffian tell Willie to stay away? Were arms going to be run into all that empty storage space in the yard? If they were, Tod and the Doyles knew all about it and were setting up an alibi. No wonder they hadn't said a word to him about their little outing.

"It was blown up."

"Good God. What was blown up?"

"The Roman villa."

"Oh, you had me frightened for a moment. I didn't think people blew things up in those days."

"It was an accident. A boat with explosives on board blew up outside the villa. Fortunately Sir Lawrence was not at home."

The fate of the villa should have been a matter of indifference to Miles just then, but it seemed peculiarly appropriate at the moment. What was going on? Only in a dream would he be dining among such freaks in the same room as Dicky Dawson and the Doyles and Tod Morris.

"No one can replace old friends. I feel deeply sorry for your tragedy."

The Countess was going into action again.

"Have you children?"

"No, I'm afraid I haven't."

"Why are you *afraid*? I have two, darling girls. Lalage makes all their clothes—beautifully." Then (leaning across Miles) "I was telling Mr O'Malley about all you do for the girls."

"Such darlings," Lalage piped.

"She spoils them terribly."

"You couldn't spoil those children. Their mother has brought them up beautifully."

"I had to. Their father is so much away from home. Cairo one day, Karachi the next, Athens, Beirut . . . I can't keep up with him."

"What does the Count do?"

"Business. Import, export. He looks very like Yasmin, my eldest."

"A perfect darling," piped Lalage, who was listening.

"And my husband isn't a count."

98

"Oh, I'm so sorry."

"Not at all. People are always making that mistake. I want you to get the right picture."

"Do you know everyone here?"

"No. I hardly know anyone in London. I live here because my children are safe. When I married I was living in Beirut, but I got out as quickly as I could. I would like you to meet my husband. He is a man of culture. I could not have married a man who lived only for business. My husband loves beauty in every form. He is the only man I ever kissed. That is a thing that worries me about England—for my girls, I mean. How am I to keep them as I was? I cannot prevent them from reading the newspapers. *The Times*—even *The Times*—has articles about matters that should not be discussed before young girls. I think if I were alone I would live in Tibet. I am deeply spiritual as Lalage will tell you."

"Uncle Sam fell asleep just then." Lalage was accounting for her sudden withdrawal from the conversation. "Has the Countess told you that she has six of Uncle Sam's paintings."

"Mr O'Malley must come and see them some day. Mr Carlo-vassi has the self-portrait. He has a wonderful collection. He is going to let us see some of his most recent acquisitions after dinner. He says that I look very like Eve in one of the paintings. He likes to tease me, I think."

The serious business of dinner was over, at any moment now old Sam would be getting to his feet. Lalage had been working on him in their corner since the lemon sorbet was served. The Countess, not having received an intelligible reply to any of her questions, had resigned herself to looking interesting. Miles sent a note to Tod Morris: "Any news of Willie?" and received it back with "Nope" scribbled on it in lipstick. In truth Miles had abandoned any hope of aid from that quarter. His mind was scuttling down innumerable blind alleys. The talk that he could not give was thrusting itself forward. He knew it would succeed in tripping him up no matter what precautions he took. He was in hell. Hell would be like this. He knew that now. Whatever he had done wrong, he was being punished for it. *Keep away from the women.* To complete the picture Daphne had only to join her brother and his wife at their table. She had a story to tell, about the time they lay down in the bluebell wood and Daphne had said, "Well, you may, but for Heaven's sake be careful", and he had failed completely to rise to the occasion and she had settled her clothes and got up in a temper.

"Ladies and gentlemen. Pray silence for the chairman, Mr Samuel Slaughter RA."

There was then an immense heaving as Sam Slaughter, assisted by his niece, hauled himself to his feet. Swaying, blinking, he looked like the oldest lion in the pride daring his rivals. He seemed to relish the applause, and glanced about him to see where it came from, perhaps hoping against hope that out there somewhere was someone who knew old Sam.

Coming out, dressing up, eating his way through that dinner with a set of teeth on which he had long since ceased to rely, had consumed his meagre reserves of nervous energy.

"Thank you," he said. "My niece . . ." But what he was going to say about his niece eluded him and the pause was becoming painful when he bent down and they had a short confabulation.

"Where is it?" he was heard to say, and she replied, "In your hand."

"Great God," he said. "So it is."

"*Miles O'Malley*. That's the man I want you to hear this evening. I'm glad he was able to come. I don't know what I am doing here. You must ask my niece. She knows everything. I did meet Alma-Tadema once. That takes me back a bit. I was a student at the Slade, and he was a grand old man. He knew his stuff all right. Don't make any mistake about that, but why anyone should be giving a dinner for him beats me. Anyhow I'm glad you did when I was still able to drag myself out to it. You will have to get someone else next time. My job is to introduce Mr O'Malley who is better known to all of you than he is to me. I hardly ever look at television nowadays. Can't see. But it can do no harm to wish you all the best of luck."

Sam was about to sit down.

"Give the toast of the guests," Lalage fluted, but nothing could arrest the old man's descent and nothing would get him on to his feet again. Aristides Carlovassi took over. Raising his glass, he said "Our guests, and I wish to couple with them, Miles O'Malley".

A round dozen rose to their feet and repeated, "Our guests and Miles O'Malley". The mass of the audience at the separate tables decided that they were not involved, and remained seated. The result was to make the proceedings at the high table seem as if they were taking place in a separate cage at the zoo. Miles, who had been thinking fast, now formed a desperate resolve. Looking preternaturally solemn, he stood up and was greeted at once with loud clapping by the hotel customers. There was a time when this was routine. No joke so flat that it did not evoke at least one hysterical laugh. He held up his arms, as he used to do, appealing for a chance to get a word in. All this popularity, his arms were saying, was killing him.

A blessed beginning. He wasn't prepared for it. Had he been, he would have forgotten all about the missing script and chatted away as only he knew how. But it was too late to change course again. He had made a decision; he would have to go through with it.

"Mr Chairman, sir, and friends. We are gathered here to celebrate a painter who died before most of us were born and whose name is only faintly remembered except among those who have made a study of late Victorian art. I hope I am right when I say that there is no particular significance in the choice of the name; indeed, I am informed by Miss Dubonnet, to whom we are indebted for the arrangements this evening, that members of the society are simply people who love beautiful things; some of whom have made collections of paintings of the late Victorian school. The society had to be called something, and I believe that the inspiration to call it after Alma-Tadema came from our chairman. He is the last survivor of that period, and I hope that he was only kidding when he said he wouldn't be able to take the chair here next year. I will now make a present of an idea to the society: let your next dinner be in honour of a great English painter, Samuel Slaughter RA, and let him take my role as your guest on that occasion. If the honour fell on me to take *his* place, I should be delighted.

"I had intended to indulge in a little reminiscence this evening, but a message was brought to me during dinner, a very sad message indeed. It announced the death of a friend. Jerry Dunne is dead, I am sorry to tell you. He was not, I am confident, a stranger to many of you here. Will you be good enough to bear with me if I visit on you some of my thoughts since I received the sad news? First of all—because the occasion calls for absolute honesty —may I say that he was not an intimate friend. People who have as much sheer drive as Jerry had—while it accelerates their rate of progress—are hard to become close to until they attain the eminence towards which they have been advancing with a concentration that leaves no room for the disinterested relaxation of friendship. We were never rivals. When the British Broadcasting Corporation decided to treat me as an uneconomic coal pit, Jerry was the first source of alternative energy it turned to. I was delighted for his sake. I could almost, I felt, have taken the credit for having shown him the way. From the moment I found myself being double-crossed by the Corporation, Jerry became as ubiquitous on the television screens of these islands as advertisements for washing powders.

"I have no grievance against Jerry on that score—God forbid —but what I want to draw your attention to is the coincidence: one Irishman replaced another on the screen that is in every home. Has it occurred to you that England is trying to make good, through television, centuries of despoliation of Ireland? Anyone with an Irish accent—and some of them are bogus ones—is given a visa to go where he pleases and a permit to say what he likes. But then I am permanently puzzled by the English idea of Ireland and its attitude towards Ireland. I speak as a friend. My debt to this country is incalculable—a hard word that 'incalculable' to say at this time of the evening. I'd like you to note that I've managed to say it twice. You are generous and long-suffering. Imagine the fate of the Jerry Dunnes of England if they proposed themselves as programme presenters in my country. There would be blood on the streets.

"The point I want to make is that Jerry died a free-lance to the end. So am I. So are all the other Paddies in the media business. If we were actuated by a common purpose, if we saw ourselves as uniquely privileged to interpret our country to the English, might we not, if we went very tactfully about it, sow the seed of better understanding?"

Miles paused for emphasis, but he was overcome by a feeling that no one wanted him to continue. His deep thoughts, now that he was airing them for the first time in public, did not seem so impressive as when, glass in hand, he had been communing with himself. He had been given all the encouragement he could have asked for when he stood up. Now people were talking to each other. There were laughs. This audience did not want a serious lecture after dinner. Nor did he really want to give one (he should be bringing in all that stuff about St Columbanus at this point but he couldn't face it). He wasn't being sincere. If he had really talked off the cuff he would have told them out there about the shameless procrastinating of the BBC and his longing to be back on the screen. For a few seconds this evening he had experienced the glow of being welcomed—a public favourite. It had surprised him; it should have heartened him, but he had thrown the chance of an evening of good fun away to maunder on about that loud-mouth Jerry Dunne. It was a desperate expedient. His dilemma, in the person of Dicky Dawson, was at that moment taking the skin off a peach. It was something he was obviously very good at. When he had taken the last strip off his own, he offered to do his wife's and swapped peaches when she accepted his offer. They might as well have been a hundred miles away, dining by themselves. There was a self-sufficiency about this modest proceeding that made Miles feel indignant. He would have liked to have pointed out Dicky to the audience and describe the humiliations he had suffered in his house and the sense of not belonging. "Protestant impudence", his mother called it.

Miles was aware that people were staring at him, and a rumble of conversation had begun in the further places where the diners had come to the conclusion that this train was running late. It was at this point Gideon Russell came into the room and looked around him distractedly. From every corner of the room waiters were descending on him.

"A friend of mine," Miles said *sotto voce* to Miss Dubonnet. Russell's arrival provided the distraction the company had been waiting for. Miles stared at indifferent faces as if inspiration might be gathered from them. He must bring this farce to an end, and find out what brought Russell here. Something serious. That was certain. The most self-effacing and unintrusive man Miles had ever met. Gate-crashing a dinner party was behaviour so totally out of character that he must have a very good reason. He had been put into a seat as a result of cross-signalling between Miss Dubonnet and the waiters who had been on the point of throwing him out. Now the audience, the welcome distraction over, turned their attention back to the speaker. Miles shared to the full their boredom, but he was at a loss how to get himself off his hook. A frantic glance at the Countess provided inspiration. If he had been markedly inattentive to her all evening and unimpressed by her charms, he had, from long training, taken in what she had been saying into his left ear even though he had not responded.

"After dinner Mr Carlovassi is going to show us some of his most recent acquisitions—"

"Only to members." The Countess sounded alarmed.

"I am sure, on this occasion, Mr Carlovassi extends an invitation to everyone. We began this evening together. It would be a pity not to see it through to the end. My charming neighbour on my right tells me that Mr Carlovassi has become deeply fond of the paintings of Russell Flint. They are in what the Countess describes very happily as the 'refined nude' tradition. Mr Carlovassi, who must forgive me for acting as his circus band, will tell you about his pictures himself. They will be on display in the reception room on the next floor, where they have a suitable background. Mr Carlovassi, the Countess tells me, sees the forming of the Alma-Tadema Society as a step towards the revival of the lost tradition of western art, going back to Botticelli and beyond. No one has done more to stand out against the rot than Sam, our gallant chairman. How are we going to bring about a renaissance of the Renaissance? That's our problem. I leave the answer to you. I feel myself being drawn out of my depth, and I am a person who likes always to have one foot at least on the ground. I only present you with the idea—throw it to you to chew over, describes it better. Ideas begin in this sort of environment. They spread if someone has the wit in front and the money behind them."

A note was passed to Miles. "Must talk to you. Urgent."

He looked down the table and saw Gideon Russell's imploring face. He felt utterly irresponsible so far as this evening's entertainment was concerned. He would stop now.

"I give you the toast of the Alma-Tadema Society and with it I couple the name of—"

"Aristides," said the Countess, rescuing him.

"*Aristides* Carlovassi."

Miles sat and tapped his fingers on the table while he listened to Mr Carlovassi delivering platitudes in a voice that sounded as if it was coming up from an oil well. He could see the Dawsons looking ever so slightly dubious, as if the joke was going on a little too long. Dicky had effectively ruined the evening for Miles by his presence, but now it didn't seem to matter. The imploring expression on Gideon Russell's face told him that something far more important than the absurdities of this dinner had taken place elsewhere. The very moment the speaker finished—he asked everyone present to come down and see his paintings—Miles got up without ceremony and moved down the table to where Russell was sitting in one of the empty seats.

"Gideon, what brings you here?"

"I tried to reach you on the telephone, but I was told you couldn't be disturbed."

"What are you trying to tell me?"

"Not good news, I'm afraid. There's been a fire."

"Where?"

"At the hotel."

"No one was hurt? Tell me."

"I don't think so, but there was pandemonium, getting all those families out. You can imagine. The fire started in the garages at the back of your block. The firemen got it under control before it got to the bed and breakfast blocks."

"The Doyles are here. Morris brought them. We had better break the news to them. I see signs of a general move downstairs. What an evening it has been. When did the fire break out? Willie was here shortly after we sat down to dinner."

"Willie was *here*?"

"Why do you look so surprised? You are in bad shape, Gideon. I hadn't noticed when you came in. I must get hold of a drink for you."

"I don't want anything, thank you. You said Willie was here. I don't understand."

"Someone sent him with a message that Jerry Dunne was dead. He had me called away from the table. He was terribly worked up about it. I don't know why. Now I understand why he didn't come back. I was cursing the poor fellow. The fire must have given him a bad fright. Everyone seems to be going. I'll catch our friends. Wait here. I wish you would let me get you something to drink."

Russell shook his head impatiently.

As Miles moved away from the table a man who was passing put a friendly hand on Russell's shoulder and said something to his companion. She looked back and smiled. Miles stared with amazement. Gideon Russell knew Dicky, knew him quite well, judging by that little scene. The Dawsons had gone before Miles had come to the end of the very pregnant Bridget's effusive greeting.

"You were wonderful, just wonderful. Wasn't he Dominick?"

"I have had bad news, I'm sorry to tell you. Who was left in charge at the hotel?"

The Doyles exchanged glances; then Dominick said Jane was. "She is well able to look after it, the same lassie, and Willie's there."

"My friend Mr Russell came to tell me there has been a fire."

"O Sacred Heart of Jesus," said Bridget.

"What class of a fire?" said her husband.

"Here he is. Mr Russell will tell you for himself. This is Mr Doyle, our manager, Gideon, and Mrs Doyle. Tell them about the fire, Gideon, and should *I* be doing anything? What's going to happen to all those poor creatures on the street?"

"I think someone should get back to the hotel as quickly as possible," Russell said. "I just happened to be taking an evening stroll when I saw a sudden blaze. It looked a mile high, and it was some time before I realized where it was coming from. Then there was shouting and screaming and people pouring out on to the road. Pandemonium. The fire brigade arrived wonderfully soon. Of course we were all kept back, but so far as I could make out the fire was confined to the rear of the first building. Your own flat is unharmed, I'd say. There were several police cars about."

"So long as nobody's killed we may be thankful," Bridget said piously.

Tod Morris took over, ignoring Russell.

"You had better go back to the hotel, Dominick. I'll drive you. Bridget, you should go to your sister's place. We will get you a taxi. I don't know what Miles wants to do."

"I want a word with Mr O'Malley," Russell said with a note of authority that Miles had never heard from him before. He was not going to be ordered about by Tod Morris. Looking at them both Miles was shocked by Gideon's pallor. He was unable to disguise his impatience with this interruption, and when Bridget said, "I'm worrying about where our poor gentleman is going to sleep this night", he ignored her. "I want a word with you, Miles." No one looked pleased with the outcome; but Russell stood his ground, and under Tod's sulky leadership the little party shambled out with further "Good nights" exclusively for Miles's benefit.

"I thought they would never go," Russell said, wiping his forehead with a table napkin lying close at hand. "Can we sit down somewhere? Over here. I'll take that drink now."

Russell led the way to a corner of the lounge. This was a new Russell. A man in charge. Left to himself Miles would not have known what to do. There were those absurd people upstairs—he couldn't face them at the moment, but he should, at least, give an explanation to Lalage for his sudden disappearance. The hotel fire was what people called a tragedy: but the more he thought about it the more pleased he was. There would be insurance money; it was what he had been secretly longing for—a miracle, a way of escaping from the Doyles, Tod Morris, and the horrible hotel. But it didn't seem the thing to say to decent Russell, who was looking like a man who had seen a ghost.

"I can't stay for long," he said. "Wife. You understand."

"What did you want to tell me? I thought our friends didn't look too pleased at being kept out of the secret."

"I don't care for your friends. Forget about them for a moment. I have something more serious to tell you."

"What is it?"

"You said Willie was here. When did he leave?"

"Let me see. We sat down at eight-thirty. He arrived at the very beginning of dinner. I remember calculating that he had an hour at least to go home and get back in. I had left my notes behind and I wanted him to fetch them. By the way, I didn't know you knew Dicky Dawson."

"I don't know who you are talking about; could we stick to the subject?"

"But, I've often mentioned Dicky to you, and you never let on you knew him. It's the most extraordinary coincidence."

"Miles, I've no time for your frivolities. Willie is dead. Dead. Murdered. I wasn't going to mention it in front of that crew, but now I'm sorry I didn't. I'd have liked to watch their faces."

"He was caught in the fire then. Poor little Willie. And to think—"

"He was murdered, I tell you."

"Who's in God's name would ever have murdered Willie?"

"I wish I knew. I saw it happen. I see you have taken it in at last."

"Go on. I want to hear what happened. I feel to blame—"

107

"I went to get the tube at Camden Town on my way here. Except for the man who sold me my ticket I seemed to be the only person in the place—you know what tube stations are like at that time of night. The eerie sound of the escalators. I was down at the bottom when I heard a voice. I thought it was calling my name. I looked up and there, sure enough, was someone standing on the top step. A little figure. I couldn't see very well without my spectacles. I had time to spare. Your 'do' wouldn't be over for a couple of hours. I could go up and see who it was. But I didn't want to. Not at that time with no one else around—I never thought of Willie. Then I saw that other people were up there and I wasn't needed. I turned to go on to the platform, when I heard a shriek, the most terrible shriek I have ever heard. Not human. And this bundle flying towards me. For a second. It fell on the escalator and bounced and came down again and slumped against the rail like a sack. It came down so slowly I was tempted to run away and leave someone else to deal with it. And then it slid under my feet. A little hunchback. Blood was running out of his nose and his eyes were wide open. That was the shocking thing. He seemed to be glaring at me. But he was dead. There was no doubt about that. A train came in, and a few people got off. They looked away when they saw us. Can you believe it? Then I went on to the platform, but the train had gone.

"I went upstairs to the man collecting tickets. He went on as if he wasn't taking me seriously until I said, 'There's a dead man down there'. He had to pay attention then. He said he would ring for help. I went back to Willie. I didn't know who he was before that, but this time I recognized him. He looked like a dead bird. It seemed a lifetime before anyone came and all the time I had that shriek in my ears. I'll never forget it."

"Did you tell the police?"

"No. Two officials came eventually. They took particulars, and an ambulance arrived. No one asked me if I knew who Willie was. They found all they needed in his pockets. I told them exactly what happened. I gave my name and address. The police will make a call no doubt. That's why I had better get back home. So long as she isn't interrupted Doreen won't notice I'm not in until the late film is over. She always waits up for that."

"I shouldn't have sent Willie back for my notes. What the hell did they matter? But at the same time it seemed terribly important that I shouldn't offend Dicky Dawson."

"Who is Dicky Dawson? You have mentioned him twice this evening."

"The man who tapped you on the shoulder just now. He had a lady with him."

"The only people I saw that I knew, apart from yourself, were the Mycrofts, clients of the bank when I was in Lewes. Nice people."

"I must be going mad."

"We must get you to bed. Try at the desk and see if you can get yourself a room here. Get them to bring you a large whiskey and two aspirins. I'll get in touch in the morning. Don't move until I come. Then I think you ought to have a long talk with my solicitor friend."

There was a room for which a king's ransom was required, but it seemed to Miles just then the best value he had ever had in his life.

In bed, with the door locked and a bottle of Jameson beside him, he felt safe. He didn't go to sleep for a long time. The thought of Willie's death, as Russell described it, was too frightening.

He wasn't responsible for it; and he must fight any morbid inclination to feel guilty, just *sad* when he thought about him, and he must try not to think about him; that did no one any good. You could see the impression the scene had made on Russell, literally put years on him. But, then, he was a sensitive sort of man and his wife with her drug problem must be a continual strain on his nerves, wondering what she would be up to next. Russell had some grudge against Willie. He showed it the only time Miles had seen them together. He was longing to ask him what it was all about at the time, but there was something about Russell that forbade intimate questions. Miles, who was incoherent in his thoughts by this time, fell asleep while he was trying to assure himself that it was inevitable if you attained such a place in the world as he had that people would push themselves forward to help you, wanting to get in on the act, hoping that some of the glamour would brush off on them.

The telephone ringing beside his bed woke Miles next morning. He took a little while to make out where he was. Russell was on the line. A police officer had called and taken a statement from him. After he had gone Russell had got in touch with his solicitor friend. He could now tell his name: Johnnie Moriarty, another

Irishman, but that wasn't to be held against him. He, Russell, had made an appointment for Miles at lunch hour—the only time the solicitor could fit him in. His office was in Bloomsbury Square.

"If I were you I'd stay where you are until it's time to go, then take a taxi. Johnnie has a very capable secretary, Miss Stewart. She will find you somewhere to put up for the present. I think you ought to consult Johnnie before you go back to your own place."

"But I haven't got as much as a tooth brush or a rag to put on except what I came out in."

"That can be coped with, but see Johnnie first."

It was curious, Miles reflected, after that conversation, how consistent the pattern of his life was. There was always someone on hand to take him over. To get him out of the hands of the Doyles called for a fire, but a few hours later he was preparing to hand himself over to a solicitor and his secretary, neither of whom he had ever seen before or even talked to. He was still by no means clear how much damage had been done to the hotel and if his penthouse had escaped. He felt strangely lethargic about finding out. It meant trouble. He rang for the morning papers. In the serious ones there were short references to the fire, saying no one had been injured. One of the tabloids had a lurid account of the plight of the families in overcrowded rooms being thrown out on the street. There were interviews with tenants, all saying very much the same thing. The cause of the fire was not speculated about but everyone agreed how suddenly it had broken out. The police had not ruled out the possibility of arson. The manager, Mr Doyle, had refused to give a full interview, but expressed relief that none of the residents had suffered except from fright and inconvenience. His own apartments had been severely damaged. The fire began in the stores at the back of the building. He had no theory about its origins, and ruled out the idea of arson as "ridiculous". Pressed for a comment on the shameful overcrowding he had said, "Would you leave these homeless people on the streets?" Miles's name had not been mentioned. Thank God for that. But it wouldn't be for long if there was any *investigative journalism* into the circumstances. It was only when you were threatened by it yourself you realized how much pharisaical humbug there was to contend with, high-minded hacks pretending that they had declared war on secrecy in high places, prepared to cover up for anyone who was willing to betray his master's business. Once they heard that he was nominally the owner of those overcrowded dens he would never be allowed to hear the end of it. Rowena must be turning in her grave at the picture of what she had let him in for when she handed him gagged and bound into the hands of the dreadful Doyles. Willie's fate was a warning. So long as the Parnell Hotel was in his name Miles was virtually a prisoner of the IRA. He must impress on this friend of Russell's how urgent it was to get him out of the hands of these people. Nothing else would have got him out of bed this morning.

Miles was pulling on his trousers and had temporarily lost balance when someone knocked on his door. A porter with a familiar lavender-coloured envelope.

"Mr O'Malley?"

"That's me."

"A letter for you."

This envelope was addressed in a woman's handwriting, the other had been typed. This time there was no lingering pleasure in the opening; he fell on it like a hawk on a rabbit.

Dear Mr O'Malley,

Mr Carlovassi has asked me to write to you to say how sorry he is to hear that you have met with such misfortune. Will you please accept the hospitality of the society and remain where you are for as long as you please? Charge all expenditure to your room number. It will be looked after. Please accept the enclosed cheque as a small appreciation of your contribution to our entertainment last evening. If you should want to telephone me, I shall be out from eleven until two o'clock and from five until eight. Uncle is here all the time, but the poor dear finds the telephone hard to cope with.

Yours sincerely,

Lalage.

The cheque was for a thousand pounds and it was signed on behalf of the Alma-Tadema Society by Aristides Carlovassi. There was something emollient about that cheque, and the signature would have made an arresting decoration on a shirt pocket. This Alma-Tadema group were bizarre, but a thousand pounds was a thousand pounds. It was a long time since Miles had handled so much ready money. Princely. A lavish compliment at a time when he needed more than encouragement. But it only solved his immediate problem. He couldn't postpone a return to his own hotel indefinitely. His dilemma was acute. If he didn't go to see the extent of the damage and how those crowded unfortunates were getting on he might be pilloried; more than likely if he went he would be seen by some snooper. People would say he was a slum landlord, a new Rachman, an IRA sympathizer —God knows what Doyle's friends were planning for the sheds at the back. The BBC must be laughing. What had caused the fire? And what a pity it had been confined to the back of the buildings. Johnnie Moriarty would need to be pretty astute to get him out of the mess he was in.

Now it was time to get ready to meet his new lawyer. The velvet-lined cloak would have to stay behind; the sombrero likewise. What a raffish impression he made by daylight.

Miles was prepared to see the name Johnnie Moriarty up in lights, and when he read Elvery, Leech and Peterson on the brass plate in Bloomsbury Square he thought for a moment that he must have taken down the wrong address. A second notice board in the entry had lots of other names on it including J. G. Moriarty BA, TCD. The man himself came out of his room as Miles went into the general office, as if he had been waiting for him—small, ferret-faced, about fifty, in comfortably untidy clothes, all smiling informality. He settled Miles in a leather armchair, but himself seemed to prefer to conduct the interview at no fixed address. Sometimes he sat at his desk, sometimes on it, sometimes he took a perambulation round the room, and Miles grew accustomed to being addressed from behind his chair.

"I suppose you know the Doyles have been arrested?"

"I can't believe it. When did this happen?"

"Only a few minutes before you arrived."

The news gave Miles a thrill of pleasure which he hoped he did not betray. He was learning disquieting truths about himself.

"Gideon tells me that you spent last night at the new hotel on the King's Road."

"That's right. Costs a bomb. But look at this." He handed the solicitor Lalage's letter. He read it slowly, his forehead wrinkling as he did so.

"I think you ought to send back the cheque and turn down the invitation. Or let me do it for you. You know nothing about these people."

"But you couldn't meet anyone more respectable than Miss Dubonnet, and she can't be in any ring or she wouldn't be making clothes for children and housekeeping for that old uncle of hers."

"She is employed by these people."

"Nothing will convince me that she knew anything about the fire."

"No doubt, but if you won't take my advice you ought to go to some other solicitor."

Miles heard his father's voice. "Of course I'll do as you say. I don't know yet if I can use my rooms. I would have gone to see for myself on the way here but Gideon seemed to think I shouldn't until I had had a talk with you. In the first place, I don't think this is a happy moment to disclose my connection with the hotel. It is a rotten place to be staying in and a repulsive one to own. I allowed myself to get into the hands of those Doyles, and it looks as if they are in the hands of the IRA. It would be hard to convince anyone that I was innocent. You have to understand I was under constant strain with my wife's fatal illness, and after she died the BBC chose the moment to put a knife in my back. I simply couldn't cope. In that situation I let myself drift; the last thing I wanted was trouble. I had had more than my share. I'll admit to you that I thought strange men hanging around the place looked suspicious, but I had made up my mind to do something about it when I had finished with my speechifying."

"What I can't understand is a man of your experience attaching so much importance to what sounds a silly occasion. Can you explain it?"

"I was very low. The circumstances of the invitation intrigued me. I really find it impossible to explain my behaviour to a man like you whose life is conducted on the basis of reason and common sense. I have to rely on impulse. My wife—my late wife, that is—called me 'the last romantic'. But she said it was a colourful way of dodging responsibilities. That's enough about myself. Tell me what I ought to do now."

"Tell the police you want to talk to them. I'll come with you. Answer their questions truthfully and economically. I mean, listen to the question and give the shortest possible answer. Stick to facts."

"What am I to say if they ask me about Willie?"

"Tell them exactly what happened. He came to tell you your friend had died. You sent him back to get your notes. You never saw him again. Gideon Russell told you about his death."

"Coming all that way to tell me Jerry Dunne was dead when I was out to dinner doesn't sound convincing. Does it?"

"Its chief merit is that it's the truth. For all we know someone made it an excuse to get Willie off the scene. He must have been in the way."

"The Doyles can't be involved in that. They were at the dinner with Tod Morris. I was amazed to see them."

"I heard about that."

"Surely that was a fool-proof alibi."

"We shall have to wait and see."

"Am I to take it that you suspect the Alma-Tadema people?"

"Why did they arrange this dinner so conveniently? I don't believe that they had a sudden inspiration to call you out of your retirement."

"I have not retired."

"Forgive me. I should have remembered. I was told your position by Gideon. What I meant to say was, if this society is a group of picture-lovers why invite you who have no connection with the arts to address them?"

"Oh, that was explained. The last thing they wanted was a serious lecture. This was a night out. After dinner Mr Carlovassi was showing his pictures to anyone interested. Besides Sam Slaughter RA (don't forget) was as much artistic ballast as the evening could carry."

"His presence, I must admit, puzzles me. I can see that they wanted the evening to look respectable and harmless, but why call on someone quite so old?"

"His niece was the secretary. Some of the ladies knew her. The Countess Melashoff who sat beside me said that she made clothes for her children."

"The Countess's Lebanese husband wasn't there, I assume?"

"No. I gather that he keeps away from England."

"I can see why your Lalage might have been given the secretary job if she needed the money, but I am puzzled by the choice of chairman, unless they were desperate. Of course, it was an improvisation. The people who organized the dinner had their own reasons. They were not looking forward to another occasion. If the old boy lasted out the evening, that was as much as they required of him. But this uncle and niece connection puzzles me. Have you visited them at home?"

"No, but I understood that they have a house in Clapham and

he has his studio close at hand in another house that overlooks the Common."

"Let me look at that letter again. She tells you that she will be not at home at certain times but uncle is on call all day."

"He is staying at home, resting, I suppose, after what must have been a late night for him."

With the manner of one who is reserving judgement, Johnnie changed the subject.

"Shall I give the police a tinkle? A man whose property has been burnt down usually gets in touch with the police. I don't want you to wait until they call on you. That would look as if you were trying to avoid them."

"Go ahead. I'm in your hands."

That was only true up to a point: Miles had no intention of handing back the cheque. Damn it all, he had earned it, and the prospect of a few nights in that opulent hotel at someone else's expense was enticing after the shabby years. He would decide about that later. He noticed that Johnnie had a note of the police number on his blotter. Had he been in touch with them already? Miles wasn't used to the ways of respectable solicitors. His legal advisers, supplied by Tod Morris, had always conveyed the impression that they were hiding from the police themselves.

"I have Mr Miles O'Malley with me. His hotel—the Parnell Hotel in Lindsay Road—was set on fire last night. He wants to talk to whoever is in charge."

Miles made a gesture of protest at the admission that he owned the hotel. It was too bald; it left too much responsibility in his lap. Johnnie should have qualified the admission. However, he was in this man's hands, but he must not let him, or anyone, persuade him that he had anything to answer for. He had behaved like a traditional Irish landlord who left everything in his agent's hands. When the agent did anything unpopular on his master's behalf he was there for the peasants to shoot. There was a logic behind the convention.

"The Detective Superintendent would like to see us right away." Johnnie sounded as if he had scored a point. Miles tried to look gratified, but he felt as if he had handcuffs on his wrists.

The Superintendent was a youngish man with a relaxed manner. The policeman who sat in with him at the interview seemed more menacing, but that may have been because he remained silent throughout.

Miles was asked his name and address and age, at which he hesitated, before saying sixty-seven. He was genuinely vague about this, as it was one of the subjects he liked to think about as little as possible. He hesitated again when he was asked if he owned the Parnell Hotel, even though Johnnie had already admitted as much, not because of last night's events but from shame at acknowledging any connection with the overcrowded temporary accommodation. He would have liked to lead into the subject gradually, to explain why, owing admittedly to his own extravagance, he had let his large earnings slip through his fingers, and how Rowena had had this plan to provide for his future, and through illness had not been able to keep an eye on the hotel, and had been taken in by the Doyles (much more than he had ever been, his being Irish made him familiar with the type). By the time she died he had lost grip, and when he needed support he had been treated miserably by the BBC.

But the opportunity was not given him. The detective blocked his efforts to put his answer into its proper setting. "My wife bought it and I borrowed from a building society to pay for my half share. My wife is dead and I suppose I do own her half share, but it is tied up in some way and I only heard recently that the building society is registered as owner of her share as well as mine."

"Are you not in the position of anyone who has bought a property with the help of a mortgage?"

"I wouldn't like to think of anyone else being in my position. It comes I must admit from leaving myself in the hands of other people."

"Who are these other people?"

"All my business affairs are looked after by Tod Morris of Victoria Villas, Kilburn."

"Can you remember his number?"

Miles gave it hesitantly because he had become vague about all numbers and names. He had no wish to make difficulties, and he was conscious of Moriarty watching his performance and not being impressed by it.

"What is Mr Morris's role exactly? Does he take a part in the running of the hotel?"

"Much less than he used to. He introduced me to the manager,

116

Dominick Doyle. He had found me the money to pay for my share from a building society he runs—the Hibernian Friendly Society. Whenever I needed advice or, indeed, anything that had to be looked for, Morris had it or knew where to get it. Latterly, I haven't seen so much of him."

"Have you fallen out?"

"Not exactly, but he knows I disapprove of taking in homeless families that the Local Authority pays for."

"Who else is on the board?"

"The Doyles have one share each. That qualifies them to be directors. But this is a formality. In practice Doyle runs the place and Morris advises in the background. Recently I have been agitating for a board meeting to be called."

"Why?"

"I feel that I am not being consulted enough. Morris is not taking his former interest, and Doyle is running the business without proper supervision. I reproach myself for having been pushed into this room renting. At the time Morris and Doyle said we needed the money."

"Can you tell me about the hotel, the layout of the premises, I mean?"

"As you probably know—"

"I want you to tell me."

"There are six houses on Lindsay Road. I live in a penthouse that we built at the top of the first pair of houses we bought when my wife was alive. There are two rooms off the kitchen where the Doyles live, the rest consists of twenty bedrooms and a lounge and dining room. At the back there are garages which used to be coach-houses with former haylofts over them. Then we bought the four adjoining houses. They have been made into rabbit warrens. A family in each room."

"And what about the back premises?"

"They are the same in each house. Doyle has plans for building. He wants to make himself a mews residence and to add rooms to the hotel. Meanwhile there is one motor-car, my BMW, which Doyle uses exclusively, in the garage and the rest is used for storage."

"Storage of what exactly?"

"Supplies for the hotel and a good deal of rubbish. Recently one of the lofts was cleaned up and let to someone."

"Do you know who that someone is?"

"Frankly, I don't. Doyle was to give a full explanation at the next meeting."

"Did it not seem strange to you that your hotel manager should let off some of your premises without even consulting you?"

"It wasn't described as letting. The hotel was being paid a rent to keep storage space available. While it was empty Doyle was obliging a friend with temporary accommodation. He had said he would make a statement at the next board meeting, and I'm bound to admit that I had shown no interest at all in the running of the hotel. So long as I was paid enough to satisfy my modest requirements I wasn't really interested. Very recently this man —John Joe, he was called, no surname mentioned—was hanging around the place a lot and I was told that he took the hotel over on the night of the fire. I was out fulfilling a speaking engagement."

"Where was that?"

"At a new hotel in the King's Road, the Aegean. I was invited a few months ago by the Alma-Tadema Society."

"How do you spell that?"

Miles told the detective, acquiring in the process a little authority, he felt. It was like acting in a play.

"Who told you John Joe took the hotel over when you were elsewhere?"

"Willie."

"Willie who?"

"I always knew him as 'Willie', but I could get you his full name if you want me to. I daresay you have it. He was murdered that evening."

"When did you hear about that?"

"My friend Gideon Russell saw it happen at Camden Town tube station. He called me out at the dinner to tell me about it. But I am sure you have his statement. He told me he gave it to the police."

"It would save time if you would confine yourself to the questions I ask you, Mr O'Malley."

"I'm sorry. I'm not used to this sort of thing."

"Could you give me a description of this John Joe person?"

"He was about thirty, rather run to flesh with a big beer belly on him. He had reddish brown curly hair worn like a golliwog. Small blue green eyes. About my own height. Accent might be Limerick. I couldn't swear. He was noticeably curt in our exchanges."

"Could you give me an account of your own movements yesterday?"

Miles looked at his solicitor but he was deliberately staring into space. The question had a familiar and threatening ring. This was not a play. It had sinister possibilities.

"From the moment I got up?"

"Yes, if you don't mind."

It took nearly an hour and at the end Miles was exhausted. He kept on making wrong turnings, as it were, and had to retrace his footsteps; and then there was the matter of Dicky Dawson, the cause of all the confusion, the cause of Willie's murder when one faced up to it. But Dicky Dawson wasn't there, only a man from Lewes who looked like what Dicky Dawson might look like now if he was still alive (which Miles wasn't sure about). He tried to leave Dicky out of the story, but he got in somehow and made Miles sound very dotty. He couldn't save himself. He looked at Johnnie in his worst flounderings, but the solicitor was always watching the progress of a fly on the ceiling.

"Where will you be if I want to get in touch with you?" the detective inquired at the end of the session. Miles was pleased with this question. It put a card into his hand.

"I don't want to go back to my own place at the moment, even if it is possible to live in it. This letter was handed to me this morning, and I thought I might take advantage of the offer it contains."

The superintendent held the letter as if it might explode in his hand.

"Are you going to accept this invitation?"

"It seems ungracious not to. Mr Moriarty has doubts about it."

"Why?"

"My client doesn't know anything about these people," Johnnie broke in. "He can well afford to put himself up somewhere until he has decided on what course to take."

"May I keep this letter for the moment?" The detective looked at Miles.

"Certainly."

Then he turned to Johnnie.

"I should be obliged if Mr O'Malley would hand in his passport while these enquiries are in progress."

Miles's hand went to his breast pocket automatically, but he knew where his passport was, with Rowena's in the drawer of her desk. He felt as if he had been slapped in the face.

"I will have to go to the Parnell Hotel to get it. Do you want it today?"

"Yes, if that's not too much trouble."

"We can fetch it now," Johnnie said. "Do you want my client to hand it in personally?"

"I will be quite happy if you undertake to do that."

Miles knew now what it was like to feel disreputable. The police suspected him of setting fire to his own hotel. They believed that the terrible people who had murdered Willie could be his associates. Now he understood why Johnnie had been so insistent that he should refuse the Alma-Tadema offer. His good name was in question. Any day now he might read about himself in the *Sun* pushing world news on to a back page.

As a television personality he had courted publicity. He would get it now nationwide. He needed no further instruction on the seriousness of his position. If the good Gideon had not put him into Johnnie's hands he might be in prison at this moment with the Doyles. To the police they were probably birds of a feather. He controlled a vile impulse to fawn on the detective, to treat him as if they were in the studio together. Wonderful friends. He was impressed by the Superintendent. He wanted to have him on his side. Miles recognized quality. But there was something neutral in his manner at parting which was discouraging. Rowena had an expression like that which she used to wear when he wanted her to cancel out some of his transgressions.

Somehow they got out and once they found themselves in the street Miles said, "I don't know about you, but I need a drink."

"You will have to wait for it. We must go to that hotel of yours and find your passport. May I entreat you to be circumspect over the next few days. You have been unfortunate in your associates. That is why I was against further involvement with any of these Alma-Tadema people. You have quite enough on your hands. The police are investigating a fire and a murder connected with it. The fire was on your property and the murdered man was one of your employees. It shouldn't be necessary for me to say that you are in a delicate situation. No one can go on avoiding his responsibilities indefinitely."

"I never wanted responsibilities. You make them sound like poor relations. My trouble is that I haven't the least idea what way I stand financially. I have grown accustomed to living free and knowing that £100 a week was being paid into my account."

"Those days are over," Johnnie said discouragingly as he hailed a taxi.

"I'm taking up an enormous amount of your time."

"Don't worry. I cancelled all my other appointments today, and you are going to have to pay through the nose for it. Gideon has spoilt you. Free confessions. By the way, I ought to tell you that his wife has gone voluntarily into one of those homes for people who want to fight their problem. He is coming to dinner with me tonight. I think he would like it very much if you joined us. Your troubles will help him to take his mind off his own."

"I would like that."

"I'll write down the address for you. About eight. Just the three of us."

The solicitor tore a page out of his diary on which he had written his address in St John's Wood when the cab was turning into Lindsay Road.

Miles was surprised to see no sign of last night's fire. A policeman was hovering round the entrance and faces, as always, were staring out of the windows of rooms in which so many former colonials and their offspring were "temporarily" housed.

Johnnie showed the policeman his card.

"This is Mr O'Malley who owns the hotel," Johnnie explained.

Miles wished his solicitor wasn't so free with this information.

"I suppose there is no objection to our going in. Mr O'Malley wants to fetch some of his clothes and, naturally, he wants to see the extent of the damage."

"You had better have a word with the sergeant. You may go through. He is inspecting the fire damage."

The foyer was its usual gloomy self. It was when he went through the kitchen that Miles could see the extent of the damage. Only the bare walls of the garages were standing. Rubble and charred wood and slates lay about in great heaps. Excavation was in progress, and Miles left it to Johnnie to explain who they were and what they wanted. The sergeant came upstairs and watched Miles taking the passport out of its drawer.

"I would like to take a few clothes," he said.

"You are not going to sleep here?"

"Not tonight."

"I'm sure that's all right."

Under the sergeant's surveillance Miles put a few clothes into a suitcase. Each garment was examined as it went in.

"Nothing to declare," Miles said.

"Have you got everything you want?" Johnnie was hinting that facetiousness was out of order. It was less than twenty-four hours since Miles had left these rooms in which he had spent the best and the worst years of his life and the rooms had died in the interval. All the familiar objects, the innumerable photographs, were like stage properties.

"Who is here?" Miles asked the sergeant.

"Staff you mean? No one, so far as I can make out. A young woman turned up this morning. She gave us a lot of help."

"Jane."

"That's right. With Jane's help we managed very well. The six hotel guests came back for their things."

"Have they all cleared out?"

"Yes. Jane locked up the public rooms. The ones packed with children are not affected. They have their own cooking arrangements, I gather."

"Don't worry," Johnnie said to Miles when they were in the taxi again. "Give me a power of attorney and I'll get this mess off your hands. The man we must get hold of is your phoney friend Tod Morris. Will you give me *carte blanche* to settle with him?"

"I'll give you *carte blanche* to settle with everyone. Do you really believe the police suspect me?"

"They suspect everyone connected with your hotel. Can I not get you to appreciate the situation? Your manager is in jug."

"But what has that to do with me? I don't have IRA connections. That isn't difficult to prove."

"We can talk about it tonight. Meanwhile we must get rid of this passport and you, I suppose, want to be dropped at your fish-pool hotel. Don't be there on the day the police raid it."

"Are you serious?"

"I am always serious."

Back at the Aegean, Miles remembered that he had never answered Lalage's letter, but when he asked at the desk he was told that a room had been reserved for him. It was a different room this time, larger and with a better view than last night's. After the gloom of the Parnell penthouse, exactly what his drooping spirits needed. He certainly had no grievance at all against the Alma-Tadema Society. It was all very well for Johnnie, he had his elegant home. These people had given him the first taste of luxurious living he had had since Rowena's day. Quite possibly there were sharks in the background, but if that were to deter one who would buy a newspaper? If he were alone in his penthouse he would now drink himself into a stupor—those souvenirs of Rowena everywhere he looked, the dread of the Doyles and Willie—Willie's ghost would haunt him. If only he knew where he stood financially he could—he was going to say 'go abroad', leaving Johnnie to cope; and then he remembered that he had surrendered his passport. Just as well. What he might have done in perfect innocence would have been construed as a confession of guilt. What an unfair place the world was. He had said that once to Dicky Dawson, as if he had made a discovery, and had been flabbergasted when Dicky said "Of course. That's what you go to a public school for—to learn that and to learn not to complain about it."

Miles was about to order his first whiskey of the evening when he saw a notice on the wall that the hotel had a swimming pool, sauna and massage parlour in the basement. A massage was exactly what he needed in his present condition. He rang up the given number and was told in the hotel's lingua franca that another guest had just cancelled an appointment. He could be done now if he came at once. Five minutes later, having charged the exercise to his room number, wearing only a bathing wrap, he was told to go through the door of a cubicle at the other side of which he found a long table covered with a sheet and Miss Dubonnet in a white cap and uniform. She gave no sign of recognition as she invited him to lie on the table. Miles was aware of his mouth opening and shutting, but no sound issued from it. He pointed to his single garment; she misunderstood his predicament.

"Hang it on the peg behind the door."

He was about to panic, but she was offering a way out—anonymous, neutral, impersonal—it was notional invisibility. He did as he was told. She then indicated that he should lie down. He hadn't been massaged for years, and then by an osteopath. In the garish setting of this hotel the ordinary rules of life didn't apply. Already last night's happenings had taken on the character of a dream. Hallucination was the order of the day. This lady with the kneading fingers was, possibly, not Lalage at all. Certainly her professional personality was very different from the twittering bird woman he met last night. That Lalage would keep up a running comment on the state of the play if she had him under her fingers. The fingers rubbing him seemed practised enough. If this was not part of a sinister plot (concealed cameras) it was relaxing and could, if he let his mind rest, be innocently voluptuous. For her he was just another slab of meat. Even so, he wished he could have offered a more pleasing prospect. Gradually his senses took over, and when she told him to turn round he hardly hesitated. The eventuality had been present to his mind. If all the stories he had heard were true this was the moment when her bona fides would be established. She could see for herself that her ministrations so far had produced nothing tangible. She was concentrating on his calves.

"Sit up, please."

He did as he was told and she began to pummel his neck muscles.

"That's it," she said a few minutes later. He grabbed his robe.

"That was fine," he said.

"Good," she said mechanically.

Their eyes never actually met.

Downstairs he noticed that a lot of champagne was being drunk. He ordered himself a glass, asked the waiter to put it on his bill, and from a point of vantage in the bar studied the clientele and thought about his recent experience. All he knew about Miss Dubonnet was that she made children's dresses and housekept for her uncle. That letter from her which he handed to the police gave the hours when she couldn't be reached by telephone. That was consistent with her being a masseuse. Why should she not be? And yet he didn't like the idea. It vexed him. She had dented her image. She must meet men who would want her to monkey about with them. He would not mention this incident, even to Russell. He would feel foolish reciting it, and if the masseuse was really Miss Dubonnet he would have to pray that *she* didn't mention it to anyone. What a feast *Private Eye* would make of the harmless incident. And he could imagine the sniggering in the BBC. Why hadn't he taken his experienced solicitor's advice? Why, come to that, had he forgotten his father's? The idea of a conspiracy was too far-fetched. No one could have known that he would ask for a massage. But there was always the possibility, and it was strange that she had not anticipated it. Possibly she was proud of her profession, and saw no reason why she shouldn't give Miles a massage if he needed one. *Honi soit qui mal y pense.* He had enjoyed it. Very much. So much that he was tempted to repeat the experience tomorrow. It had been, in spite of all his hesitations, the most delectable pleasure he had had for a long time. It awakened his interest in Miss Dubonnet which had receded when he encountered her in the flesh. Quite extraordinary to think that within such a short space of time the rather genteel lady with the bird notes should be let loose on his bare skin. She had distracted him from his worries. It was extraordinary, considering the pickle he was in, that he could be nourishing voluptuous fancies. Had a waiter not inquired if he would like to order dinner he might have forgotten that he should have been on his way to St John's Wood.

Johnnie had a regency house. He let Miles in and led the way into a book-lined study where Gideon Russell was sitting up very straight in his chair nursing a sherry glass. He looked slightly embarrassed. "Johnnie has taken me over," he said. "I was telling him just now that I couldn't have faced the night by myself. It was an awkward coincidence. My wife had decided to go into hospital today, and I wasn't going to alter her plans, but I must admit I'd have been grateful if it could have been any other day. I had the police with me this afternoon for more information about Willie. What with one thing and another I've been having quite a time."

He looked tired certainly, like a man to whom long arrears of sleep are owing. Miles was so accustomed to treating him as a listening post that if they were in their usual setting he would hardly have noticed.

"My wife is staying with her mother in Scotland at the moment," Johnnie explained, "and I'm very grateful for Gideon's company. He is a wonderful man to have in the kitchen. I never met anyone with such perfect judgement in the scrambling of an egg."

"I have an interesting item of news," he added. "Mr Tod Morris has been looking for me all day, and proposes to call on me here before I go to my office in the morning. I pretended to be put out by his importunity, but I was delighted. I want to talk to you about this, Miles, later on. I think Gideon has had as much as a man can stand. We will pack him off early to bed."

"I would go mad listening to the voices of the grown-ups downstairs," Gideon intervened. "We are all in this together, and the only thing I dread is inaction. What do you think Tod wants to talk to you about?"

"I can only guess. For one thing I don't know whether the police have caught up with him as yet. They will want to question everyone connected with the hotel, but he might be seen as watchdog for the building society. That wouldn't excite immediate suspicion. The fact that he took the Doyles out to dinner doesn't constitute a crime, but that—and I suppose the police know about it—is the only suspicious circumstance so far as he is concerned unless they have a dossier on him. And even that might give the impression of the man who is everyone's friend. I should think he is a sure mark for ten tickets at least in every raffle drawn within a mile's radius of Kilburn."

"Does Gideon know the police have taken my passport?"

"Johnnie told me. I was horrified until he said it was only a matter of form."

"If the news gets out I'll be labelled as a crook. How would you feel if it were you?"

"I was labelled once as a crook myself, so I *can* tell you. That's how I met Johnnie."

"Against all my advice, he took the knock for someone else. He had a clear-cut explanation." Johnnie sounded angry.

"I was slack. I should have kept a closer eye on my junior. And it would have been the end of his career if I had let him take the rap. There was a young family to consider. I was promised that my pension wouldn't be affected. I was glad of the opportunity to get out. Doreen's troubles were beginning. It suited me to escape from the nine to five routine."

"The last white man," Johnnie grumbled. "Gideon would have made a perfect subject for Conrad. Don't you think so, Miles?"

"Absolutely. Right up his street." He hoped that Johnnie wouldn't pursue the subject. He thought Conrad had worn a beard, but that was all he could have contributed to a discussion about him. He was longing to tell his friends about his massage adventure. But there might have been the father and mother of a row. Johnnie might even have thrown up the case. Where would he be then? Besides, Russell had this picture of him as a fallen giant. The story would have to bide its time, and wait for another audience.

Russell described his talk with the police. He told them that his wife was hooked on cocaine and that he had seen Willie talking to her and suspected him of being a pusher. "I had only seen him on one other occasion, when I was with you, Miles. You said he worked in your hotel.

"I didn't like having to bring in your name, but the Willie connection would have come out sooner or later and I decided that I must not edit my evidence."

"Quite right," Johnnie said.

"They grilled me about the murder naturally. It seemed too much of a coincidence my being there unless Willie was following me. The police wanted me to describe the people who threw him down, but I had only the impression of vague forms. Remember, I had no idea at the time that it was Willie. Recognition came afterwards, I explained that to the police."

"Willie was a strange mixture: he loved gossip but he was a complete innocent," Miles said. "He never had anything to do with drugs. That I'll swear, but he could have been used as a go-between. It would have made him feel important. If he had been given a quid and asked to deliver what was described to him as cough-mixture, Willie would have suspected nothing and been charmed by the excuse to call on anyone, quite apart from the little addition to his wretched wages. But who was the pusher? I don't like the Doyles, God knows, but I don't believe that they are in that business."

"What about guests in the hotel? The police will have some fun looking through the register."

"To tell you the truth, Johnnie, I never took much notice of our clientele. They were mostly bed and breakfast types, and I only caught a glimpse of them occasionally. It was necessary for morale to be able to tell oneself that one didn't wholly depend on those overcrowded poor creatures in the adjoining houses. When I think of my television friends with their swimming pools and tennis courts I wonder where I went wrong. In principle, I was moderate and sensible."

"Say no more until I have seen our friend Tod," Johnnie interrupted. "We will know much more, I hope, by lunchtime tomorrow. And here I must get at you again, Miles, about your present choice of abode. You are in with a shady crowd. People who feel safer in Beirut than in London must have something gruesome to hide."

"Gideon was all in favour of my staying there last night."

"That was in a crisis. I don't like to see you putting yourself under a compliment to these people. They paid you handsomely, why should they want to make themselves liable for your hotel bills?"

"She said—"

"Who is *she*?"

"Miss Dubonnet, the secretary. They had heard about the fire. Surely that was humane behaviour, and it should be taken in the spirit in which it was offered."

"All my instincts are against it," Johnnie said.

"You sound just like my mother."

"Your mother was probably a very sensible woman."

"Would it help if I were to offer Miles a bed? It will be a come-down after the Aegean Hotel, but it might be convenient at the present state of the game. Johnnie's missus is coming back the day after tomorrow, and I'll be going home in any case. I'd be very grateful for your company at the moment."

Gideon's was the obvious solution. Johnnie looked greatly relieved. Miles accepted warmly, but a vision of that tidy side-street of uniform bay windows and trim front gardens seemed astringent after his recent imaginings. It put paid to the prospect of Arabian nights. Johnnie returned to the fray.

"I hope Tod will confirm my impression that this is a drugs case. It has nothing to do with the IRA. Undoubtedly the Doyles have friends in those circles, and Tod, I daresay, knows more than he would ever tell me or the police about our bomber friends, but all that business about the stores and the circumstances of that fire are much more suggestive of drugs than weapons and ammunition. I think the police share this view. Gideon was talking to Jane, the girl who was left in charge. She has quite a story about dubious characters who stayed at your hotel and who used to send Willie on messages. If I were you I'd go and see the Detective Superintendent again. Take Gideon with you. That will make a good impression."

So, much arranged and Gideon showing signs of exhaustion, Miles asked if he might call a taxi. Gideon, it was agreed, would come to the Aegean in the morning and they could go from there to the police together.

"I want to make a good impression and show them the kind of company I keep," Miles said. At any other time this would have been said in sourness, but Miles was feeling curiously elated. Excitement meant as much to him as to a child. It was what he missed most since television gave him up. How much he realized now when his life was in total disarray, and he found himself revelling in it. To be under police surveillance, to have had his property set on fire, two of his employees put in prison, another murdered—it might all have been seen as a threat to the health of a man who had been in steady physical decline and required a gradually rising intake of alcohol to get him into a condition to meet even the routine demands of the most eventless day, but it was not so; he had forgotten a time when he always felt like this, dismissive of difficulties, curious about the people around him, eager for the latest diversion (there was always a fresh one). He would, of course, have preferred to get this stimulus from a decision by the BBC to act like gentlemen; but if it came to a choice between present danger and the routine he had developed —trips to the betting shop, monologues in Gideon's ear, videos in the lonely evenings—he had no doubt which he would choose. Terror every time. It was, therefore, vexing to have to give up the possibilities of adventure of another sort in the Aegean Hotel.

The last fare had left his *Evening Standard* in the taxi. Miles picked it up and glanced through it casually. As he was throwing it down a paragraph caught his eye. It was headed *Let Erin Remember*:

There was a notable turn-out of celebrities in the entertainment industry at the funeral this morning at Marylebone Cemetery of Jerry ("Pot") Dunne (49) the controversial commentator on television and radio whose mid-morning half hour for harassed housewives on B.B.C. Radio One was responsible for one of the Beeb's most congested letter-boxes. Jerry Dunne could always be relied upon to serve up those indispensable condiments without which programmes of this sort might become too bland. There was never any danger of blandness when Pot was around. He would have seen to it that there was always a liberal dose of pepper in the chocolate sundae. A large Irish contingent was present to see the irascible Pot off and *de mortuis* was the order of the day. The pall-bearers were all from the old sod. I saw Terry Wogan (47), wearing black glasses, Frank Delaney (25), Eamonn Andrews (99), and Henry Kelly (21). There seemed to be some breakdown in arrangements. After prayers were said at the graveside by Father

Aloysius Dunne (54), a brother of the deceased, all four of the pall-bearers started to address the mourners simultaneously, and when none showed an inclination to give way there was a spontaneous stampede towards local hostelries. Very reminiscent of the Pot's own programmes. A telegram of condolence from the Holy Father was read out by Father Aloysius during a short lull in the proceedings.

Miles had the sensation of someone who comes across a plot against his life that he always had when he saw the name of someone he knew in print, but after having read the paragraph for the third time—Johnnie had been liberal with the port—Miles laughed aloud. He had been trying not to think of Jerry Dunne ever since the insulting reception the offer of his funeral services had received, even though he had used Jerry's death as a way out of a difficulty when he was stuck for a speech. Not including him in this party was intended as a public snub to Miles. He saw that at once. It was worth a snub if it meant not having to see "Miles O'Malley (67)" in that news item. He took the page, folded it neatly, and put it in his pocket. He would read it again before saying "God bless everyone" aloud when he was settling down on his pillow. He said it as a child when he slept with his bedroom door open, and had resumed the practice since he began to sleep alone.

Miles had pictured himself as the policeman's friend when he came in with Gideon to report that Mrs Russell had been getting drugs from someone in the hotel, and was deflated when he was told to wait outside while Russell made his statement. The Detective Superintendent wanted a word with him afterwards. He was questioned again about the letting of storage space. How was it possible for Doyle to make an arrangement of that kind without mentioning either the rent or the name of the person to whom the letting was being made?

"I was told it was to a friend and that all the facts and figures would be put before us at the next meeting. You must understand that I had left everything in Doyle's hands. It suited me because I had my own job to look after."

"I understand that you have been out of work for some time."

"Certainly, but I was hoping for a return to normal, and you must bear in mind that I inherited this position. The hotel was my wife's idea. The Doyles have always been in charge of it. I have made a point of not interfering. It suited me to know that I could depend on a certain modest income. I had given up any kind of social life. My needs were few. I blame myself now for not having taken a more active role."

"Did you think there was anything suspicious about the storage proposition?"

"I knew the place was empty. That is what puzzled me. Who would want to pay an allegedly high rent for storage space that he wasn't using?"

"Did you have any knowledge of drug pushing?"

"Where?"

"In the hotel."

"Absolutely none. I wouldn't have allowed it to happen for a moment."

He was let go at last. Gideon was waiting for him. He was wholly taken up by the problem that Doreen, his wife, presented. The police wanted to interview her. How was it to be managed without upsetting her just at the moment that she was trying to take a stand against her addiction? He was only half-attending to Miles. It was now lunch-time. They were close to their old haunts, but in the new chapter Miles could not do less than suggest an Italian restaurant in Camden Town. When they arrived he asked for permission to use the telephone.

Johnnie sounded as if he was waiting for the call.

"I have splendid news. Our friend will accept fifty thousand for spot cash. You owe him much more than that on the mortgage, but speed in his case is of the essence—he wants it by the week-end. I have lots more to tell you. Come and have breakfast with me."

"Do you want us both?"

"No. I'm afraid, I must leave Gideon out of this. I'll explain when I see you. This might be an inquisitive telephone so I think we had better wait to talk until we meet."

"How am I to lay my hands on fifty thou?"

"That's my problem."

"Johnnie seems to think that he will get me out of Tod Morris's hands," Miles told Gideon when he rejoined him. He felt such relief that he found it hard to return to Gideon's sombre mood. If Johnnie could get rid of Tod Morris, he would get rid of the

131

Doyles, then the six houses could be sold and he would have a fine capital sum to live on.

Money wasn't everything, but spending it could be fun. When he got his passport back, he would take a trip abroad, change his whole manner of life. The BBC might be interested in a travel feature. It was worth suggesting. Even if it were only to Ireland, Telefís Eireann might very well come in on a returned exile programme. He was full of rich ideas and in no mood to listen to Gideon's sad talk.

"I'm off," he said. "I have to collect my things in that hotel, and I have a few things to do in town. If I get to you around seven or seven thirty, how will that be?"

"I'm there all the time. Suit yourself."

Gideon watched his friend's retreating back with misgivings. "I wonder what he is getting up to? There was a wild look in his eye," he thought.

Miles was not sure himself what he was up to; all he knew was that he had smelled freedom from afar and with his nostrils full of it he found even the thought of the air in that house with the bay windows intolerably stuffy. He was irked by the weight of gratitude with which this serious man had encumbered him and he wished they could return to the time when all Gideon asked for was to be allowed to listen while Miles communed with himself aloud. He had until supper-time to enjoy his liberty; after that he could give attention to pressing problems, by which he meant his own problems.

Now, when he entered the portals of the Aegean Hotel he gave the hall porter a confident greeting reminiscent of the days when he knew the christian name of the head waiter in any restaurant that was in fashion. There was a note in his pigeon hole telling him to ring a number. The message had come soon after he went out this morning. He decided to make the call from his room. Telephone messages had become enormously important recently. Things were happening again at last. If there were nothing else in prospect this afternoon he might look in house agents' lists for somewhere to live. The fire had brought home to him the madness —there was no other word for it—of that whole hotel arrangement. Rowena, bless her heart, had meant it all for the best, but she was a dying woman, even if she didn't know it, and towards the end reverted to her Stockton-on-Tees origins, where she felt at home. When he saw his rivals in luxury houses in Bucks and

Surrey—the stockbroker belt—while he was a prisoner in the hands of a gang, there was no doubt about that now, on Lindsay Road, he was amazed at his stupidity. As he sat down on the bed to make his telephone call his eyes ranged over the prospect of London and he had a lifting of the heart. It was laid out there for him, to be reconquered. His exile had seemed final; now he felt like the ancient Roman he had read about at school who retired to his farm but was called back by his people, unable to manage without him. But before Miles managed anything he must get some new clothes.

There was a certain dandyism about the manner in which he picked up the telephone, as there was about the lighting and holding of his cigarette. He nearly let both aids to elegance fall when he heard Miss Dubonnet's voice.

"Oh, Mr O'Malley, how kind of you to call. I hope you have fully recovered after the truly terrible time you have had. Are they making you perfectly comfortable?"

"Indeed."

"Mr Carlovassi says that he doesn't want you to take it as a hint, but he would be very grateful if you could let him know sometime when you expect to be leaving. He has a friend from Bagdhad coming next week. Do you think you will be out by then?"

"I am leaving today. I came in to collect my belongings. I am going to stay with my friend Gideon Russell."

"I wish I had known that. I sent an invitation to you care of your solicitor for the private view of Uncle's exhibition. Mr Carlovassi has arranged it all. I am most grateful to him. We are working like demons at it."

"This *is* a surprise. Where is it to be held?"

"In the studio. That has been cleaned up for the first time in over sixty years. All sorts of things are turning up. There's a man installed at the moment making frames. That is why Uncle has to work at home. It puts him out, poor dear, but I tell him it's worth it."

"I wish you had told me about this. If invitations are going out you must have been making preparations for weeks."

"I was sworn to silence. Mr Carlovassi never likes to disclose his plans in advance."

"I am bowled over."

He was. Miss Dubonnet was continually surprising him. She

was a bright, efficient, little bird of a person having nothing to do really with Lalage, the Alma-Tadema goddess whom he pictured looking like an advertisement for some very superior brand of talcum powder. That was the Lalage who had massaged him in his reconstruction of that encounter, not the Countess's dressmaker. Miles's imagination was capable of transforming anything or anyone into the ideal he was looking for at the moment. The masseuse might have been some faceless woman on whom he planted the desired features. Not for the first time the confusion arose from his passion for identifying people, creating personalities for complete strangers. If he saw Miss Dubonnet alone in congenial surroundings over a pleasant meal this matter which fascinated him in his luxurious moments and threatened him when he felt low could be resolved for ever. At the worst, Miss Dubonnet was probably grateful enough not to be reminded of the things she sometimes had to do for money. They might enter into a mutual defence pact, preferably tacit.

"Wouldn't it be good for you to get away for a few hours? What about dinner some evening?"

"That sounds delightful. We might go to Ormond's Wine Bar, which is quite near and I am told is excellent. But now I really must get back to work or Mr Carlovassi will have my life."

Miles sat with the receiver in his hand. She had rung off, frightened by Mr Carlovassi, perhaps. He had been flabbergasted when she answered the telephone, but she had put him at his ease at once by her friendly matter-of-factness and, if she *had* been pounding his fifteen stone weight of naked flesh as recently as yesterday, her professionalism was perfect. Why could he not accept the situation with her tact and good sense? It was in part vanity. It was in part a struggle to preserve an idyll. That kneading of his not too solid flesh should have been a hilarious send-up of his latest day-dream but he was reluctant to let it go. He was still intrigued by Miss Dubonnet—Miss Dubonnet as Lalage, that is to say. Was she entirely innocent? She had hinted at disagreeable possibilities where this Mr Carlovassi was concerned. Helping Mr Carlovassi might mean anything. Did he own this hotel? Lalage made him sound as if he was the manager. In that case she might have been standing in for the regular masseur. She provided a Universal Aunts service for this mysterious group: dressmaking, secretarial part-time, and massaging, at a pinch. Stirrings, primordial stirrings, were prompting him to make use of the few hours left to rehearse the pleasures of yesterday. When everything was in the lap of the gods, why not throw this in as well? The temptation would be less when he was not living on the premises. This must not become an addiction.

He could see the number of the massage parlour from where he was sitting. The same voice answered when he rang and said he was to come down to the basement at five o'clock. So far so good, in the meanwhile he must decide whether to call Lalage's bluff. He had hardly said this to himself when he felt ashamed. Of course she would behave in exactly the same manner as yesterday. It was professional etiquette. A doctor didn't enquire after a patient's bowels down the length of a dinner table. Lalage's handling of the situation had been exemplary. It was a pity she was so birdlike, spoiling the picture Miles painted with his luxuriant imagination. Bird-like or not, it would be pleasant to have her working him over to remember on winter evenings.

He was outside the cubicle at five minutes to five; his heart trembling a little. But there was no turning back now. The room had not changed but the masseur was a Chinaman, and he had a wall-eye.

Gideon had been to Marks and Spencer: the outcome was covered in silver foil in his refrigerator beside a bottle of Spanish wine. He was looking rather pleased with himself. "This is the first time I have given a meal to a guest in this house," he explained.

Miles had his own reasons for encouraging his host to run the conversation, and when Russell asked him about his afternoon Miles demurred. He wanted to hear what Gideon had been up to. "I hate to think of you giving up all your time to my affairs."

"You must not think of it in that way. I am more deeply involved in this business than you imagine." Miles said nothing in reply to that, assuming it was one more example of his host's self-denying disposition but, under the influence of what Miles decided privately was sourish wine, Gideon became confessorial.

"You must get the picture right. For five years or more my marriage has been in ruins. My wife became an habitual liar. Have you any idea what that means? Normal conversation ceases to have any meaning. I am not a romantic figure. I was considerably older than Doreen and we couldn't have children. Each of us had something wrong in that department. Perhaps it was a blessing. At first I couldn't make out what was happening to Doreen. She became so secretive. She hadn't been like that. Then I discovered she had a man friend whose existence she was hiding from me. Later I found out that he was supplying her with cocaine. We had a show-down about it. And just at this time I had my trouble in the bank. At first I was satisfied to get out. Looking after Doreen was a whole-time job. But I didn't do that as well as I thought I had. One of her peculiarities is to stay up all night, or most of the night, and go to sleep in the middle of the day. I found the atmosphere so lowering that I don't think I could have carried on if I hadn't hit on the idea of going out at the time Doreen was asleep and betting on the horses. It was something that had always appealed to me. I never went in deep, and my boring sort of nature saved me from the usual gamblers' traps. I was patient and prepared to wait to recover my losses, and I had always been a good judge of form. I aimed at making around a thousand a year free of tax this way, and I did, almost invariably. When I came home Doreen was usually still asleep. Life began for her with the six o'clock news. It was not much of a life for either of us, but at least it coped with our problems.

"She might have been safe if it had not been for her mother. So far from being grateful to me for taking her daughter off her hands, my mother-in-law made it plain that her child had made a disastrous match and, I daresay, had her own version of my reason for early retirement. Insofar as she admitted that Doreen had a drug problem, she explained the cause—the appalling dullness of her life with an elderly, impotent, confirmed gambler. There was, of course, a modicum of truth in the accusation. She had Doreen to stay from time to time, but mother and daughter had never got on, and Doreen always came back after a row and final parting. A pattern was formed, a dreary and recurring one; but to be candid, I think I would have cut my throat long ago if it hadn't been for those flittings from the nest. One is taking place at the moment. Sometimes Doreen cheats. The trips to the mother are covers for a return to the drug habit. She swore to me that she could always be cured by hypnotism. It was making a fool of me. You have seen what the drug does to her when she drinks whisky on top of it. I was grateful to you for not saying anything that day."

"There was nothing to be said."

"That rarely stops people. I wanted to discover who her

contact was. Then one day I came home early—racing had been cancelled—and I saw Doreen talking to a strange-looking, hump-backed figure in our porch. They saw me. I was on the opposite side of the road and had to let a lorry pass. By the time I reached the gate the visitor had cycled away. I was only able to get a glimpse of him. Doreen is as cute as a fox, and she anticipated a question by complaining that she had sent for someone to examine the television set which had been behaving temperamentally and the shop had sent 'a fool of a man who knew no more about television sets than I did.' You were with me when I saw that man again. You told me that it was the famous Willie. You can see what a fix I was in."

"Willie thought he understood about television sets. He offered to help when my set played up on me. I let him once, and he finished it off completely."

"I still think that I was being given a doctored story. I brought the name of your hotel into the conversation and watched her reaction. She looked at me from under her eyelids in a way she has when she is suspicious, and then pretended not to have understood what I was talking about. When you began to tell me of strange goings on in your yard I hadn't known what to make of it and suspected your IRA theories might have some foundation, but the Willie incident gave me other ideas. Whatever Doreen may be up to any time, I don't see her working for Irish terrorists. She is far too much of a coward, for one thing, and no terrorist worth his salt would trust her with a secret. I had listened with interest to your preparations for the Alma-Tadema dinner, but when you asked me to find out what I could for you about these people and I made enquiries among my former bank connections, I was advised to give them a wide berth. The Aegean Hotel was owned by a group who had understandably been getting what they could out of the Lebanon for some time past. The hotel was only a side-show, and the group had international ramifications.

"Why at this time of day were they asking *you* to address them? I asked myself. I was no more convinced by the given explanation than I was by the Alma-Tadema Society. I also discovered that old Slaughter is on the rocks. That is not strictly relevant, but as you seem to be fascinated by his niece I thought I should keep you up-to-date.

"Nothing is known to the discredit of either of them (that is from a bank's point of view). They own a substantial house, full of lodgers. How Miss Dubonnet got in with the Aegean Hotel crowd I have not been able to discover. She makes herself generally useful apparently. The notion that the dinner was a plot to ensure your absence from the Parnell Hotel on a particular evening entered my mind. You had complained to me about strangers on the premises and Doyle's reluctance to explain their presence. Your place was to be used to store drugs in, and whoever was in charge wanted you out of the way when the drugs were coming in. I had decided to drop in at your hotel when you were out making your speech and ask as casually as possible if you were at home. It would give me a chance to cast an eye around and see if anything suspicious was going on. I told Doreen after tea that I was going out for a stroll and took myself off to the Parnell Hotel. There was a NO VACANCIES notice on the door; but it was open. When I came in I saw Willie lurking in the background. He came over to me at once, but before either of us could get a word in, a man came up from downstairs and pushed Willie aside. I recognized him from your description of the stranger in the yard. The hotel was closed for repairs, he said. The door should have been locked. Had I not read the NO VACANCIES notice? His manner wasn't so much rude as truculent, like a policeman telling a loiterer to move on, not at all like a hotel receptionist at work. I said I was a friend of Mr O'Malley's and had called as I happened to be passing.

" 'Mr O'Malley is out to dinner.' No power on earth was going to stop Willie from telling me that. I asked if I could see either Mr or Mrs Doyle.

" 'The Doyles is out as well.'

"John Joe—if that's the man I was dealing with—tried to kill Willie with a look. Then he turned to me. 'The place is shut; there's no one in, I'm telling you.'

" 'May I leave a note for Mr O'Malley?'

" 'I suppose so. Have you got a pen? The door shouldn't have been left open. No one's allowed in while repairs are going on.'

" 'May I trouble you for a sheet of paper and an envelope?'

"He would dearly have liked to hit me, I could see that. From the expression on his face I might have been asking for something locked away in a safe. Willie surfaced again. I could see he took pride in his office. I was given what I asked for and wrote 'Every good wish' and signed it and gave the envelope to Willie (I wonder what happened to it?). Then I took myself off. I had seen enough to convince me that some dirty work was going on, if only from the manner in which this John Joe ruffian seemed to have taken over. I had no doubt that the right thing was to tell the police. I had been told lies. I discovered that when I was writing the note and saw what looked like a permanent guest on the stairs. He went back when he saw us talking, and I don't think the others saw him.

"I asked myself, as a friend, what should I do? Mind my own business? Or advise the police to keep an eye oń the hotel? It wasn't an easy decision. I was tempted to ring you up, but you mightn't have wanted to be interrupted at your dinner and might have thought it was an occasion for me to use my own initiative. After much thought I went to the police station off the Kentish Town Road. The visit was a disaster. If I had confined my statement to what I had seen at the hotel, I might have made an impression; as it was, when I described your movements, I could see I was being taken for a crackpot. Complaints about the Parnell Hotel are fairly frequent, I suspect. There was a weary air about the officer who took down my statement. I went home then and tried to watch television while all the time I was thinking how I ought to have handled the police. They might well have decided that my message was not an urgent one. I should call again and urge them to look in this very evening. I told Doreen I was going out 'for something' and made for the police station. I had to pass the hotel on my way. The blocks let out to the homeless were all lit up, and this made the others look like a tomb. A few feeble lights were on in the rooms of, presumably, the few guests who couldn't be pushed out. The principal rooms were in total darkness. I arrived at the hotel as a van shot out of the side-road leading to the rear of the premises. It very nearly ran me down. At that moment, as if someone had dropped a match into a petrol tank, the buildings at the back went up in a sheet of flame. You know all the rest. Forgive me if I have been long-winded. As I suspected, the police hadn't taken me very seriously, but one of them must have decided to take a precautionary look at the precise moment that the van was going to be unloaded. The fire was a distraction. My guess is that it had been ready and waiting so that in the event of a search the evidence could be destroyed. The van got away. It must be somewhere. I am prepared to bet anything I've got that some of your friends at the Alma-Tadema Society could tell you exactly where to find it."

"And the Doyles?"

"I don't think so. They were to get a rake-off for letting the premises, but they are only small fry."

"Tod Morris?"

"A bigger fish, but he lives in a complicated world of wheeling and dealing and never knows—and doesn't want to know—anything definite about what is happening in the undergrowth. He recommended the hotel to the drug importers, I have no doubt, and introduced the Doyles to his friends, but he would maintain that he had no idea of the nature of the material that was being stored. 'Something very precious, I understand. I thought it more discreet not to inquire.' That, I fancy, would be his explanation of his performance."

"And Willie?"

"An innocent. I agree with you, but he would have regarded the police with the same inbred suspicion that he would the IRA or anyone who pushed people around."

"You must regret the impulse that made you talk to me that day when we were making our innocent bets. I have given you no end of trouble ever since."

"All well worth while if it leads us to the stuff in that van."

"I am having breakfast with Johnnie in the morning at eight o'clock. I haven't been out of bed at that hour since I gave up wearing short trousers."

"If Johnnie gets you out of the hands of Tod Morris and the Doyles, what are you going to do with yourself?"

"I have that all planned. Provided the hotel sale leaves me enough, I shall get myself a pad at a good address. I hadn't a hope of getting back where I belonged while I lived in that Lindsay Road dump. It was mad even to have contemplated it. I realize that now. Rather late in the day, you might say."

"Do you ever think you might get married again?"

"I wouldn't wholly rule out the possibility. It would be a comfort in the long winter nights."

"What a deeply frivolous person you are."

"What do you mean by that exactly?"

"I envy you. Did it ever occur to you to end your days in Ireland?"

"Are you serious?"

"Always. I have listened to you talking about yourself quite a lot. I get the impression that you were very happy with your first wife before television raised its ugly head."

"I didn't know the sort of animal I was. I wasn't fully alive."

"Now that is what I mean by a deeply frivolous remark. You were a married man, successful in your business. How can you say that you weren't fully alive until you were on public exhibition?"

"Oh, I thought I was very much alive at the time, the life if not the soul of the party, with a job that suited me in many ways—I could never have sat down behind a desk. But I always felt that something was missing, and I only knew what it was when I found myself in a television studio—the opportunity to make a contact with thousands of people. After I found my vocation, ordinary life became terribly dull. I didn't want to live it up socially. Ideally, I'd have liked to be on telly all day and come home to relax and watch my performance. I did try hard; no one can deny that. I was alive to my weak spots, and I worked on them, and where I couldn't effect a cure, I learned what the traps were and how to avoid them. For example, if you watched me on screen regularly you'd discover that I always turned my right profile to the camera. Little things. I believe that one of the reasons for my success was that, however trivial what I was doing might seem, I took it as seriously as a priest saying mass; and that is no affectation. I believe that television is taking over the roles of the church and the press. While church attendance is going down, look at the television charts in comparison. Did you ever notice how it imposes its own standards, cuts everyone down to screen size? Very soon the country is going to be governed by television. A good picture on the screen—it needs only one—can change foreign policy. I want to get back. I would sell my soul to get back."

If Russell had been looking forward to a discussion about the present situation he was disappointed. Miles drank a great deal of his whiskey while he reminisced. He was avoiding painful subjects. All too plainly he expected to hear tomorrow that he was about to escape from Camden Town and everything that went with it. At midnight he decided to go to bed.

"Have you an alarm clock you could lend me? I have to be up at an unearthly hour."

"Don't worry. I'll wake you. I am always up at six."

*

Johnnie's breakfast table was crowded with old-fashioned treats, but what caught Miles's eye to the exclusion of everything else was a lavender-coloured envelope lying beside his place. It was addressed to him care of "John F. Moriarty Esq. B.A. T.C.D." Miles grabbed it, begging his host's pardon while he opened the envelope with the clumsiness of a lover. Inside was a printed invitation to a private view of an exhibition of the paintings of Samuel Slaughter RA in the studio at the rear of 999 Clapham Common (North Side). There was a note in Miss Dubonnet's hand, "I hope you will be able to come. It was so very kind of Mr Carlovassi to give Uncle this surprise."

Miles had to meet his solicitor's quizzical gaze although he put it off as long as possible.

"Contemplating another after-dinner talk, are you?"

"No. In fact this is rather touching. Read it for yourself."

Johnnie continued to look sceptical, pursing his lips as he read the covering note.

"You will accept, I daresay. I shouldn't drink too much if I were you or come home with any of the cast-offs. I see the Countess Melashoff is to open the show. I hope that doesn't put your nose out of joint."

"I can't understand why I wasn't told about this."

"Perhaps because they were shy. But it indicates what a hold this crew has on you that you haven't yet asked me about your own business. My bank will lend you the money to pay Morris off. The necessary deeds of release will be ready on Friday. There was no formal trust, I discovered. The hotel was put into the name of the Hibernian Friendly Society so as to prevent you giving the place away without Tod Morris knowing about it—that is, so far as your wife's share was concerned. Your half, as you know, is subject to a mortgage, but that will be released now. It is none of my business to know why Mr Morris is in such a hurry. I do know it is very much in your interest to take advantage of it."

"God bless you. That's all I can say. And what about the Doyles?"

"Morris believes they won't be charged. Nothing was found on the premises. They were out at the time of the fire. John Joe, who might have compromised them, is probably eating his breakfast at this moment somewhere on the Emerald Isle."

"And the van?"

"There is no proof that it wasn't full of holy medals. I am sure

142

the police believe the Doyles had a hand in whatever was going on but I don't think they have enough evidence to prosecute. And I am convinced that you will be handed back your passport. As soon as I can settle with the insurance people you will have your hotel to sell, two empty houses and four overcrowded ones. You ought to get quite a lot of money for them all. The Doyles will be looking for something out of it, but we can deal with that when it arises. If I were you, as soon as you get your passport back, I'd go for a good long holiday miles away from all that squalor. You will come back like a lion refreshed."

"That sounds like good sense. But I must see what my new agent thinks about it. He may advise that this is not the moment to be out of reach—"

"What a man you are. A new agent? I can't keep up with you. My taxi will be here any minute now, can I drop you anywhere?"

Miles turned down the offer. He wanted to get away from advisers.

"How can I ever thank you for all you have done for me?"

"Don't worry. You will be staggered when you see what I am charging for it."

"I must hide somewhere," Miles said when he heard that the Doyles had been released from custody. He tried to be jocose talking to Johnnie, but he had been dreading a confrontation with them and he was not at all confident that Johnnie would be able to get the couple off his back. He saw himself being forced out of the property and accepting some pittance in exchange for his freedom, but Johnnie was buoyant.

"They are coming in one fell swoop to my office on Friday —Tod Morris and the Doyles, all three of them, prepared to talk business. Nice if we could plant a bomb for the occasion. A proud day for the office. I shall have it blessed after they leave."

"Are you going to hold a company meeting?"

"That is the idea."

"I couldn't face it."

"You don't have to. I'm sending you a power of attorney enabling me to act in your place. I think the omens are good. I have a preliminary report from the auditors which ought to provide me with sufficient stick. I calculate that it will take at least two hours to deal with them. Come round here at six and I'll tell you what happened. I don't trust telephones at the moment."

"Will they expect to go back to the hotel, do you suppose? And if they do, how are we ever going to get them out?"

"Go to a good film; put your feet up. Forget about the Doyles. I should tell you that Tod Morris was my source of information. He is just as anxious as you are to get rid of them."

Miles went to the Zoo instead of the pictures for no better reason than that he had never been there before. The animals were a distraction and he could walk about. In a cinema he would have had to sit still. He couldn't trust himself. The Zoo, at least, offered no temptations. He had been trying to ration his whiskey intake, and apportioned the afternoon so that he would not have time for more than two whiskies before he called on Johnnie. Approaching the office in Bloomsbury Square he asked himself what he would do if he were to meet the Doyles on their way out. Inside he was safe because Johnnie had arranged for him to be shown up to his secretary's room so that he would not have to pass through the public office.

Johnnie was waiting for him.

"That was good timing. Your friends left less than ten minutes ago."

"And?"

"And everything is Okay. Better than Okay in fact."

"Tell me all about it. My God, what a man you are."

"Sit down there in that uncomfortable chair. I always believe in putting my clients at a disadvantage, you may have noticed. I'll not weary you with the details. There were technical difficulties to be got over. For example, I had to get them to transfer their shares and give me formal resignations. Otherwise the company business and all its tiresome formalities would have been round our necks for ever. The books have been impounded, but I got my own accountant to look at them on your behalf. He has done wonders. I don't like to think what he is going to charge you. The hotel has been earning thousands ever since it took up the disreputable temporary accommodation business. The Doyles have taken a modest ten thousand a year each for their services, the idea being that a large surplus would accumulate and at some time in the future, when the homeless are housed, the savings would be there to modernize the hotel."

"That's what I always understood."

"Doyle lodged the surplus in Tod's friendly society."

"I knew that."

"In his own name. Did you know that? You drew a princely £100 a week and huge sums were charged up by Doyle as your extras. Whiskey, I suppose. You could have floated a battleship on your weekly intake. But even with that, thousands of pounds are due to you. And you know where they are?"

"In the bank, I suppose."

"In the Friendly Society in Doyle's name. The income tax position is chaotic, but we will get that sorted out. I persuaded Tod—without much difficulty—to sign his resignation, and the Doyles likewise when I said I would sue on your behalf if they didn't. I hinted that the Director of Public Prosecutions might be interested to see the papers. I had been trying to find out more about the Friendly Society. It is registered under the Friendly Societies Act for the admirable purpose of aiding lapsed priests to purchase their own dwellings, but something funny is going on. The right hand of that Friendly Society doesn't know what the left hand is doing. I persuaded Tod into releasing the sum you owe on the mortgage. He is off in the morning and—listen to this—the Doyles are going with him. Whatever that man may have done he will receive sufficient punishment."

"Where are they off to?"

"I didn't ask, and they didn't offer to tell me. We weren't meeting as allies after all. When I told them that they were going to get nothing out of the sale I thought Doyle would produce a gun, but when I asked where the money was that he had tucked away in his own name he started to bluff. I am quite certain that you have been robbed and robbed again, but I knew that your freedom was more important than money and when we get that hotel off your back you will have enough to keep you in reasonable comfort."

Miles grasped the lawyer's hands; the tears in his eyes were perfectly genuine. No one had ever done him such service; he was a free man. It was too much to take in. He could have said all that. What he could not have said was that, for all this lifting of weights and severing of chains, there was a sadness still at the centre of him. Freedom, it seemed, was not enough. He would have thought this news would have made him deliriously happy, but the sensation was more like relief after pain: it left him in a condition to get on with life, but it contributed nothing towards that process, and removed a first class excuse for doing nothing. All right: the Doyles were off his back. All right: the horrible hotel was going to be sold. All right: he would have sufficient to live on in decent comfort for the rest of his life. He could prefix "All right" to a long list of desirables but not to anything he really cared a straw about. Swan Tours to Greece with Gideon and his (DV) reformed wife, regular attendance at all the cultural events he read about with dismay in the Sunday papers, a suitable home for an ageing celebrity—thank you very much. He wanted redder meat than any of that.

What he wanted was to be back on television screens, doing his thing. Otherwise he was merely waiting for the cart. The news that he really wanted to hear could come only from his new agent Harry Hutchinson. He got the name from a gossip column (where else was he to get his information?) and there was no doubt this Hutchinson character was well in with everyone who mattered. That was the sort of agent he needed. He had asked for an appointment, and it was chilling, after the first gush of welcome, to hear that he would have to wait for three days—and no suggestion of a meeting over lunch. No celebration of his arrival. Hutchinson, perhaps, had been hearing the BBC's side of the story. Miles could trust himself to remove any false impressions made by those tricksters. Damn it all; it was not as if he were some newcomer looking for any opportunity to prove himself. There were twenty and more years of work on tape to demonstrate his skills, his adaptability, his genius for getting on with people. It came—Rowena told him on an occasion when they had made love instead of dressing to go out to lunch with a collector of fob watches—from his quickness to arrive at the place in the most diverse types where all humanity meets. He wasn't put off by rudeness, which is so often defensive. He was not unduly impressed by great talent or learning or the clerical dog-collar. He had found that he could do a most effective clowning act with such people. He never forgot that in the studio they were on his home ground, before an audience who were watching the modern equivalent of throwing Christians to the lions. Whatever television was, there was no substitute for it.

Johnnie, who thought he could read his client's mind, saw that there was still a pebble in his shoe, but he had other clients clamouring for aid and he got rid of Miles with a tactful compromise, recommending his secretary, Miss Stewart, as the nearest thing to *Whitaker's Almanac* in skirts, if he ever wanted to call her for aid. Several of his clients left their lives in her hands.

Miles had seen the lady and remembered that Gideon had mentioned her with respect. The idea did not appeal to Miles. Miss Stewart, he felt, would put him away safely in a filing-cabinet.

The meeting with his agent that was to herald a new dawn had not been encouraging. Even after two last-minute postponements Mr Hutchinson did nothing to conceal the impression that time given to Miles could have been more profitably employed. Throughout the short interview he took calls from people to whom he seemed to be devoted, and when he turned back to Miles at the opposite side of the desk he had always forgotten where the conversation had left off ("You were saying"). It was not the reception a distinguished new client was entitled to expect. At first Miles attributed the neglect to brashness. A young man had got on too well too quickly and still had a lot to learn, but those snatches of telephone talk were the sort Miles knew very well. He had mastered the manner early in his career. It was "beautiful people" talk—success and insincerity embracing one another. When Mr Hutchinson lent his attention to Miles he seemed unable to grasp what he was expected to do, even though Miles had begun by laying his cards on the table.

"I've come to you because my previous agent seemed to be unable to get any move at all out of the BBC."

"What move were you expecting?"

"A clear statement of what they were offering. It was understood that there was to be some revision of the terms of my contract. I was suffering from over-exposure—I would be the first to admit it; but no one came forward with any suggestions. In the end I had to suppose that no message meant bankruptcy in the ideas department at their end. I urged my former agent to put up suggestions—a travel series seemed the most promising. I was very high in the ratings, but the fact that I was still some distance from the top suggested that a change in packaging was required. That terrible little man Conway Foster was supposed to be working on a plan, but he was far too busy with his own power struggle to give full attention to anyone else's affairs. I wonder if the public realizes what a miracle it is that anything appears on their screens when you know as much as you and I do about the cat and mouse atmosphere in which the poor buggers are trying to put out programmes."

"What exactly is your position at the moment?"

"The same position as Job's."

"I don't understand. I seem to recall that boils were his trouble."

"After being patient for so long I feel I must do something to help myself. Their policy seems to be quite brutally to starve me out. They want to reduce me to a condition in which I'd be grateful to do street interviews. I would put it down to ethnic prejudice—"

"Mr Hutchinson looked interested at last. "I had no idea you were—"

"My being Irish, I mean; but the Irish do very well on television and radio. Frankly I think the British public lets itself be taken in, but then I can't understand how someone like Russell Harty—"

"Could we keep to your own problem? So far as I can understand the position, you were under contract to the BBC. When the contract ran out they didn't renew it. I want to get down to basics. After that it will be time to look for explanations."

"Strictly speaking what you say is correct, but when I was signed up by the BBC the idea that the contract would not be renewed was never contemplated. I don't want to sound conceited, but such an idea at the time would have seemed absurd."

"What do you suggest? What have you got in mind?"

"I shouldn't have to come back like some novice. I still see myself in an on-going situation with the BBC. If I were to get tied up with another authority I'd feel the Beeb had a grievance."

"Have you had any offers?"

"No, to be quite frank, but I think my position is fairly well understood."

"You wouldn't be the first to cross the divide."

"I'm aware of that, but in my case it would be like a sex change."

Mr Hutchinson raised his eyebrows, but asked for no elucidation.

"I'm glad to have had this opportunity for a chat. I'm sorry I haven't more time to go into your case. I have this lunch date and you know what traffic's like. I'll think over your problem and drop you a line if I can come up with something. Have you ever considered the possibility of going back to Ireland? There seems to be a one-way traffic at the moment. You might be the man to reverse the trend. Set the fashion. It might be worth thinking over.

I really must be going. It was a great pleasure meeting you at last."

On his way out Miles let fall a pleasantry to the girl at the reception desk, which she didn't bother to pick up. In his heyday little attentions to underlings had been very characteristic of Miles, what Rowena called "part of his act", but it came naturally to him. He couldn't buy a postage stamp without establishing an instant relationship with the face behind the grille, or feel an address or telephone number was sufficient for the performance of any business transaction, however trivial; one had to supply a name: "Ask for Joe Lynch and be sure to say I gave you his name", even if no more than the purchase of a ticket was involved.

This girl examining her finger nails took no doubt a jaundiced view of random male salutes, but if Miles's visit was rated as news in the office she would have looked up at least. Hutchinson had been formally civil. Miles knew the type, so lately arrived that it only wanted what came hot from the oven, terrified of being saddled with "left-overs", enormously impressed by names in the news, a sitting duck for confidence tricksters—a type of gentry that flourished in the entertainment business. Miles was offering him vintage port, he was looking out for wine that sprayed the room when the cork was drawn. Miles had been on the brink of taking offence when Hutchinson made the suggestion about his going back to Ireland. It was a roundabout way of advising him to throw his career in the trash can.

In the street a sudden flood of misery overwhelmed him, so that when the taxi he had hailed drew up at the kerb he could think of no address to give the driver and stood mute beside the door.

"An Irish pub," he said at last.

"That's a tall order, my friend."

"The Archway Tavern, then."

In the taxi he cursed himself. At this time of day (or at any time of day) the last place he wanted to go was the Archway Road. This difficulty with names was getting worse. Was there some treatment for it? He hoped that sleek young man hadn't noticed it when he started to talk about slipping standards in the BBC and wondered what—Reith, he meant to say—would have thought about it, but couldn't think of the old boy's name from Adam and only got himself off the hook at last by saying "old granite face". On this insane journey to the last place he wanted to go, he found himself thinking of Ireland. There had been love there. He had existed in his own right. No one had to tap a barometer before deciding what manner to wear for him.

Miles recovered his spirits at once when a man who was doing a crossword puzzle at the bar got down and came over to ask for his autograph. They went through the familiar pantomime.

"From your accent I'd say you came from the midlands."

"You're right. Cavan."

"I'd call that north, part of the ancient province. Making the six counties was a crude piece of surgery."

"You can say *that* again. I didn't know great men like you bothered their heads with matters at home. Wining and dining over here, I'd have thought you had left all that behind you. By the same token, I haven't seen you on the box for ages. Someone was telling me you had retired. You had made your pile. I was sorry to hear it. None of us is getting younger, but I'd have thought by the look of you there's the odd caper left in you still."

Miles ordered the good fellow a large Jameson, and having attached him to that gave him a run-down of his case against the BBC. His new friend was too busy trying to catch the eyes of acquaintances—drawing attention to his privileged position— to make a perfect audience, but after the slick careerism of Harry Hutchinson Miles found comfort watching this loafer looking as if he was taking part in a miracle play, as whiskey followed whiskey and he heard himself being urged to hurry up and finish what was in his tumbler.

"Fancy meeting the likes of yourself in the Archway. I'd have expected to find you in the Ritz with some American floosie."

"You've got me all wrong. I want to do something for Ireland before I've finished with them over here."

"I'll drink to that. I see a good friend of mine, just come in. I'd like you to meet him. He comes from Longford—Athlone. Do you know Athlone by any chance?"

Another breakfast with Gideon was made awful by a lavender-coloured envelope which Miles refrained from opening until he had finished his muesli, but he was uncomfortably aware of a peevish face on the other side of the table as he read:

Dear Mr O'Malley, I have run into problems that I cannot disturb Uncle with in his present condition. Greatly daring I am writing you this in the hope that you might spare me an hour of your valuable time on Wednesday afternoon. I could come into the city, but if it were possible I would prefer us to meet at the studio where the pictures are now hanging. I am prejudiced, of course, but I really think they look impressive, and I feel quite proud for Uncle's sake. The studio is behind 999, near the church, one of the Queen Anne houses. You come in by the same gate. The entrance to the studio is posted on the drive.

Curiosity and funk fought a pitched battle in Miles's heart and mind. He was in this lady's power to an extent that he could not measure. Having his passport taken by the police and being questioned like a criminal were unpleasant, but no charge that the police could conceivably bring against him would have such a lethal effect on his morale as any leakage to the press by Miss Dubonnet. She had the power to make him a laughing stock, and like many of his countrymen he would prefer to be fried in oil than to become an object of ridicule. He was more in her power because of her reticence than if she acknowledged that she had rendered him those services. With his powers of self-deception —as witness Dicky Dawson—there was always the possibility that the lady with the soothing oils had not been Lalage, but how was he to bring himself to say to her, "You have never massaged me, by any chance, have you?" Although to hear her say "I have never had that pleasure" would be blessed relief. He wasn't rational about this matter, but he knew where he was vulnerable, and there were people—some of them his own countrymen— with scores still to settle with him. Brian O'Boil, for instance, who was always insulting when they met at the Embassy. He wrote a vainglorious book and sent Miles an advance copy, Miles had not acknowledged the gift. Brian, lost to shame, wrote and asked him if the book had arrived. Miles sent back a picture-postcard with a second class stamp on it of a goat grazing on a rock face in Connemara and the brief message: "It did".

There were the likes of O'Boil out there waiting to plunge in avenging knives if the opportunity arose.

"I'm going to Ladbroke's," Gideon said, after hovering for an hour. When the door closed behind him, Miles dialled 674 3676.

"Oh, Mr O'Malley. How nice of you to call."

"I only wanted to say that I will meet you at the studio at whatever time you like to name on Wednesday."

"You are really too kind. I'll be there at three o'clock sharp, and I promise not to keep you for long. I'll tell you what it's all about when I see you."

She sounded as if she was speaking under some constraint —her uncle in the room perhaps. Miles didn't ask any questions. Never had he met any woman who seemed quite so respectable as Miss Dubonnet. Her image brought up a recollection of the pantry off the kitchen in the Dawson deanery—all those bottles of preserved fruit with their tidy tops and neat labels.

He had been curious for a long time about Sam's studio. If someone had told him it was a myth, he would not have been greatly surprised; but here it was on a November afternoon, covered in Virginia creeper, looking like a ship that had by some miracle come to harbour here. The large skylight was the only outside evidence of its purpose. The building took up a large portion of the garden and was screened from the Common by the house in front. Panels of stained glass were let into the *art nouveau* door on which Miles, as always, knocked much harder than was necessary. This was one of his mannerisms which gave an impression of aggressiveness; it came in fact from the effort required to take any decisive step. Ideally the door should have opened itself, thus sparing him the responsibility of making a decision afterwards or (who knows?) being asked to accept its consequences. Lalage, looking wind-swept, opened the door after a slight delay, but her bird face beamed when she recognized her visitor.

"Mr O'Malley—"

"Miles, please."

"You are so kind. Do come in. Sit down if you can find yourself a chair."

Her doubt was justified; every chair in the large room had been commissioned to prop up a picture; there were pictures on screens, walls, easels, but the studio was dominated by one enormous canvas. It hung from the balcony of what might be described as the upper-deck which stretched across the whole length of the studio at its further end and was reached by a flight of wooden steps at the side. The subject was Trooping the Colour, and the immediate impression was of a picture-postcard blown up to billboard proportions. The youthfulness of the Queen dated it. There was an eerie fascination in the sheer scale of the whole performance even though the principal figures were as stiff as wooden toys. In the foreground, sitting on their fathers' shoulders, children of all nationalities were waving little Union Jacks. These almost brought the picture alive. On a pavement the picture, apart from its size, might not have attracted more than a passing glance; hanging here, it was the pictorial equivalent of a roll of drums.

"Golly," said Miles.

"It is rather wonderful, isn't it?"

"Amazing."

"I found it hidden away behind stacks of old canvases. There was some row about it at the time it was painted. Uncle thought it would make a sensation at the Academy Summer Exhibition that year—it's the first Trooping of the present Queen's reign—but there was some objection to it. Don't ask me to remember. Living with uncle one moves from row to row. I think that's why people tend to quarrel over the same things, it requires less energy: one knows the routines. This one ended with the canvas being rolled up and stuck in a corner. Let me find something for you to sit down on; you will spoil those smart trousers."

Miles had seated himself on the step between the two levels on which the studio was built. While Lalage poked in drawers he had an opportunity to look around him. Most of the pictures followed the familiar Slaughter formula: brown cows, green fields, black clouds. (It had been good enough for Constable, he liked to say.) The element of surprise was one that Sam had dispensed with early in his career. But the exhibition showed that he had attempted other things. There were many unfinished self-portraits and decorous nude ladies tossing spring blossoms about and frolicking with cherubim. Miles looked at one of these and then at Miss Dubonnet.

"That's my mother," Lalage said. She had found a cloth and was spreading it out for them to sit on.

"She had a graceful figure. Do you feel sad about selling it?"

"I have a very good small portrait of her that Uncle gave me. I would never part with that. I don't know how much time you have—"

"I took the afternoon off."

"I hope I won't keep you for so long, but I am desperately worried, and I have no one else to talk to."

"I'm at your service."

"It's Mr Carlovassi. The exhibition, as I told you, was his idea. I was so pleased for Uncle's sake; he has waited for recognition for so long. Mr Carlovassi has been tremendously businesslike and went to no end of trouble. Don't take any notice of the chairs; there are two more screens due in good time for the exhibition. I am counting on the picture of the Queen making quite a sensation. Invitations have been sent out to all sorts of people and if the Friends of the Arts Society turn up at the opening on Saturday there will be queues across the Common."

"What's your trouble then?"

"Mr Carlovassi has disappeared. He works, as I think you know, from his new office in the Aegean Hotel. His secretary found a note to say that he would be in touch and to tell anyone that mattered he would let them know just as soon as he got back. I rang his flat and got no reply. Mrs Carlovassi is never in London. Whenever I enquired about her he said she was with her mother. That meant somewhere on the Italian Riviera. The Countess was to say a few words at the private view. The President of the Arts Society very kindly agreed to speak at the official opening. He was trying to unravel the complicated story about the Queen's picture, he told me, to put the record straight. Between you and me and the frying pan I believe that it was thought undignified at the time to show an unauthorized picture of Her Majesty.

"I am not worrying on that score, but I want to know what's going on. The Countess gets cross if anyone enquires about Mr Carlovassi's movements but the fact is—and I'm a person who loathes gossip as a rule—you can't go to the Countess's place without meeting Mr Carlovassi coming out or, when you are leaving, Mr Carlovassi coming in. I asked everyone else before I thought of troubling her. I had to in the end from sheer desperation. The *au pair* answered. She is even more bewildered than I am. The Countess left yesterday, said she wasn't certain about her movements, asked the girl to take especially good care of the children, and handed her a cheque for a thousand pounds to keep the house going for the moment."

Miles recognized the place where he might come into the story. He had been piqued to see the Countess preferred to himself as the sayer of a few words, and at once sentences began to form themselves in his mind. Slaughter be blowed. The picture of Trooping the Colour would appear in every newspaper in the country on the front page, and he must get his few words in. It was exactly the sort of opportunity he had given up praying for. Sam would not be able, at his age, to stand the strain. Excitement might be stimulating at first, but he must be protected against himself. He could rely on this champion. It would be a two-winged operation, bringing Sam belated fame and Miles back on page one. There was no conflict of interest. The media would be grateful to Sam's spokesman. One clip of the old boy mumbling and mouthing would be picturesque. Much of it would, frankly, be a bore. Miles would step in before that could happen. The Queen's picture would be connected with him in the public mind. T-shirts would follow. He would enjoy watching that agent's face—across a restaurant table—always—after this.

"Are you very uncomfortable?"

The question pulled Miles up. He had to come back from his rambles.

"Not at all. I like it here. I can look round, but to tell you the God's honest truth, I can't keep my eyes off the big picture. The Countess won't be there on Friday, you were saying."

"Well, it seems rather unlikely."

"That leaves you in a hole. I'm surprised at the Countess. You have been such a good friend to her. Now I can tell you what I wouldn't have dared to under the old regime. I never cared for the woman. I shall never forget that cleavage: it was like the Grand Canyon."

"The Countess has been a good friend to me, I am sorry she won't be here but the only speech that matters is the President's at the official opening on Saturday. Old Lady Cotterington is coming on Friday and it will be quite enough if she says a few words. She was painted by Uncle when she got married. It was during the General Strike of 1926. They have been friends ever since."

Swallowing the temptation to sulk, Miles put on his weighty manner.

"I think you ought to make sure that the picture of the Queen gets off to a flying start. The thing to do is to find a reliable local photographer and give him *carte blanche* to take any pictures he pleases on the day of the private view before anyone gets in. I, if you would entrust me with the task, would have a piece ready for the papers. Both would go in together. The matter we shall have to decide is how to present the information. We must remind the public what a picturesque figure your uncle is; then we must have a titillating reference to the painting: WHO PREVENTED THE PUBLIC FROM SEEING THE PICTURE OF THE QUEEN AT HER FIRST TROOPING THE COLOUR? I see that as a headline. After that, I should think it is only a question of tipping off the police."

"Why the police, for Heaven's sake?"

"Crowds. There could be a traffic problem. I don't suppose the pictures are insured. I'd cover them for a hundred thousand at least if I were you. I'll contact my agent and see what the chances are for television coverage. You were talking about worry just now. You ought to be walking on air."

Miss Dubonnet's hands were wrestling with each other as if one represented hope, the other experience.

"But if all these wonderful things won't happen, and, please Mr O'Malley—Miles, I mean—don't raise Uncle's hopes. I can't bear to see him disappointed yet again at this stage. He has become inured to disaster and, if you will forgive me for saying so, what I have dragged you all this way to discuss is far more like what really does happen than your rosy picture. I mean, it actually has happened and I have to deal with it before I can do any rainbow-chasing."

"Ah, there, if you will forgive me, is the commonest mistake in the world. A great general ignores setbacks, he looks for his enemy's weak spot and attacks again. Let us forget Carlovassi and his Countess. I am not enamoured of either of them and am not the only one who thinks they take advantage of your uncle's distinguished position in the art world and, I venture to say, your own *savoir faire* and good nature."

"A great general has resources to draw on. Uncle only has what I get him from social security. That doesn't go far when he has the house and this studio to keep up and all those dependents. I don't know whether you are aware that we have three of his former models living with us, and at least as many more treat him as a last resort when their other sources run dry."

"But why does he put up with it? Why do *you* put up with it, if I may ask?"

"I can't change him now. He says that he models his life on Dr Johnson's who he believes was the only English saint. Johnson used to have his house full, a blind old lady and other unfortunates. Uncle says these women gave the best of themselves to him when they had it to give and he is not going to let them down now."

"Hard on you, isn't it?"

"I'm used to it. Mummy always looked after him while she was alive, and when she went I took her place. At the time I grumbled a lot because I always wanted to do physiotherapy. I can turn my hand to most things and I've been making do ever since. Mr Carlovassi only came into our lives when I met the Countess. He came to the studio and bought some of Uncle's pictures, and said it was a shame that he wasn't better known. It was then that he formed the Alma-Tadema Society and I met you because Uncle mixed you up with Eamonn Andrews and hoped you were going to put him in the 'This is Your Life' programme."

"Eamonn jolly well ought to. I'd speak to him about it if I could be certain that he didn't suspect me of hinting that it was about time I figured in the programme myself."

"Oh, I was not suggesting—"

"It would be utterly reasonable. I was only explaining."

"That is of no importance. My trouble is Mr Carlovassi's disappearance. It was he who insisted on holding this exhibition. He got frightfully excited when I discovered the picture of the Queen. It was then he decided to invite half the world to the opening and all the rest of it. He ordered champagne and waiters for the private view, and I can't tell you what else. On top of that was the framing. He insisted that the frames should be uniform. In some cases that meant reframing pictures which were already in perfectly good frames. Then—I've only just thought of it —there will be a huge bill for printing and newspaper advertising. I dread to think of what all that will come to. I told Mr Carlovassi at the time that I thought he was overdoing things a bit, but he refused to listen. He told me he knew exactly what he was up to, and it was well worth every penny he was spending. It would all come back. I couldn't attempt to describe his elation when he saw the picture of the Queen. Talk of loyalty—he slavered at the mouth."

"It couldn't have been from loyalty. Wasn't he born in Beirut or Baghdad or some other disorderly part of the world?"

"Quite so. I was surprised until I saw the reason. He was like someone in a story who had decided to give a party to impress people and was slightly nervous about the probable result, and then a message came that the Queen was coming, and *on horseback*, for the occasion. Try to picture that. It's not so much that he is a snob. He doesn't know the ropes well enough. He is terribly anxious to be regarded as respectable, and his dream of Heaven is to be part of the English establishment. That should stop me from worrying. He would never allow himself to get into debt and injure his credit. The idea is ridiculous, when you think he owns a hotel."

"I'd be grateful if you wouldn't dwell on that. It is no guarantee of anything. Let me assure you."

"I know. I know. I was thinking of your troubles when I was bothering you to come and listen to mine."

"If you are sure Mr Carlovassi will meet the expenses, why are you so anxious?"

"Because I suspect that there must be some very good reason (I mean *bad*) why he should run off like this and take the Countess with him. He gave me the impression of a man with many secrets. I would have been glad, I don't mind telling *you*, not to have become so dependent on him, but Uncle had been such a problem. I don't like being so much in Mr Carlovassi's debt. I dislike his attitude to women for one thing. If I knew you a little better I could tell you things—"

"I feel as if I had known you all my life. Don't hesitate—"

"I'm rather old-fashioned, I'm afraid. It is rather curious because Uncle, although he is beautifully chivalrous to women, has never been conventional in his behaviour. He has always loved women and been kind to them. He needed them so much, you see, and more and more as his hope of fame dimmed. They represented the principle of beauty. There were always new ones when the old ones began to fade, but there was never any trouble so long as Mummy was there. She managed things for him with such tact. She had all the poise of a great lady. They made an impressive pair at the Academy every year, I can tell you. He always insisted on taking her."

"If Mr Carlovassi gave the orders for the expenses of the exhibition I cannot see what you are worrying about. In whose name did you order things?"

"It was done on that Alma-Tadema account. Mr Carlovassi used it for all his art dealings."

"Stop worrying then."

"I can't because it was all done for Uncle's sake. Mr Carlovassi was getting nothing out of it."

"He strikes me as being a man who has a very good practical reason for anything he does. If my prophecy proves correct it will be time enough to think about paying expenses when the exhibition closes. I can't see how you can fail to make money out of that painting, and I am sure it will help to sell the others."

"You are most encouraging and, of course, I shall be more than grateful for your help. I wish, though, that I could get over this eerie feeling I have, as if Mr Carlovassi had gone away for ever. He is not a good man. Have you time to come home and have a word with Uncle? He would be delighted to see a visitor, I know, especially such a distinguished visitor; you won't be offended if he finds a little difficulty at first in putting a name on you. Sometimes he thinks I am Mummy; we are quite used to it at home, but I thought I should tip you off."

Miles enjoyed the stroll across the Common. Lalage put her arm into his. It was a gesture of trust; she was telling him about the arrangements at 87 Rodenhurst Road. He was half-listening; the side of him that Rowena used to call "Instant Miles" was roughing out the talk in the studio tomorrow, but he caught the drift of the narrative and sensed a certain shyness about the home scene for which she was gently preparing him.

"Rose is really very conscientious, and can be relied upon in an emergency. Lynette is hopeless. Her eyes were her whole stock in trade, and she will turn them on to you—she does to every man—but she will not expect you to take any notice. Edwina is the oddest of the lot. I can see the point about the others, but I cannot understand what Uncle ever saw in her. He calls her 'the black one'. Fortunately she keeps herself to herself, otherwise I would die from depression sometimes. Mummy, just before she died, said how sorry she was leaving me in charge of this collection. Was there ever anything like it? I must show you Mummy's portrait. I have it in my own room. It really shows what Uncle could do when he was inspired. My mother, as you will see, was very beautiful. She had TB before they discovered the cure. I think Uncle gave me the picture because it makes him sad to look at it. Everything makes him sad nowadays. He used to play Chopin quite well on the piano, but he hasn't played for years. It makes him sad too. The only music we are allowed in our house is Gilbert and Sullivan and the record is cracked. I don't know whether you have guessed already, but Uncle isn't really my uncle. There's a lot I could tell you if we knew each other a little better."

"I think we are getting to know one another pretty well."

"You know what I mean."

"I think I do. I've a lot to look forward to."

Lalage's little introduction was a wise precaution. From the moment she turned the key in the lock heads came out of doorways and Miles was surveyed with unconcealed curiosity by ravaged faces. Lalage made the introductions. "This is Miles, Rose." "This is Miles, Lynette." "This is Miles, Edwina." When Miles's television identity was recognized, cries went from ground floor to upstairs landing and back again but Lalage pressed on.

Sam's roar when she knocked on his door suggested rude health. He was lying on a small four-poster, propped up by innumerable cushions. The walls of the room had been painted gold a long time since. With claret coloured curtains and black rugs on bare boards, the result was theatrical and seedy in roughly equal proportions.

"Uncle, I've brought Mr O'Malley to see you. He has been admiring the pictures. I'll let him tell you about them while I go down and get us a drink. We have something to celebrate."

The old man was staring at Miles and paying no attention to what Lalage was saying.

"Haven't I met you somewhere? Don't tell me. I remember very well, but where it was exactly defeats me—brain's going; memory's going; time I was dead."

"We spoke together at a dinner recently at the Alma-Tadema Society."

"Did you ever hear such nonsense? If you would only give me a chance I'll tell you. I do know you. I remember the face. Name is on the tip of my tongue. I mixed you up with some television fellow. Lalage gets very cross with me. Well, how are you, anyway? It was nice of you to drop in."

"I had to come. I was knocked over by that picture of the Queen."

"Rode you down, did she?"

"It will make a huge impression."

"Well, that's something. To tell you the God's honest truth, my boy, I couldn't give a tinker's curse. They talk about the advantages of old age and the pains of old age, but they never mention the apathy of old age. I'd bear pains and aches gladly if I could give a damn about anything."

"You'll be the talk of the town. Trooping the Colour is quite important enough to be shown by itself. I was telling Lalage that it will be on the front page of every newspaper in the country."

"I must say you are full of interesting information. What I want to know is who's going to look after that pack of women downstairs when I'm gone? I should have been dead years ago, but I can't expect to go on for ever. I must die sometime. They are all pretty long in the tooth themselves. I hope you don't think that was a very ungallant remark of mine; even so, they ought to last a bit longer than I shall. I don't know what I thought I was doing when I took them in originally. Lalage's mother used to look after the whole show. You never laid eyes on her by any chance? Beautiful. She was beautiful, I tell you. Lalage is a very decent girl, but she can't hold a candle to her mother."

Lalage, followed by the old ladies, who looked as if they had pulled down their bedroom curtains as clothes for the occasion, came in, eager-eyed.

"I could only find brandy," Lalage said.

"It isn't the time of day for brandy," said Edwina.

"It's always the time of day for brandy in my book."

"Good for you Sam," said Rose.

"To the artist, to Sam, to Trooping the Colour." Miles held up his glass.

All present said "To the artist". It had a certain gravity about it.

Lalage had to rush to the artist's aid when he began to hold his glass sideways.

Between them all they very soon finished the bottle. An animated discussion broke out among the ladies as to costume and how they were going to get to the private view. Rose was evidently the one with a wardrobe, and it was soon apparent that the more fetching items in all the ladies' outfits were going to be supplied by her. As to transport, on such a day Sam, it was agreed by all, should arrive with Lalage in a taxi. Any appearance of a circus was to be avoided. If it was raining the taxi could be sent back for the others. Miles promised to come half an hour before the opening to see that everything was in order at the studio. A local caterer was supplying staff to "push the plonk round" as

Rose said. Miles was sorry now that he hadn't looked more carefully at Sam's pictures. Rose, in particular, must have been fetching when she was young. She was of a more cheerful disposition than the other pair, who kept up a running battle. Sam closed his eyes after a while with a certain deliberateness. It was a signal. The old ladies scattered. Lalage came down to the door with Miles.

"You have been wonderful," she said. "I am so anxious to make sure that this is going to be a triumph. The poor dear has waited so long, and he is very tired."

They shook hands. Afterwards Miles wondered why they hadn't kissed. He kissed all women at partings on door-steps unless there was some overwhelming objection. He decided that it was because of the unresolved mystery in their dealings with each other. That would have to be cleared up before he could feel wholly at ease with her.

Walking to the tube station Miles was gratified by the number of glances of recognition he received. One old lady leading a pair of Yorkshire terriers actually smiled at him conspiratorially, and a much younger woman looked back over her shoulder, and he knew she was asking her companion if that was Miles O'Malley. He would never cure himself of this need for reassurance. If only the people who hesitated to ask him for his autograph knew how welcome they were they would have been incredulous. Everything was working out so nicely. Trooping the Colour was the answer to many problems.

Cyril Chancellor was a very young man with a very new camera. So far fame had eluded him, but the *Clapham Courier* had used some of his photographs, and in an interview with the editor at the office door he had been told that if the *Courier* ever rose to the luxury of employing a full-time photographer his candidature for the post would receive sympathetic consideration. That had been sweet to hear, and its sincerity was demonstrated a few days later when he received a message, on coming home, to ring up the editor. Which doing, he was told to cover a preview of a local art exhibition. He was given very precise instructions. There was a hand-out which would give the necessary biographical material. He was to leave that and the catalogue in the office when he was delivering the photographs. There was no reporter available to cover the show. An attempt to interview the artist had broken down. If possible, a picture of him should be supplied with the copy. The story had some local interest, and would be followed up later in the week.

Cyril was given the telephone number of Miss Dubonnet who was in charge of the exhibition. She promised to have the artist in the studio at least an hour before the private view. There was one sensational picture. Miss Dubonnet preferred not to discuss it on the telephone. Miles O'Malley, the television celebrity (who was available for interview) had written a piece about this. Cyril would be given a copy. Lady Cottrington was to have spoken a few words, but she unfortunately had fallen victim to the prevalent flu bug. Mr O'Malley would stand in for her and take the opportunity to add to what he had to say in his printed statement. "I think the *Courier* has the chance of a coup," Miss Dubonnet said. Cyril Chancellor thought so too.

The weather was very kind that afternoon. Sam rose magnificently to the occasion, and was lamblike when Lalage was putting the final touches to his appearance. Miles was quiet, but it was the quietness of one who finds the omens are good and is waiting for the something wonderful to happen.

Chuckling to himself, unable to conceal his pleasure, Cyril left the studio at six o'clock. Sam made a challenging subject for a photographer—Lear on the blased heath, Lot with his daughters —the photographic possibilities were endless. Miles became irritated at last by the photographer's exclusive preoccupation with his subject. He had expected to be included in some of the pictures in his own right. When he hinted as much the young man said, "Consider yourself a listed building, I suppose." Everything about the fellow, from his hair style to his canvas boots, offended Miles. He put up with it for the old man's sake (and to please Lalage) but his temper was stretched by a blanket ignoring of his presence and his suggestions. He had the excellent idea of a photograph of himself standing in front of the picture while Sam explained the points of the horse to Lalage. Cyril pretended not to hear when Miles made the suggestion.

Meanwhile the private view was showing how desperately publicity was needed. Sam was there. Lalage was there. Rose, Lynette and Edwina were there, two servitors to dispense the champagne, of which Miles had taken it on himself to order the broaching of a bottle, were there. Otherwise, since the photographer had taken himself away, there was nobody there. There was some furtive glancing at watches, then Miles said to Lalage that he thought she had made a mistake in keeping the picture of the Queen a secret. If the editor of the *Courier* had known about that a week sooner the news would have gone round. Lalage was starting to argue when two middle-aged women apparently suffering from long-term neglect of adenoid trouble came in. Lalage rushed up to them brandishing catalogues which they refused to take as if unwilling to be involved in the proceedings. Admittedly they did stand for quite a half a minute before the great picture.

"That's the Queen," one said, the older one.

Then they left.

That set the pattern for the afternoon. Admission to the private view was by invitation and the shy stragglers who came in and, as a rule, went away at once after gawking at the royal picture, all had invitation cards in their hands. Miss Dubonnet never asked to examine them. Whoever these law-abiding people might happen to be they were not anyone for whom the champagne had been ordered, nor were they offered any or treated like people who were present by invitation.

Sam was the first to strike. "I want to go home. Why are we all standing round like this?"

"No one is going to come now," said Lynette. "Come on Lalage, let's go home."

In her small Fiat Lalage could accommodate only the old man, and that with much groaning. "See you in the morning," Miles said. It required courage. The waiters said the champagne was not returnable and left, unable to conceal their contempt for the proceedings.

The old ladies helped Miles to tidy up, and a place to hide the champagne was found in an oak chest on which they sat in silence until a taxi arrived. Miles accompanied the fluttering threesome home, but declined their invitation to go in. They would all meet again in the morning at the official opening. Miles had done his best to raise their hopes during the drive. Saturday morning in November was more likely to find the public out of doors than a Friday evening. Clapham was a long distance for many to come after dark. The President of the Arts Society would give the opening a distinction. He had been most kind in his eagerness to honour his revered old friend. But the three ladies, shivering in their draperies, were all too obviously on the verge of tears. Nothing had changed.

It was Gideon who drew Miles's attention to the photograph of the Slaughter picture on the front page of the *Guardian*. Underneath there was a large caption and a directive to turn to the last page where the art expert said that he understood that the picture of the Queen was painted in 1954 before Sam Slaughter had been made an RA and as such entitled to unload his pictures on the Academy's Summer Exhibitions. It was rejected, and it would be interesting to see whether the hanging committee at the time had shown good judgement.

Miles, who had come down late to breakfast, with a bad head and in a bad temper, picked up his *Times* and found the picture lower down than in the *Guardian* but still on the front page. The story was shorter, but the fact that the public exhibition would be opened by the President of the Arts Society this morning was highlighted. There was no sarcastic speculation as in the *Guardian*.

There was a shop at the corner of the road run by an Indian and his family which opened at six in the morning and closed shortly before midnight. Thither Miles shuffled in his slippers and a feast met his eye. From the cold *Telegraph* to the most lurid of the yellow press, every newspaper on the counter reproduced Sam's painting on its front page. Miles had not taken to Cyril, but he would have embraced the boy if he had been present. He had played his card with consummate skill.

Miles was disappointed in one respect: he had orchestrated Sam's success, but his own connection with the great man was mentioned nowhere. He had intended that the news would have been given in an extract from his speech at the private view. The fact that he hadn't made one was irrelevant, the text was with the newspapers. He could only hope that he might meet some gossip columnist at the official opening. He was so preoccupied with his own position that Lalage rang up before he had telephoned to her.

Her uncle had had some difficulty about taking in the sensation he had made, she said. A neighbour had brought in the *Daily Mail*.

"Go out and get them all. Every one has the picture. You could paper the wall with them. I was just about to call you."

"Come a little early this morning. We might do justice to the champagne. I am only worried about one thing, if there is a crowd—and I know it is only an 'if'—Uncle will need my help—talking to more than one person at a time has become such a bother to him. Someone else ought to be there to deal with purchasers, sticking on red spots, not to say taking down names and addresses. I was wondering if you—"

"Gladly, Lalage, if you were in a hole, but I had been hoping that I might keep myself free to discuss the big picture with the press or, indeed, anyone who is interested. I don't want to hear about a possible rich American buyer who had to hurry away and found no one to talk to him about it."

"I can probably manage on my own. I'll bring an exercise book and let buyers write down their names and addresses. I wonder if Rose would be up to it. She is quite sharp in some ways. Lynette won't be able to take her eyes off the men. She would be hopeless. Edwina would be frightened to death, and anyhow she can't spell. We are all babes in the wood really. Uncle's last exhibition was twenty years ago, with five other painters. It was in the Brummel Gallery. They have some of his pictures still, but he hasn't heard from them for years. Perhaps we should have let them organize the exhibition. What do you think? It did occur to me when Mr Carlovassi mentioned his plan, but he wouldn't hear of it. He likes to work on his own."

"It is too late in the day to be thinking of that. Has Sam made up his mind what to ask for the big picture, or is he leaving that to you?"

"He has a story about Landseer—the stag man—selling a picture on opening day at the Royal Academy for £10,000. His imagination will not soar beyond that."

"My advice is to say the picture is reserved and mention no price at first. Then we can see who is genuinely interested and hope to play them along. Don't let us be rushed into anything. You will see what I mean if you go out and buy *all* the newspapers. They will make you dizzy. I should think you will be answering the telephone non-stop from now on. I would like to be there to see Sam's old face. He is already as famous as the Falklands. Ten thousand pounds. Pah! I'll go to the studio straight away. After I have dressed myself, I mean. I have the key you lent me."

Telephone conversations could be heard all over Gideon Russell's thin-walled house. The lavatory by some freak of plumbing acted as a loud speaker. As a convention, when either man was talking on the telephone, the other left the room. Miles would have liked, because he was in a hurry, not to have had to pretend that his host hadn't heard every word of his conversation with Lalage, but with Gideon the decencies had always to be scrupulously observed.

"That was Miss Dubonnet to tell me about the picture. She didn't know that it was in the other papers. I am so pleased for the old man. I wish I could persuade you to separate Lalage and her uncle from the Aegean Hotel connection. As she said herself just now, they *are* truly babes in the wood."

"She works for Carlovassi, doesn't she? She was the one who dragged you into that circle. Willie would be alive today if you had never met Miss Dubonnet. Has that ever occurred to you? I am quite prepared to believe that her uncle is harmlessly disreputable, but why you should mix yourself up with these people while the police have you under observation defeats me."

"Come and talk to me while I am dressing. I have to get myself ready for the opening this morning. If the President of the Arts Society is going to attend and speak, where could I find myself in more respectable company? Carlovassi and his lady friend have hopped it. Evidently at short notice. The fuss about the Queen's picture may bring a crowd this morning, and they will find it hard to cope with. What I wondered was whether you would come along and help me. If people want to buy we must be businesslike. The old man is the problem. He is quite unpredictable. One never knows how much attention he may need. If you had been at the private view yesterday your heart would have bled for all of them. They don't belong in the world. Has it ever struck you that I am the dangerous friend, nor poor old Sam Slaughter and his elderly troupe?"

"I regard you as worth the risk, but I don't want you to involve yourself with these people. Every instinct warns me against them. I couldn't be so hypocritical as to go and pretend to support them."

"Not even for my sake? I would give anything to think you were looking after picture sales while I was handling the world press."

"Twice is enough. But I wish your friends all the success in the world, if only they would leave you alone."

"You sound just like my father. Would you mind getting off that chair? You are sitting on the shirt I had hoped to wear."

Gideon returned to his newspaper. He hated not to be on good terms with his great man, but he had had the fright of his life from this friendship, and Miles seemed wonderfully casual about it. Exasperated, he took himself off to the betting shop before the taxi came for Miles. In the interval Miles tried on the hair piece he had come across when looking for sticking plaster. It looked rather well, he was surprised to see. It seemed to belong. He would keep it on.

"Thank God you have come," was Miss Dubonnet's greeting when Miles made his appearance in the studio. "The telephone never stops ringing, people wanting to know where Clapham is and newspapermen with sly voices asking impertinent questions. I told them all that you would be here at the opening if they wanted information. I left Rose at home to keep an eye on Uncle. They will come on by taxi later. I'll have to look after the President and I suppose there is a Mrs President. Neither Lynette nor Edwina is capable of lifting a hand unless there's a glass in it. Lynette ought to be able to cope with anyone who wants to buy a picture. I can't be in three places at once and you won't want to be interrupted if you're talking to people."

"I don't want to miss all the fun," was Lynette's response when Miles said he had found a job for her.

"It isn't difficult, if anyone wants to buy a picture they must pay at least a quarter down as a deposit, then you put a red spot on the frame, write their name against the number in the catalogue and take down their address. And—I was forgetting—give them a receipt. Everything is on the desk."

"And if they start to bargain?"

"Don't listen to them. The prices are on that notice on the back of the door."

"And if they want us to reserve a picture?"

"We may do that later on in the exhibition. Not today. We must cash in on the publicity."

"If they start talking to me about the big picture, I won't know what to say."

"Refer them to me."

Lynette rolled her eyes like two gas-filled balloons round the room while receiving her instructions; when Miles had quite finished she concentrated her gaze on him.

"Now, tell me that *all* over again slowly. I'm not sure that I quite took it all in. *Slowly*, remember. I never had much of a head for figures."

People were starting to arrive before twelve o'clock. The President was strictly punctual. Sam had been strategically posed before the big picture and when the President was led up to him by Lalage several cameras clicked and there were requests for one more pose. Miles, who had constituted himself master of ceremonies, was piqued not to be in either picture, but a cameraman recognized him and he was snapped talking enthusiastically to the President's wife. He caught Lalage's eye. She was radiant. Perhaps she was thinking that her life had, after all, been worthwhile. The President on arrival spoke of a lunch engagement in some more fashionable quarter of town. After the photographing session he made eye-signals to Lalage. She clapped her hands (Miles had offered to relieve her of the task) and told the rapidly-crowding room that the President of the Arts Society wanted to say a few words.

To smiling faces he likened Sam kindly to St Pancras Station; a landmark which if it were not there would leave Londoners with a feeling that something irreplaceable had gone out of their lives. "Needs a million spent on the roof," Sam said aloud. The speaker went on to say kindly tactful things about the paintings, but made no reference at all to the picture of the Queen. Miles had gone so far as to make signals in its direction, hoping that he had caught the speaker's eye, but the President was not to be diverted from his script and ended with "*ad multos annos*".

The Latin tag seemed to give Sam peculiar pleasure. He leant forward and touched the President on the sleeve, then removed his hand and looked at it as if in its excitement it had gone too far. By this time the studio had become so crowded that it was impossible to see the pictures. The President, who had been looking anxiously at his watch, now made a determined exit. Lalage shook hands and was about to thank him for his good offices when she saw him thrust aside by a middle-aged man, violently red in the face.

"I can't get my car in or out of my drive. If something is not done about it at once I'm calling the police."

"I am very sorry, Mr Parsley. I'll see to it at once."

Life had resumed its normal pattern. Lalage went in search of Miles whom she ran to earth eventually on the balcony where he had improvised a press conference.

"What do you have to say about the comment in the *Evening Standard*?"

"I don't read the *Evening Standard*."

"Well, you ought to. It says the picture was turned down for the Summer Exhibition by the hanging committee at the time as a fake."

"I don't know what you mean by 'a fake'."

"A blown-up photograph pinched from the *Illustrated London News*."

"Three of the figures in the foreground are here today if you would like to meet them. Nothing but the jealousy of colleagues prevented that picture being the picture of the year."

"Miles, you will have to come here for a moment. Mr Parsley who owns number 999 is in a filthy temper. He says his drive is blocked with cars. He threatens us with the police. Will you make an announcement? Tell all drivers to take their cars on to the road. I never thought of this. I can't talk to anyone at the moment, Lynette."

Lynette's eyes had never worked so hard. She was not going to be put off.

"I have the most wonderful news. I've sold all the pictures except the big one. I told anyone interested in that to talk to Mr O'Malley."

"And have they paid?"

"Take a look at that. I have never seen so many bank notes in my life."

Lynette with a certain sense of theatre had run up the steps when Miles was requesting the visitors to take their cars out of the drive and whispered the triumph in his ear.

By lunchtime the tide had begun to turn. A kind neighbour had offered to take Sam home. Edwina who had done nothing to help so far and had developed hiccups was given a sandwich and a cup of coffee and left downstairs; the rest of the party sat round a table in a small room under the balcony which had been used in its time for many purposes. Lynette was the heroine. She showed the party a bag full of notes.

"Thirty thousand pounds. I counted them twice."

Rose asked Lalage's permission to touch the bundle for luck.

Lalage was the only one present with any experience of picture-selling, but her routines were not a useful precedent. There was never a rush by Sam's purchasers, neither did they pay in cash. Perhaps £1,000 for the larger pictures and £500 for the smaller ones had been too little to ask on this occasion. Knowing dealers were probably laughing at their bargains. Rose who, as Miles pointed out, had no experience that entitled her to give an opinion, took that view. He had himself been approached by several possible purchasers of the big picture and told them that offers would be considered. In the light of the sell-out today an auction might be the most satisfactory solution.

"They are coming back at six to collect," Lynette announced casually.

Lalage gave her most poignant call. "But they can't do that. You didn't say they could, did you, Lynette?"

"I'll tell you how it happened. The first buyer wanted ten pictures. When I asked him for a deposit, he said he had the money on him to pay for them, and would it be all right if he were to collect them this evening when the exhibition closed? I told him it would be open all next week, but he wouldn't listen to me. He had come all the way from Yorkshire, and he didn't want to have to make two journeys. He showed me the money. I looked for you, Lalage, but you were so busy talking to the President I couldn't attract your attention. The only one I could reach in that crowd was Uncle Sam. He was quite delighted. 'The sooner the better' was what he had to say, and I agreed with him. After that a man wanted five pictures and he also had the cash and he also wanted to collect them today. Having said 'yes' to the first one I felt that I couldn't say 'no' to him. There was a queue of buyers by this time, all wanting to collect today, and I was so pleased that I'm afraid I agreed and raked the money in."

"People will be coming to see the big picture. So long as that is on view I don't think it matters quite so much," Miles said. He was feeling euphoric. "Yesterday we were neglected by the world; today we are grumbling because there is this unprecedented run on Uncle Sam's pictures. We are going to have to do a lot of thinking about the big picture. Now we can concentrate on that."

"I'm not going to worry," Lalage said. "We can put red spots on some of the ones we have at home and stick them round the place."

All afternoon there was a steady stream of visitors. Most of them looked only at the Queen but others went dutifully round the exhibition. The question of buying didn't arise as every picture except the Queen had on its red spot. When Lalage told one of the visitors that the pictures had been bought by people who wanted as many as ten in some cases, she said: "They must have been bargains then." Lalage talked to Miles about this; he sat with her at the desk during the afternoon. The three old girls had had enough, and in their different ways were proving tiresome. It was a relief to pack them all into a taxi. "We mustn't be greedy," Lalage said. "Uncle used to sell quite well until he was made an academician, then he felt it was *infra dig* not to put a high price on his pictures, and after that he sold very few. I'm worried about the picture of the Queen; it was done by blowing up a photograph, and when the picture came before the hanging committee someone pulled the *Illustrated London News* out of his pocket and showed the photo. There was a fierce argument about the ethics of the proceeding, apart from the artistic question. The vote was given against Uncle. His pride was greatly hurt. He said that he had done nothing portrait painters weren't doing every day. He had been naughty; it would have been all right if he had taken his own photograph. The group in the foreground was his invention. That might have saved him from a charge of stealing their picture, but it would have been dicey if the owners of the magazine had brought a case. They didn't because the Trooping didn't appear in the exhibition. All this publicity has been wonderful, but I will be glad to see the last of that picture. It has never brought Uncle anything but trouble. Did you notice that the President made no reference to it? I thought that was very significant."

"We don't know his reasons. His chief concern was to get to his lunch in time. That might well have persuaded him not to bring up an old controversy. I must ask Johnnie about the copyright question. Sam has never admitted the plagiarism, I presume. And it is not as if the picture was produced by some faking process. He painted it all on to the canvas in oil. The fact that there was a huge reproduction of the photograph to guide him is neither here nor there. Everything he copied was seen on television screens in thousands of homes. And the foreground is undeniable Sam, with those women. We have them as exhibits if it comes to law. I don't know what we are worrying about—a snide paragraph at most, and they have become so *de rigeur* everyone forgets them before the next meal. But I agree with you, if someone makes a substantial offer for the picture it might be as well to take it. An evilly-disposed person might spoil an auction."

"I feel gloomy all of a sudden," Lalage said. "A few minutes ago I would have said this was a golden afternoon; now I get the impression of snakes in the grass and vultures on the trees. I know that I should be as pleased as Punch. Do you think that nice friend of yours, Mr Russell, would advise what I should do about investing the money? I shall have my work cut out stopping Uncle Sam from giving it all away."

"Gideon is a funny chap. I don't think he would like to accept the responsibility. I should tell you he has a poor opinion of your friend Mr Carlovassi and he disapproves of my connection with him."

"But you have no connection with Mr Carlovassi."

"I came to his dinner. He organized this exhibition. He put me up at his hotel."

"There is nothing wrong in any of that."

"Gideon has made enquiries, and from what he has learnt Mr Carlovassi is bad news."

"He has gone away. He may never come back. I don't know anything about his business affairs; but I will admit that there have been occasions when I asked myself how much longer I could put up with Mr Carlovassi. There are things I could tell you if I knew you a little better—"

"You have often said that to me. Aren't we friends enough by this time for confidences? I can promise you that nothing you tell me will go any farther. And we are both quite grown-up. Nothing shocks me now."

"Mr Russell doesn't approve of me then."

"I never said that."

"He doesn't approve of your helping us. He never came to the exhibition. What has he heard against us, I wonder? Have you asked him?"

"He has troubles of his own. Also, you must not forget what he had to go through on the night of the dinner. You sent me the invitation in the first place, and Gideon sees all our disasters as stemming from that invitation. He doesn't like some of your friends."

"Neither do I, but this exhibition—"

"Mr Carlovassi's idea—"

173

"Makes me free. If you knew some of the things I have had to do . . . the straits I have been in. Having those women in the house has made it impossible to get out of our muddles. Uncle—some day I will tell you much more about him. It will explain a lot that must puzzle you at times. I don't blame you. What was I saying just then?"

"You were telling me that you have had your troubles. I think you can forget about them now. What about handing over the studio to the three ladies? You could then flat your other house and live comfortably on that and the money from the pictures."

"Your Mr Moriarty might recommend a stockbroker?"

"No trouble about that. Now what else is on your mind?"

"Nothing tangible, nothing I can put into words. Perhaps I don't know how to cope with good luck."

Miles felt cheated by Lalage's tone. He was prepared to encounter practical difficulties, but this note of sadness seemed out of place.

"I'm simply frightened."

The conversation was interrupted by two men in dungarees. They came in, then stood and looked around as if they had been sent for to do repairs and were searching with trained eyes to see where the damage was. Lalage asked if she could help them. One produced a receipt and said, "Pictures for Norris."

"He bought numbers one to ten inclusive. I'm afraid they are not hanging in consecutive numbers."

The men set about their task very quickly as soon as Lalage pointed out the pictures.

"Are they going to a gallery?" Miles enquired of one of the men while Lalage was getting the other to sign a receipt.

"Can't tell you, mate. We are just carriers."

Another couple arrived within ten minutes. The spokesman in this case was Irish. He produced his receipt and said he was told to make sure that the five pictures he and his mate were collecting were some of the smaller-sized ones.

"Sounds like loaves of bread when you put it like that," Miles said.

"I've seen you before. Used to be on the telly—weren't you— when I first came to England."

"Where are you living now?"

"In the Birmingham area."

"A change after Limerick, don't you find it?"

"How did you know I came from Limerick?"

"I know Irish accents."

"I wouldn't be certain where you came from, but you put it on a bit posh, don't you?"

As they seemed to be getting on well Miles put out another feeler.

"I'd be interested to hear what happens to the pictures. Are they going to a dealer by any chance?"

"That's something you'd have to ask my boss, and he is in California at this moment in time, as they say."

Leaving, he was good enough to give Miles a nod and a wink.

The next couple hardly spoke at all and were tense in manner. They were taking ten of each size and refused to give any written acknowledgement. "We were told to show our receipt and collect."

"What happens if the purchaser says he never got them?"

"I have to go by my instructions."

"He has shown the receipt for payment. I wouldn't fight with him over it," Miles said when referred to.

Everyone had gone and Lalage was wondering whether to shut shop when a couple arrived for the last five pictures.

"We thought you were not going to make it," Miles said. Neither of the men took the slightest notice of him.

"These the pictures?" one said. Lalage had stacked the last five close to the door.

"May I see your receipt?"

"I'll give you a receipt when you give me the pictures."

The spokesman was a short tub of a man with large sad eyes and a two-day growth of beard.

"We have no proof of your identity," Miles explained.

"The name is Brooks. We were told to collect five pictures."

"I'm sure it's all right," Miles said to Lalage.

This was taken as the starter's pistol. The men fell on the pictures and were out and in, in and out of the studio in a few seconds. They did not waste time in any acknowledgement, and the roar as the driver revved up the engine followed by a hideous scrunching when their tyres cut a swathe in the meticulously raked gravel on the angry householder's drive was pure cinema.

Not a word was spoken by either Miles or Lalage then. They were sharing the same thought, and it was only when Lalage looked up at the clock and then began to collect her belongings and the bags of money that Miles ventured to speak aloud.

"I didn't like that."

"Better lock up carefully," Lalage said.

"Have a nice week-end." Miles was talking to the Queen's picture.

"I'll drop in tomorrow and see how she is," Lalage said.

"What a day."

There was something mildly conspiratorial in their manner, like children who have seen something they know they shouldn't be looking at. Inside Lalage's little Fiat they both gave a sigh of relief.

"A return to the womb," Miles said. "I hope you feel safe at last."

"Not with all this money. The idea of its lying around at home until Monday scares me stiff. I'd be much happier after I dropped it into the bank's night safe. I will scribble a note to the manager. After that I shan't have a worry in the world. The bank is on the south side of the Common. It won't take us more than a few minutes. There is always some little matter to be attended to, some precaution to be taken before one is free to do what one wants. Have you noticed that, Miles?"

He had shown some signs of irritation at the time it took to write the note to the bank manager.

"There has always been someone in my life to look after them for me."

"You have been lucky."

"Things go wrong just the same."

"You have done more to help me and Uncle—but that is the same thing as helping me—than anyone. This morning we were as poor as church mice—poorer, indeed, because banks don't let church mice run up overdrafts—and this evening I am looking forward to all sorts of things—a Hoover that works, a toaster that doesn't burn bread, an upper plate for Rose, the one that she has doesn't fit—I can't begin to count them all. I have always wanted to give Uncle a pair of silk pyjamas. I can get him two pairs now. With his own money—I know that—but he gets so fussed when he sees money it is much nicer for him to pretend it is mine."

"We mustn't forget that your friend Mr Carlovassi masterminded the exhibition. And we mustn't forget cheeky Cyril. He alerted Fleet Street."

"But the *Clapham Courier* was your idea. Don't try to stop me being grateful to you. I don't like having to be grateful to Mr Carlovassi. If I knew you a little better—" But they were outside number 87 Rodenhurst Road and Lynette in the window was rolling her great eyes as in Sam's picture when she posed for Andromeda chained to the rock as the sea-monster approached. On its way to Birmingham at this moment.

"What is it *now*?" Lalage sighed, but Lynette was exaggerating the nature of the disaster. Sam had been complaining loudly because he couldn't find a clean pair of under-pants. Edwina had locked herself into her room, and Rose, in Lalage's absence, was trying to cope.

"You see what I mean," Lalage said to Miles, then ran upstairs making, approximately, a dove sound.

Gideon Russell laid his bets in his usual deliberate manner and started to walk home. He no longer went into the pub; now he, too, collected the day's winnings when he arrived at the betting shop on the following morning. Life in these little ways had changed for Gideon since his wife went into the home and Miles had introduced his more self-indulgent habits to his friend. Nothing was said about rent, but Miles, by random injections, raised Gideon's standard of living to a height that was going to be impossible to maintain when Doreen came back. Before that they would have had their Mediterranean trip, a second and much more ambitious honeymoon—thanks to Miles; life had been transformed since Miles came into it. Whatever he had been able to do in return Gideon saw as small and dull in comparison. Miles brought excitement into his life. At close range he might reveal chips in many places, but he remained for Gideon the only great man in his life. Where he had met bigwigs in the world of commerce everyone had a badge telling who he was pinned to his coat. Miles's badge was his face; no other identification mark was required. That was fame, not greatness; the latest child-murderer had *his* face spread over the newspapers. But Miles was famous because he could entertain people. It was a glorious gift. Try as he might, Gideon had never raised more than a rictus when he left off being his sensible self. As people hate most their own faults in other people, they admire most what they cannot achieve. In Gideon's case, making people laugh. No one ever singled him out in a crowd unless it was to borrow something from him.

It was only anxiety on Miles's behalf that had made him disagreeable about Miss Dubonnet. He disliked the Carlovassi connection. Gideon had been told nothing specific about him, but he was known in the City as someone who left a trail of trouble in his wake. He was impossible to pin down. He moved fast. All the instincts of a bank official made Mr Carlovassi taboo. Who Miles chose as his friends was his own business. At sixty-seven he was not to be ordered about. Gideon became regretful, apprehensive —if he lost Miles's friendship that would be the worst calamity of all. As Miles had said, it was harsh to condemn Miss Dubonnet and her uncle (he was an RA after all) because a city slicker patronized them. City slickers had done that since the world began. If he, Gideon, didn't look out Miles might stop confiding in him and get more deeply embroiled with these people. There was only one thing to do: smarten himself up and attend the opening of the exhibition. It didn't matter if he were late for the ceremony, so long as he put in an appearance. He provided himself with one of the spare invitation cards that Miles had left lying about. He was ready to go when the telephone rang. Doreen. She had had a bad night. Would he come and take her out to lunch? Come early, she didn't want to miss "The Archers". The great thing was to get a glimpse of her Gideon. Then she knew everything was as it should be.

He sighed, but he went. Lunch in a café was not memorable, and Doreen kept on looking at her watch. "The Archers" were important to her; something else that she could be sure of. She had tested her Gideon and he had proved his reliable self. That was all she asked, and she was sorry he had to go to the expense of a taxi.

Going to Clapham he took the Northern Line. There was a long delay at Stockwell, and it was after five o'clock when he left the tube at Clapham Common. He had told himself more than once not to be a fool, to go home, but now it had become a game with his conscience. He must make this gesture of atonement to Miles. He was nearly there and was crossing the road when a van came out of the drive of number 999 and made straight for him, or so it seemed. He stepped back as it skidded, righted itself, and roared off. He watched the van's retreating back and cursed his short sight. He couldn't see the number.

*

178

Miles was growing impatient. He could never look at books without discomfort and the bound volume of *Punch* that was laid out on the coffee table held his attention only long enough for him to wonder how the jokes could have ever amused anybody. The room was in keeping with the occupants of the household. There were two sofas of an uncomfortable shape draped with shawls, chintz, lace curtains, brocade; the floor was covered with rugs in various degrees of dilapidation. There were stools of different sizes spread about, but only one chair, so low that anyone sitting on it would give the impression of being on the ground. A Venetian chandelier hung from the ceiling. Nowhere any sign of Sam's art. The walls were decorated with framed prints of Royal Academy pictures that used to be given away with Christmas numbers of magazines. None of them by Sam. All portraying a world in which adults were perpetually in evening dress and children in party frocks except for baby, in the arms of the smiling nurse in immaculate uniform. The world of *Peter Pan*. An enormously respectable world into which as the sounds of women's voices on every floor proclaimed, Sam would not have fitted comfortably. Lalage might well have, Miles decided when she appeared at last wearing a sealskin cloak, apologizing for having kept him waiting. They should have set out in a hansom to retain the period atmosphere, and Miles's feeling of inadequacy increased when he squeezed himself in beside her in her shabby little car. He thought of that BMW in the garage of the Parnell Hotel. Even if he had it here he would have had to ask Lalage to drive it. But when they were settled in the Ormond Wine Bar and he saw that at two tables someone recognized him and word was getting round, he felt a renewal of confidence.

Lalage was indeed birdlike, but the beak was fine and delicate. It gave an intent look to her face and matched the bird eyes which never rested for a moment. As soon as Lalage sat down those eyes had taken note of everyone in the room and what they were wearing. Her sapphire silk blouse would have done a bird of paradise proud. Miles had never noticed before that she had a bird of paradise figure. He could not fail to notice that she had taken trouble with her appearance for this modest entertainment. It touched him. Things like that touched him; they were as close as his imagination could get to the tears of things.

He looked at the wine list and would have ordered nectar if it had been on offer; at the same time he realized that what he was sharing with Lalage was not the triumph of the picture sale but an unspoken acknowledgement that they were now in an open conspiracy after playing parts that someone else had written for them. Miles could see reproving fingers raised: "We told you to keep away from these people". What he had proved for himself was Lalage's innocence. He had never been wrong about her, and if he had stepped into trouble again, she was in it with him. There was a certain constraint about the conversation until Lalage without any preliminary, as if they had been discussing the subject, said "Why *two* men? It was particularly absurd where there were only five small pictures to carry."

"In case there was any trouble, I suppose. There may have been a third at the wheel. We never saw what they were driving."

"Why were they in such a hurry to collect? Everyone knows that—except in very unusual circumstances, and even then only in the case of a single picture—one doesn't advertise an exhibition and then let the pictures be taken away before it is over."

"You are forgetting the Queen's picture, Lalage."

"Even so. And it doesn't explain why *all* the purchasers expected to be able to do it; they *all* remained as anonymous as possible; no one came to collect his own picture; they *all* used faceless carriers and—this, surely, was very odd—the purchasers didn't seem to give a damn about the pictures they were buying. They bought them as one would buy rubbish bags. Didn't you feel in your bones that something very suspicious was going on?"

"In a way; but I was conditioned to that. The drama about the Queen's picture rather went to my head. I was prepared for anything, and the move to buy up all the pictures while they looked like bargains was understandable enough. After all we must not forget that if the Queen's picture sells for a big sum Sam's reputation with the general public will get an almighty boost."

"What I can't get over is the way it was done, as if the pictures were being sent to gas chambers. How could I explain to anyone that I have no idea of the identity of the people to whom I gave Uncle's pictures? We had the money, of course, but even so. Why did I allow myself to be ordered about like that? It is curious, you will admit, not to be able to explain one's own behaviour."

"I supported you."

"But you had no responsibility. I can only explain my slackness by the fact that after waiting so long, and when Uncle needs the money so badly, I couldn't run the risk of letting such a sum slip through my fingers. And, like you, I was in a state of euphoria."

"But why do you let it get you down? You can give any grumblers their money back."

"It isn't as simple as that. Even at the time I wondered why Mr Carlovassi was giving so much personal attention to the exhibition. As a rule he left all such matters to me. For example, the framing of the pictures: he insisted on looking after that himself and had it done in the studio by someone I never heard of. I got a shock when I saw the frames. They had such a funereal appearance, rectangular coffins. And I noticed that one picture had been cut down to fit the frame. That really annoyed me. I was told to give specific instructions to anyone with a key to the studio to keep away: the framer—whatever his name was—couldn't be disturbed. He was being paid on a time and material basis. That was very like Mr Carlovassi. He had never lost the strict ways of his youth where relatively small sums of expenditure were concerned.

"When Uncle went down one day to look for a missing pipe the framer was very rude to him. He came back in a tearing rage. He threatened to call the exhibition off, but in a couple of days he had forgotten all about the incident. He forgets everything. He was quite pathetic this evening. He has convinced himself that the Queen wants to buy her picture, and he was asking me if there was any way of finding out what she could afford. He is prepared to give her a bargain."

"Tell me, Lalage. Do you see Mr Carlovassi behind these mysterious purchases? If he is a man who likes to make bargains and if he is persuaded that Sam Slaughter is a neglected artist, he may have been shy of being seen to grab them, so he set up this complicated machinery instead. For all we know the pictures are now reposing in his house."

"You are forgetting he has run off."

"With your Countess?"

"I don't for a moment believe that he left on her account. He had other good reasons for going and he invited her to come along and as she doesn't like the idea of his being at a loose end she went. I'm sure she was genuinely sorry to leave the children."

"We did nothing that was wrong. There were pictures for sale and we sold them. We were not expected to cross-examine purchasers about their motives. The only legitimate grievance anyone can have against us—you notice I include myself in this—is that we advertised an exhibition and let so many pictures go before the exhibition was over; don't let that spoil our evening. While I was waiting for you at Rodenhurst Road I had the most promising idea I've had for ages. Attend. That drawing room must be the same as it was in your mother's time."

"Oh, since long before that."

"All the better. It is the perfect setting for Sam. In a television studio they would fake it up but they would put in such predictable period touches that they would give the game away. People are going to be curious about Sam. He is an obvious subject for a television programme.

"The only difficulty would be keeping him going in an interview. Have you noticed how the oldest inhabitant items on television tend to seize up? If we get a sympathetic director who could use me as someone he can turn to when things are going too slowly, someone who can fill in the blanks, as it were, the programme might well be a howling success. We must choose a time of day when your uncle is at his best. A voice over can give a good deal of the background so that we can concentrate on Sam's personality in single shots. And he will look magnificent. No doubt in the world about that. I don't see why you shouldn't be in the programme. You know more about him than anyone."

"Who would want to see me?"

"You are fishing. I can see you very much at your ease in the drawing room when we come in. We should begin before that with a shot of the house and me knocking at the door. In real life, as we know, three heads would then be seen leaning over the banisters. Here is the first big question: should we bring the old girls in? If so, do we explain who they are? It would raise audience ratings a hundred per cent if we did. It's a wonderful story. But you are the one to say. I should think Sam is past caring."

"I wouldn't rely on that. He has always been inconsistent. One of his firmest convictions is that people who accept honours have to pay for them by becoming respectable. That, he says, is why so many dreadful people are given titles. It is the equivalent of muzzling a dog."

"Castrating it, I'd say."

"I'm sure you would. You must let me do my things my way."

"In general you don't see him refusing to take part in such a programme?"

"He would revel in it. But the television people would need to hurry; his doctor has been very discouraging lately. When I asked if going to his exhibition might not be too much for him, Doctor Preston said he might as well enjoy himself whenever he could. It wouldn't be for long. I didn't pursue the subject. But you ought to bear in mind that we can no longer anticipate more than a day at a time."

"I'll get on to my agent first thing on Monday. He is an extremely pushing character, and I expect he will see that we are really on to a winner this time. I had never realized what marvellous eyes you have. I don't think I've ever seen them properly before. No one could look into them and not speak the truth."

"They have managed to. Frequently. May I put your remark down on my list of compliments? There is plenty of room. It isn't very long."

"Don't be cynical. I am finding this evening wonderfully reassuring, and I don't mind telling you that I was feeling very uneasy indeed at the end of the day's work. That inspiration for a programme about your uncle lifted my spirits. There is nothing like having shared a grim experience to bring people together. The comradeship that came from it took a positive line when I got the idea for a programme in your drawing room. I have had another idea: if your uncle is not going to use it any more, would he rent me the studio? We could have the greatest fun doing it up and looking out for the right kind of furniture. I am never going back to that rook's nest on Lindsay Road. The rent coming in regularly might suit both of you better than a sale. Suppose I were to take a five year lease with an option to renew? Think about it."

"You don't let the grass grow under your feet, do you, Mr O'Malley?"

"That 'Mr O'Malley' is positively insulting."

"Don't be insulted. I was brought up to respect the great."

"You are laughing at me."

"I am not, and you must remember how I met you as a celebrity who would draw attention to our little dinner."

"Don't remind me of that disastrous evening. I say 'disastrous', but I don't really mean it. When I set out for the dinner I was living virtually in a slum, surrounded by crooks, my career in a shambles, without a friend in the world except a man whose name I didn't know I ran into in a betting shop. I needed dynamite to move me, and the first explosion went off that evening. And now, look at me, having dinner with a woman who has the most perfectly shaped fingers I have ever seen—I have quite a thing about hands—and my hateful hotel is going to be sold and the people who were robbing me have run away and here I am discussing a new nest—"

"The people at the table behind you are listening to every word you say."

"I don't care. At least they ought to get the story right; they are hearing it from the horse's mouth. Enough about me. I want to know more about you, and as the people behind you are, by the signs of things, going to copulate at any moment they won't hear you even if you were to sing what you have to say."

"You want to hear my secret?"

"Yes, please. I have a question—"

"Let me tell you the secret first. Uncle Sam is my father. You don't look surprised."

"How lucky he has been in his daughter. After what you have told me, I can see that you have to be protected from your own good-nature. What you were saying about Mr Carlovassi just now is very interesting. Now that I know so much more—"

"Not everything."

"I wouldn't be so presumptuous as to assume that I would ever know *everything* about you, but there is one question that I have wanted to ask you for ever so long."

"And what is that?"

Before Miles could frame his question the waiter came over to the table. "Miss Dubonnet?"

"Yes."

"Someone on the telephone. Says it is a message from home for you, madam. Will you take it?"

"Certainly."

It was bad news. Miles was sure of that. And Lalage had gone white-faced to the telephone. Sam might have taken a really bad turn—ringing her up at a restaurant was going rather far if there wasn't an urgent reason. Suppose the old man had kicked the bucket—what then? What had he (Miles) said to Lalage? It was important to remember exactly. Rent the studio. That, certainly. It could be turned into a bachelor residence full of character. But had he not spoken of her helping him to choose the furnishings? What might she have deduced from that? What had he meant to imply? He asked himself that question now, as on occasions in the past, when what had been a pleasing prospect threatened to become a slice of life. In fairness to himself, he thought, on these occasions, he should be allowed to start again with a clean sheet. After all, it isn't until a fancy becomes a fact that one can really know what you want to do about it. What would happen to the three former models? Was Lalage supposed to house them for the rest of their lives? Surely, in a welfare state, there was some way of transferring the cost of their keep to the public? One step at a time; he knew that he was coming to the parting of the ways with Gideon. The business of the picture sale bore out his prophecy of what would happen if Miles kept up his Alma-Tadema connection. So be it. He had had enough of life behind lace curtains. With luck Gideon would have his wife back with him by the time Sam's studio was ready for occupation. It was the sort of background that Miles needed at the moment. He would give Lalage a generous rent. They would be living within a quarter of an hour's walk of one another. Once again a woman was there when she was needed. He saw his father's face with its familiar rueful expression. It reminded him that he had failed once again to get round to asking Lalage that embarrassing question. There was always some interruption. As now, this call.

Lalage came back then. Her face set. "I must go home at once."

"Is it bad news?"

She nodded. He saw her lips tremble. He didn't ask her any more questions, but beckoned to the waiter. They drove to Rodenhurst Road in silence. Lalage stopped outside the Clapham South tube station. "You might as well get your train. There's no point in your coming back. No one can help him now."

"I'll ring up when I get home and find out how you are. May I come round in the morning? I would like to help you if I can."

"That would be very kind, if you can spare the time."

He gave her his first kiss. She didn't notice. It fell off her face.

He would have liked to have said something. He felt inadequate in the situation. He was never at his best when feelings were too deep for words, and Lalage had really loved that old cod. In the tube train he felt angry with himself and perplexed by his inadequacy. Gideon was still up when he came in, and in a state of high excitement. As a rule when they had both been out he would begin by asking Miles how he had fared; this evening he pushed Miles into a chair.

"A most extraordinary thing, unless I am suffering from hallucinations. I was late going to the exhibition because Doreen wanted me to have lunch with her. I got there eventually just before it closed. As I was crossing the road on the Common a van nearly ran me down. I caught a glimpse of the driver's face and I could have sworn he was the man who was driving the van on the night of the fire. I hadn't time to put on my glasses to see the number, but I rang up the police and gave them a general description of the van and the driver. It is the most extraordinary coincidence. I wanted to see the exhibition, but the powers that be must have been determined I shouldn't. I had to stand around waiting for the police to come. They examined tyre marks and looked about. They took me for a scaremonger I suspect. By the time they had finished I decided to call it a day and took myself home where I have been waiting to tell you my story ever since. How did your day go? I hope the exhibition was a success and you sold lots of pictures."

"All of them except the big one, but that isn't really in the sale. Tell me more about your mysterious driver. Was he alone, could you see?"

"I wouldn't like to swear to it. For one thing I have very short sight without my spectacles; I should really get bi-focals. Besides, it all happened in a flash: one moment he seemed to be intent on running over me, the next he was haring off down the road. There was just this split second when the van was very close that I thought I recognized him. I never felt more sure of anything. What I can't make out is whether the fellow is trying to kill me or do I just happen to be always in the way when he is in a hurry?"

"Describe him more fully. I'll tell you why in a moment."

"Dark, thick-set, not much hair, needs a shave, late forties, might be more, blue shirt, no collar. To me his face looks fierce, but that may be from the impression I get that he wants to drive over me."

"What time was this?"

"About half-past five."

"You can't be all that short-sighted if you can take in as much as that in a passing glance."

"You look at people very hard when you think they have tried to kill you. Last time I saw him under a street light. This afternoon he was as close to me as you are."

"But still you say that you couldn't swear whether he was by himself or not."

"I do think there was somebody else in the van, but you must understand I was right up against this face. I concentrated on it. The next moment the van swerved across the road and all I could see was the back and the very dirty number plate. How I cursed—I surprised myself—when I could only make out the letter 'M'."

Miles wasn't listening. He was trying to make up his mind how much he would tell Gideon. He was only being superficially cautious; he knew himself well enough to know that once he began a story he couldn't stop until he came to the end of it. Gideon sensed this and fetched the whiskey bottle.

"A rather sad thing has happened this evening. I took Lalage Dubonnet out to dinner to celebrate; she was called to the telephone in the restaurant to be told the old man was dead."

"I am so sorry. That is really sad news. I hope not before he had heard of his success."

"I don't know how much he was taking in recently. Lalage was upset, I could see, that she wasn't there at the end. I felt very much in the way."

"One always does on these occasions. What will happen now?"

"She lives in this extraordinary ménage with former models the old man took in for charity. I shall have to try to persuade her to consult Johnnie about her position. Of course we don't know what arrangements Sam may have made in his will. Fortunately there is today's windfall, and I am confident we can get a nice price for the big picture. I had the idea of selling it to a charity which could put it up for auction. A flexible price could be arranged, I fancy. I think Lalage ought to be all right so far as money goes. There is something else that you are too polite to mention. You must wonder to yourself sometimes about my getting out before Doreen comes home."

"The thought has never crossed my mind. At any time you are a very welcome guest here. You mustn't be rushed into anything. Whatever you decide upon now should be for keeps. It's time you settled down, my boy."

"I have a tentative plan: we won't go into it now. I have something more important to tell you. That man you describe could be one of the carriers who came today to take away the pictures. A man who came about the time you mention answers to your description. He was more truculent in his manner than the others. I have been feeling very uncomfortable about the whole lot of them. I was in a false position. A dealer should have been running the exhibition. No one had any idea there would be such a crowd. I felt even worse about the business when tough guys working in couples came just before we were closing and collected the pictures. They said they were working for carriers, and none of them seemed to know anything about their clients. I was too pleased by the success of the exhibition and old Sam getting all that lovely dough to be the one to raise difficulties. It was Lalage who made the point that two men were not needed. The purchasers had hardly looked at what they were buying. It was all wrong, somehow. I wish I knew what was going on."

"Were the pictures in cases?"

"No. The framer supplied cardboard boxes for them with a lot of padding. The pictures were glazed. All we had to do was slip each into its own box."

"You said the pictures were glazed. Is that unusual?"

"I should have thought so for contemporary paintings. Of course Sam regarded himself as an old master. Even so."

Gideon had been listening with his mouth open. "Do you see it all now?"

"See what?"

"You were selling thousands of pounds worth of drugs today. What money passed was only bird seed. You must get on to the Drug Squad at once. You could be in real trouble this time. I'll ring them up and say you are going over now. There's not a moment to waste."

Miles left ten minutes later by taxi for New Scotland Yard. He knew who to ask for. Gideon, as usual, had been as thorough as possible. Sitting back in the taxi Miles thought of Lalage. They had been in this adventure together and here he was on his way to tip off the police, to clear himself, without any thought for her. If he succeeded in doing that he would leave Lalage under suspicion, and he was as sure of her innocence as he was of his own. He tapped on the window behind the driver's head.

"Before we go to New Scotland Yard I'd like you to take me to Clapham—87 Rodenhurst Road. Go to Clapham South tube station. I'll direct you from there." What a night for old Sam to choose to die. It was going to be difficult to persuade Lalage to do anything to protect herself, but there was nothing she could do for the old boy now. She must be persuaded to come at once to the police with him. They would make common case. He wished he knew a little more about her involvement with Mr Carlovassi. Now that he was exposed as a dealer in drugs—and evidently on a grand scale—he was a dangerous acquaintance. How much did she know? Gideon, damn him, had been right. Wavering as always, as if he was unable to retain his balance in an upright position, Miles was on the point of telling the driver to turn back, that he had changed his mind again, when he thought of himself in the cubicle in the Aegean Hotel, laid out like meat on a slab waiting for ministering hands. That vision recalled him to his duty. When the taxi turned into Rodenhurst Road Miles told the driver to stop before they arrived at 87. "I won't be long," he said. "Wait for me."

The curtains were drawn in every window, but lights were on all over the house. No one, apparently, had as yet gone to bed. Miles knocked gently and rang; rang and knocked again; waited, then knocked more authoritatively; rang three times in quick succession—his ear against the door now—then he gave a long rude ring. He listened. Not a sound from within. He remembered that when Lalage gave him a key to the studio today there was another latchkey on the ring. He took it out and without much hope tried it in the keyhole. The lock turned.

The hall looked as if an invading army had recently passed through. The garish light and heavy silence were a macabre background to the devastation. The drawing room was on his left. He opened the door and stepped in cautiously. Here the scene was chaotic; every drawer in the room had been pulled out and its contents strewn about the room. Cushions were ripped open, covers torn off sofas and chairs. China on the mantelpiece had been swept off and lay in pieces on the floor beside the fireplace which had been used recently as a privy. The next room, he remembered, was divided in two for Rose and Lynette. Outside the door was locked, but the key was in the lock. When he turned it a faint shriek came from inside. He supposed from Rose, who was lying on the bed, her scanty hair loose, one eye closed, a stocking in her mouth. He removed the gag. "Rose, are you all right?" She could only stare at him. Every drawer and cupboard here had been ransacked, and the room was strewn with the contents. The scene in the next room was the same, but Lynette was lying on the floor. She screamed when Miles removed her gag and tried to lift her up, and screamed when he asked her a question. She had come out of the raid better than Rose who had started to moan quietly. Miles knew that it was useless to question them, but he was frightened by the silence upstairs. He went back into the hall and called out Lalage's name, and when he got no reply, Edwina's. He wanted them to know they were out of danger. He was going out to consult with the taxi driver when he thought he heard a sound of someone moving upstairs and went up to investigate. In the first room he entered Sam was lying in state. His hair and beard had been combed; he was wearing a silk dressing-gown, and his bed linen was immaculate. No unfriendly hand had been laid on him, but the disorder in the room was even greater than downstairs, and there were signs of someone having lifted floor boards. There was similar chaos in the next room, where there was nobody; but when Miles tried to turn the handle of the bathroom door he found it locked from inside. He knocked. No answer.

"This is Miles. Who's in there? Are you all right?"

He heard a whimper. The next door was ajar. The disorder here was on the same scale as in Sam's. No piece of furniture had been left standing. The contents were piled up on the bed and pitched on the floor. It was only when he went round to the far side of the bed that Miles saw Lalage. Wearing only stockings, she lay in blood-soaked sheets, her face hacked out of recognition. What happened then was done in a trance. He lifted the body on to the bed—amazed at its weight—and spread the first garment that came to hand over what had been Lalage's face. Only then did he hear the continuous loud knocking on the front door. The noise paralysed him with fear at first. Then he remembered the taxi-driver. He needed someone. The driver must be told. He was amazed to find himself clear-headed and cool.

When he opened the door two policemen were standing outside.

"Put your hands up," one of them said.

It was not a time for joking; Miles was outraged at the coarseness of the man.

"Put your hands up," said the second policeman.

"You won't be told a third time," said the first policeman.

As Miles put up his hands he saw that they were covered in blood.

*

In all the circumstances a very kind letter from Jean. She had read about the Clapham horrors and could imagine what Miles must have had to go through. She knew very little but she had been outraged to hear that he had been arrested. If there was any help from home that he needed he had only to let her know and she would organize it. He was never out of her prayers, and she was listening every day to the news from England to hear that all charges against him had been dropped.

There was always a kind woman. He thanked God for that. The idea of shaking England off had occurred to him during sleepless nights. Jean's letter opened a door. He had not been charged by the police. The taxi driver had been told by someone in one of the neighbouring houses that something very peculiar had been happening at 87 before he arrived. Very frightening noises had been heard. The ladies in the house were notorious and given to screeching during domestic disturbances, but this had exceeded anything that had ever been heard before. This neighbour had sent for the police. The police moved quickly. When the door of 87 was opened after a long wait by Miles O'Malley, his face and hair were covered in blood. They thought they might be dealing with a desperate man and took no chances.

The doctor had seen Sam Slaughter earlier that evening, and his death was not attended with suspicious circumstances. The police doctors were satisfied, after consulting with her usual physician, that Rose had died of a heart attack. Lynette, unpredictable at the best of times, had not recovered from the shock. She had lost all contact with reality, and was unable to give a coherent account of what had happened. Edwina, the detached one, had taken herself early in the evening to see *Amadeus* at the cinema. She went by tube from Clapham South to Camden Town for that purpose. When she came home and saw the appalling mess the house was in she had knocked on her friends' bedroom doors and receiving no satisfaction had locked herself into the bathroom. When she heard Miles's voice she had been too embarrassed to disclose her identity. She had no idea that Sam was decorously laid out in one room and Lalage a mutilated corpse in another. Her characteristic incuriosity about the concerns of others in the house spared her considerable unpleasantness.

Miss Dubonnet's death was caused by a hatchet, found in her room. Miles's fingerprints were on it, but he had admitted to picking it up and putting it down again after he had lifted Lalage

191

off the floor. Why had he touched anything in the room before the police had made their search? An impulse. He wasn't quite sure what he was doing. He had been out with her only that evening. It seemed heartless to leave her lying on the floor. He admitted that his behaviour had been incautious and not calculated to help the police with their enquiries. But he was under a fearful strain.

The first police interrogation lasted for five hours. Miles said that he would not answer questions until his solicitor was present. He was not at all confident that Johnnie would take him on again in the circumstances. Johnnie arrived unshaved but willing and the interrogation began. As Miles recounted the events of the day his confidence began to return—the grimness of the police faces and getting out of his blood-stained clothes and other indignities convinced him that he was on his way to the scaffold. There, perhaps, like others of his countrymen, he was destined to make his mark on history.

When he told the police about the picture sales he felt that he was on trial before Johnnie, but as the story unrolled his confidence mounted. That incident about lodging the money in the bank night safe could not only be verified, but it explained the furious search in the house, on the supposition that the raid was made by some of the men who had taken the pictures away and came back looking for their share of the loot.

The time that Miles left the restaurant with Lalage could be confirmed, and that he had gone back to Gideon. The only occasion when Miles saw any change of expression on his solicitor's face was when he heard this and thought of that safe port in troubled seas. Then his eyes lit up for a fraction of a second. Up to this Miles was able to explain his actions, but after leaving Gideon's house in a taxi bound for Scotland Yard, what had caused him to direct the driver to go out of his way to Rodenhurst Road? He had never made up his mind about this, but he worried at the truth.

"I wanted to take Miss Dubonnet with me. To go to the police on my own in the circumstances seemed to imply that I was detaching myself from her. That conclusion might be drawn. It would have been quite unjust. I was and am convinced that Miss Dubonnet knew nothing about the drug sales. Like myself she was unfortunate in her associates."

Here Miles broke into tears. He quickly pulled himself together. He had been subjected to awful experiences. He did not need to feel ashamed, but he saw Johnnie looking at him, questioning his sincerity no doubt. The detective pushed the water carafe in his direction.

"I'm sorry about that," Miles said.

That was only the first of endless seemingly interminable sessions. He got very tired, but as he had a clear conscience about the criminal aspects of the matter he stood up to the ordeal well. What was beginning to undermine him was the way in which the officer in charge of the case began to repeat questions that had been often raised before and fully answered. This brought in an element of unreality at first. But when Miles began to say, "I have already answered your questions about that", his interruptions were ignored. If this treatment went on he would crack under it. He was more suggestible than most people. He would begin to believe he had done anything if he was encouraged to go on talking about it for long enough.

Miles was very anxious to hear about the Trooping the Colour picture. Sam left everything to Lalage in his will, and as she didn't make one, it all passed to the aunt who had brought her up. Lalage would have wished him to have had that picture, Miles knew, but how was he to convey that to the old lady? She said she was not to be bothered by anybody, and left everything in Johnnie's hands. When Miles mentioned the subject Johnnie fell in with his roundabout approach and reassured him about old Lynette and Edwina's welfare, even suggesting that Miles should drag himself to Streatham or somewhere at the other end of the world to see them. "They'd be delighted." As to pictures. He didn't know what his client had decided. If Miles was so anxious to help he could write to the old lady and send the letter to Johnnie's office. He would send it on. Miles wrote—twice to be exact—and never had an answer.

Having nothing else to do but discuss his uncomfortable situation until the hidden villains were unearthed, and to keep a grip on his sanity, he returned to his old regime. He went back to the betting shop without Gideon now, but he soon found himself the centre of a friendly group in the convenient pub. On his way out in the mornings, as on his homeward preamble, as one connected with two murders and a drug scandal he was the object of gratifying attention. It was like the old days. There was a stir when he arrived at the pub, and even in the betting shop harrassed punters would give him a quick glance of recognition. He was not slow to report this to Hutchinson, but his agent held out no hope of any success in the war of attrition with the BBC, even hinting that Miles was no longer a suitable person for family entertainment.

Johnnie Moriarty rang him up with the news that the police had decided not to prosecute, and sportingly proposed a celebration with his wife and Gideon Russell. Not an hilarious prospect, but well-intended, no doubt.

"I wish there were a Mrs O'Malley to make up our numbers," Johnnie said.

This would be the first time Miles had met Johnnie's wife. Russell talked about her with awe, and was beside himself at the dinner prospect. When Miles pressed him for details he confessed to never having laid eyes on the lady.

"Surely you must have run into her at those conferences you were having with Johnnie when we first became acquainted."

"Conferences?"

"Conversations or whatever you like to call them."

"We used to meet at the vet's. We are both cat-lovers."

"You never meet him now?"

"My cat died."

"I wonder if he will tell us this evening about how matters are working out for our Clapham friends. When I asked about the pictures he became very cagey. Damn it all, if it hadn't been for me he wouldn't be doing this Clapham business. I wonder if he ever thinks of that."

"Johnnie is very strict, I believe, about keeping office matters in the office."

"He talked about my business at the vet's, you gave me to understand."

"I was telling him, and I never mention names."

Miles was in better temper when Johnnie greeted him and the delighted Russell in his book-lined hall.

"I don't think either of you gentlemen have met my wife," he said, gently propelling them into the drawing room where a slim woman was standing with her back to the fireplace. She came across the room to shake hands. Miles had decided to wear his spectacles this evening, and he did not have to make his usual approximations. Mrs Moriarty was not the commanding Irishwoman he had envisaged, but English, tall, with hair defiantly and prematurely white, wearing a white silk dress and a garnet necklace. She was, at a guess, forty. Miles recognized her accent —he was an authority on English accents—hers was standard upper-class. This made him angry. None of his women had spoken like that. No wonder Johnnie was beaming. His frank pride in his wife was only an aspect of his acquisitiveness. The pictures and furniture in the room—Miles had never noticed them before—were obviously collectors' pieces. It simply wasn't fair. It wasn't fair that he should be mulcted for thousands of pounds to help fill this little man's treasure chest. His rage passed as quickly as it came. It was largely against the way the world is run, and Daphne in the old days snubbing him.

What a superb creature she is, he thought, shaking hands that had never done a day's honest work, looking into violet eyes that were giving nothing away. And then he panicked. If Johnnie at that moment had not started to play about with a bottle of champagne, Miles would have run away. He had met this woman before. A long time ago, but she could not have forgotten him. His face was public property. She gave no sign of recognition. He might be mistaken; he had met so many people, and as he grew older the habit of fitting names to wrong faces had grown on him. From Johnnie's manner it was clear that he had never heard a word about their first encounter. Avilda was her name. He remembered that. Why did Johnnie call her "Puss cat"?

Miles had been making a winter sports programme, the sort of thing that suited his talent for clowning and his natural bent for making a better than average shot at any new sport. The guests in the Swiss hotel were delighted, on the whole, to be included in the programme. Some were not. The Conservative Party, Miles christened them. He was sorry that a very pretty girl in one of these groups held out against his blandishments. Avilda looked exquisite against the sparkling snow, he told her when he found himself beside her. "I wish I could return the compliment," she said. He loved a challenge like that and rose to it at once. "We want a contrast. Everyone is looking so boringly happy. If only you and your party would join in it would lend us the authenticity we are missing at the moment." She said nothing then, just went away.

That evening charades were played after dinner at someone's suggestion. Miles threw himself into the plan. He was surprised to see the girl coming forward and he tried to get her on to his side. She turned down the offer. The game took its predictable course and the audience was cheerfully uncritical. Then there was a final scene in a television studio. Loud clapping and cheering greeted the appearance of Avilda in a man's suit, stuffed with a cushion, her nose painted red. When she said: "I hope yees are quite comfortable out there", no one doubted whom she was taking off. She was a good mimic. At first Miles looked apprehensive, then delighted—but delight didn't last for long. On the platform were the Archbishop of Canterbury, Greta Garbo and Mr Gromyko. A good deal of preparation had been put into the scene. Each of the celebrities insisted on reversing roles and asking "Miles" the questions. Garbo wanted to know if any woman could resist him. The reply was drowned in an explosion of laughter. They had heard it before. Among these people he was a private joke. Miles was painfully conscious of curious glances in his direction. The girl had gone too far. The older guests must have thought that he did the sensible thing when he slipped out of the room while the clapping was going on.

Avilda's party had left the hotel when Miles came down for breakfast. He never saw or heard of her again. He was too busy and prosperous just then to allow anything disagreeable to occupy his mind for long, and a time came when he had forgotten why his heart never rose at the mention of Switzerland and why it never occurred to him to take a winter sports holiday.

Avilda was not more than twenty, and that encounter took place almost twenty years ago. The girl had been cruel, but not without provocation. In a penitent mood Miles might have agreed that she had taken revenge for some of her sex. She had certainly demonstrated the good sense in his father's warning.

He did not think that he was capable of going through the evening without alluding to the past. It was better to bite on the bullet at once. "I think we have met before," he said as they sat down in the octagonal dining room. His hostess seemed to consider, then she said, "I think your memory is at fault."

If that was how she wanted to play it he was perfectly happy to join in. They discussed theatres, operas, ballets—he was never getting anything right. He thought of President Reagan in a similar situation and muddled on. When she was talking to Russell on her other side he was able to study her face. An exquisite jaw line, he decided. The Avilda he knew was covered with a layer of puppy fat.

The lighting was subdued, the over abundant silver and glass glowed and sparkled. Johnnie's face glowed as he looked complacently (Miles thought) at his Avilda, his sparkling diamond in its appropriate setting. Her name was never mentioned; her husband used a range of endearments. Miles was tempted to let a quiet "Avilda" fall and watch her reaction, if only to establish that his imagination had not taken advantage of his memory again. He bided his time; after a sticky start (Russell was too obsequious, for one thing) the evening, under the influence of Johnnie's wine, picked up. He must have been observing the state of the game and broke in when Miles was struggling with the name of the tenor he had last heard in *Rigoletto*. Conversation became general. Russell made the joke that he had brought to the party perfectly polished and was gratified by its attentive reception.

"What splendid pictures you have," Miles said. There were lights under them all. He said it involuntarily because the subject brought up a grievance, and he was relieved when Mrs Moriarty didn't take him up on his remark. Instead she proposed an adjournment to Johnnie's study where coffee and liqueurs were waiting for them.

"I'll lead the way," she said.

Johnnie put his hand on Miles's shoulder, steering him. In the hall he paused as if he had suddenly remembered something he wanted to say. Before he could speak Gideon rushed past to open the study door for his hostess. From where he stood Miles could see a roaring fire in the grate in front of which a sofa table was spread with preparations for coffee and liqueurs of sinister colours. An Italian inlaid marble mantelpiece made a worthy background for Avilda (if she was Avilda) when she stood in front of it. Over the fireplace hung an enormous picture. It had not been provided with a spotlight as were the other pictures in the room.

Russell was the first to speak. "Isn't that the picture there was all the fuss about?"

"It is not my cup of tea, I'm afraid," Avilda said, "and it looks so out of place over the Bossi chimney-piece. But it is rather fun in its terrible way. The trouble will be to find the right place for it."

"You shouldn't look a gift horse in the mouth, my precious."

Russell saw the possibility of another joke in Johnnie's remark and started to work on it.

Johnnie's friendly hand was back on Miles's shoulder. "A present. I know you took a great interest in that picture, and I meant to tell you. I was overcome by the old lady's 'mark of appreciation', as she chose to call it. You must forgive me; you know how busy I have been lately. Don't mind what Susan says. Her Majesty will have a kind home.''

Miles's friends were anxious about him in his present position. At sixty-seven it was time he settled down. There must not be another Miss Dubonnet. The final Mrs O'Malley should, before any other qualification, be a woman unknown to the police. Miles, still eminently suggestible, when writing what had become a weekly account of his prospects to Jean, asked her if she ever thought about the possibility of their doing "the Darby and Joan act". He couldn't entertain the notion so long as there was a prospect of his having to stand in the dock on a murder charge. However preposterous it sounded, that was on the cards. "I do manage to get around," he wrote (he had fallen into a facetious manner in their correspondence, in contrast with her undisguised anxiety on his account). It couldn't be for three years (he told himself). He had still this hope that the BBC would make an offer. He was about to ring up the supercilious Hutchinson to give him a prod when the telephone rang. This didn't happen very often. Only the small circle of his intimates had his number. When he answered, a girl's voice told him to hold on for Beatrice Dixon of the *Sunday Chronicle*. The name was familiar, and when she came on the line her voice sounded familiar.

"I have just heard the good news," she said (familiarity was her business). "No one ever believed the Crown could have a case. If there had been a prosecution the police would have had to hold back an army of protesters outside the Old Bailey, with me at the head of them.''

"You are very encouraging.''

"I am only talking horse sense. Is there any chance of our lunching together today? I want to discuss the prospect of your giving the *Chronicle* your story. I daresay you will be flooded with offers, but I would be rather leery about them if I were you.''

"My agent—''

"I have a rather dim view of agents, I'm afraid. They are like divorce lawyers; they make people fight who would, left to themselves, get along perfectly well.''

"My agent—''

"I have no objection to agents putting the final shape on

198

agreements, but I'd much prefer us to talk man-to-man at this stage and get the bones of the thing settled. We can leave the nitty gritty to the agent. Who is yours, by the way?"

"Harry Hutchinson."

"I have never heard of him, I must confess, but they swarm like locusts. I am sure we will get along famously. I have a table for us at Claridges at one fifteen. I thought I had better seize it, just in case. I've always wanted to meet you. In flannel nightie days you were one of my pin-ups."

"I don't wear flannel nighties."

"Oh, you Irish. No use trying to keep up with you. See you at lunch then."

At the very beginning, when the outlook was threatening, he had heard the phrase *sub judice* very often, but that was the time Miles might have expected approaches from newspapers. Johnnie, no doubt, had kept them at bay. Beatrice Dixon sounded like a toughie, but Miles looked forward to the lunch. He was pleased not to bring in the agent at this stage. That young man was inclined to get above himself. After a conversation with him Miles always felt like a geriatric. It would be pleasant for a change, to surprise him with a glamorous offer. The *Sunday Chronicle* was a rag, but it had a huge circulation. From the television angle it would do more for him than any of the "posh Sundays". He was sure the Dixon woman would make a lavish offer; what the agent would have to look after would be questions of copyright in the book which would inevitably follow the Sunday serialization. He needed someone at the moment like Beatrice Dixon, someone energetic, vulgar, bracing—someone, above all, unconnected with the past. He felt guilty to discover how resilient he was, how soon the sap rose in him again. He tried to conceal the truth from Gideon who still felt obliged to talk to him as if he was in an emergency ward. For decency's sake Miles restrained his urge to put his recent experiences to profitable use when his friend, out of concern, showed infinite compassion in protecting him from all callers anxious to have the talks Miles was longing for.

What was he to wear when lunching with the lady from the *Sunday Chronicle*? If his costume were to reflect the buoyancy of his mood he should put on one of his recent purchases. (When the exhibition was in the wind he had spent an extravagant morning in Moss Bros to whom his figure presented no problem that their work-rooms couldn't cope with.) There was the crushed-strawberry suede jacket in which he looked vaguely Georgian when he took off the sombrero which had become part of his legend. The trousers were a subtle shade of grey, and it was an opportunity to wear the butter-coloured brocade waistcoat and matching cravat. Was it a little too much? At the moment, perhaps. His scarlet-lined black suit gave a cloak and dagger effect that wasn't the right note either. His problem was to reconcile the Regency buck with the man of feeling. If only Rowena were here to advise. He never used to have these problems. She understood him so well.

After his recent experiences, was it not extraordinary that he should be bothering his head about what he would wear? Russell had called him "deeply frivolous". Perhaps he was. Perhaps that was his secret, why he had survived. When he thought about Lalage—and he tried not to—there was always behind the horror the reassurance that an embarrassing secret had been taken to the grave. It astonished him how, after one night of teeth-rattling, that first sight of her battered face was fixed in memory as if it had been seen by somebody else. The prosaic fact was that he hardly knew Lalage. They had had only two conversations, both of which had been broken off before they became even approximately intimate. He had automatically excised from memory that moment when he had all but asked the taxi driver to turn back and go straight to New Scotland Yard. His father's received wisdom was asserting itself then, but he had done the gallant thing. He shouldn't blame himself now if he found that life was bursting to begin again. He would never forget Lalage, but it would be morbid to fight against nature's homeopathy. Now it was at work absorbing him in the task of dressing up to go to lunch with Beatrice Dixon. All bust and bad language, he imagined her. Broad in every sense. He even pictured himself with her on Brighton pier when it was being battered by breakers, with that voice beside him creaking like a ship's mast in the storm. Exactly the voice Miles wanted to hear at the moment. He felt a sudden rush of gratitude to God for His unfailing supply of voices when he needed one to urge him on. In Beatrice's case it was not so much the voice as the message. He was eminently suggestible —Rowena's voice led him into television and into the hands of crooks who had bled him alive. Lalage's had led into horrors unspeakable, but provided him with the wherewithal for what might prove itself to be his last great opportunity. Beatrice Dixon was leading him on to that. He had hardly shaped the thought when the telephone rang—the *Daily Mail*. He replaced the receiver; the telephone rang again, and after that again and again after that—Fleet Street had got his number.

He told every caller to contact his agent. That struck him as a sophisticated way to give Hutchinson some exercise, and when that young man had sorted out these enquiries he, Miles, would produce Beatrice from out of his hat. Perhaps it might, after all, be more sensible not to close at once with her offer. Better far to take her into his confidence and let her play the final round with that uppish young man. That decision led to another. He decided to wear his Donegal tweed suit with tie to match. This return of confidence—yesterday he couldn't get himself to concentrate long enough to address an envelope to his bank—was exhilarating. He would have time if he went at once to get a haircut at the unisex shop round the corner. He had previously looked askance at such establishments, but looking at the window of this one recently he envied a man, of his own age at least, looking like a tabby cat in the sun while an interesting-looking foreign girl was snipping at his ludicrous sideburns. She might be free. As he was leaving his apartment he saw an envelope on the ground and picked it up. The letter he had written to Jean—a hundred years ago, it seemed. So much had taken place this morning. He slipped it into his pocket.

At three o'clock he left Claridges in a taxi with Miss Dixon. He had insisted on taking her back to her office after a good lunch and more wine than was wise at that time of day. If he hadn't drunk quite so much he would not have insisted on undertaking her transport. She had been tremendous. He had imagined a massive blonde, a comic postcard stereotype, and was surprised to find her small, dark and leather-skinned. Her voice was out of all proportion to her stature. She was one of nature's drill sergeants. Australian, rough and kind. She had been all over him until he disclosed his bargaining plan. That, she said, was holding her up to a Dutch auction. She would be buggered before she would let the price be pushed up and then invited to top it. He had agreed to fix the deal over lunch, and she liked men who stuck to their word.

"I am going to find it hard to face my agent."

"So long as he gets his fee he is not going to mind. Let's say fifty-five. I'll offer him the round figure and when he asks me to improve on that I'll hum and haw and then come up with the other five. What do you say to that?"

"I'm perfectly happy."

"Is it a deal?"

"It's a deal."

"Good." Then she began to talk rather boringly about the decline of standards in Fleet Street since she arrived wide-eyed from Sydney. Miles wasn't listening. He very seldom listened to this sort of talk. It was like any free hand-out, going from hand to hand and then into the litter bin, so far as he was concerned. He felt in his pocket for his keys and his fingers met the letter to Jean and he remembered the Darby and Joan bit. That was out of date now. He took the letter out surreptitiously and tore it across under the table.

"I told him he could bugger himself," Mrs Dixon was saying when he tuned in at last.

Outside the *Chronicle* offices, he gave their deputy editor a sloppy kiss. It clearly surprised her. She made another reference to Miles's nationality. He went upstairs with her to her offices and heard her telephone conversation with Miles's agent. "He is here with me," she said. "He wants a word with you." She handed Miles the receiver.

"What's going on? They are all on the line. Let me tell the woman she will have to wait. Why should she be allowed to take a short-cut? You should have refused to discuss her offer. What do you think an agent's for?"

"She was the first to make an offer. Fifty thousand for me, five for you. I'm perfectly satisfied. What I want *you* to do is get in touch with the BBC. We are on a winner at last."

"I wish you would forget about the BBC. You have a wonderful opportunity to sell a story to the press. Their tongues are hanging out, and you go and give it away to the first female who offers you lunch."

"Miss Dixon is a friend of mine. I'm going to hand you back to her. Tell her to send you the contract."

There followed a short conversation. Beatrice was smiling when she put down the receiver.

"That's all right then. I don't think you would have done very much better. He will huff and puff for a while, but I wouldn't break my heart about that if I were you."

Miles left the *Sunday Chronicle* offices well pleased with himself. It was a luxury to have made his own decision about his own business. Bugger Mr Hutchinson, as that little terrier of a woman would have said. A good sort, but not destined to play a part in his future. He regretted the kiss. Force of habit. Before he left the office she asked him if he was going to write the story himself. The *Chronicle* would be telling its readers in the morning that it had lived up to its reputation. If Miles liked the idea there was a very bright young journalist, Pam Werner, who would take him down on tape and do whatever editing was required. If there was to be a book she might be very helpful about that. Miles knew that he was listening to God's voice now. Pam Werner. Of course he would be very happy to take advantage of the offer. Pam Werner. What role was she destined to play in his story?

"We pay her, but of course if you make a book or a film out of it that's between you and Pam."

"That is between you and Pam." He liked the sound of that. He repeated it aloud as he walked towards Ludgate Circus. He had a sudden impulse to go into St Paul's. In those lofty surroundings he would sort out the high drama of his day. Pam Werner would ring him up this evening or early in the morning. Beatrice would arrange that. He was surrounded by Vestal Virgins.

The wonderful boy was singing in St Paul's. His hymn records had been top of the polls. It was a phenomenon of recent weeks, and not the sort of news that Miles was taking in at present. The cathedral had discovered the largest source of income that it had ever known and many were claiming to see the hand of God in it. Miles had been in St Paul's on business more than once, but that was a long time ago, and he had only a vague picture of the interior in his mind.

Richard Dawson was well aware of the treat that awaited him at St Paul's as he left his solicitor's office in Lincoln's Inn and, finding himself with a long stretch of morning ahead of him, decided to walk to the cathedral. It was an unseasonably beautiful morning and the excursion suited his mood. Everything had gone very well for him this trip—life was entirely satisfactory at the moment. The great decision to move to Bath had justified itself tenfold. A bridge circle had welcomed in a charming couple who played a first class game. Richard (Olivia hated the diminutive "Dicky") found that his clerical background still, as she amusingly put it, "turns up trumps". He was already a power in the vestry. Seventy on his next birthday, he could still hold his own in men's doubles at tennis, and his golf handicap, having slipped to nine, showed every sign of sticking there. The Dawsons made regular raids on London. Olivia liked to see her sister; Richard did a round of his advisers—a little tooth trouble this trip—and they both enjoyed the opportunity to go to the Albert Hall and see a few theatres (the girls were going to a matinée at the Haymarket this afternoon).

Richard walked down Chancery Lane and into Fleet Street. There his attention was caught by the window display in a bookshop. He played with the idea of going in and buying Olivia the one about the Queen. Why had the publishers put such an unflattering photograph of HM on the jacket? He thought of her always as the near-child who had been summoned from Africa to become queen, and he was a man with whom old impressions died hard. In this picture the Queen looked like her formidable great-grandmother. This was the first cloud to pass across the blue sky of Richard's morning. He turned away to resume his walk, and as he did so nearly bumped into a pedestrian, a bulky figure in a tweed suit, with a game-cock's feather in his hat. But oddly familiar. It was only when the man looked back that Richard recognized Miles O'Malley to whom he had so often been tempted to write but had been held back by shyness. One couldn't pick up old threads like that easily, and they lived in such utterly different worlds—always had, but childhood makes for unlikely combinations sometimes. If Miles recognized him the result was unflattering. He broke into a run, making, in Richard's opinion, an extraordinary spectacle.

Jean was troubled about Miles. Swallowing pride, she had held out her hands to him when he looked to have reached the end of his tether. He had responded in his typically frivolous way, but left her with the possibility of his return to cherish, provided he wasn't sent to prison. What a terrible mess the poor old silly had got himself into this time. His cool assumption that their reunion was only entered on a list of options maddened her for a day, but when she remembered the horrors he had witnessed she put his indecent levity down to the after-effect of shock. She was grateful to this mysterious Mr Russell who played the role of keeper and decided that here was a real friend. She wrote to him. Gideon cautiously answered. Then she decided to come over to London —she had friends to stay with—to try to make Mr Russell's better acquaintance. Of course, all the time, from the moment she set foot in London, she wanted only to get to Miles and take his foolish head in her lap. She had spoken on the telephone this morning to Gideon who, after much hesitation, suggested a meeting next day in the restaurant attached to St James's, Picca- dilly, to discuss the situation. She had to occupy herself mean- while and at a friend's suggestion she went to St Paul's to hear the boy with the marvellous singing voice. One was expected to put a pound into the collection box, but Jean was advised that women had to restrain themselves otherwise they emptied their purses. The boy had come straight from Heaven.

She crossed Ludgate Circus circumspectly, looking in all direc- tions before she accepted the green light as decisive, and was waiting on the island before venturing across the final strip of roadway when she saw behind her the awkward figure of an elderly man, dressed for a walk on the moors, running across the road. She waited where she was. His outline was familiar: the way his head hung to one side and those jack-knife legs. It was Miles. It could be no one else. And she knew that he had seen her. "Watch out," she shouted. He had started off against the lights as if he were an ambulance or a police car.

There was a bookshop beside the *Sunday Chronicle* offices. Miles liked books in a shop window, but felt threatened by them in a private house. There was a picture of the Queen on the cover of one. He could have done without that at the moment. There was a coffee table book about the islands of the Pacific with stunning- looking girls on the cover—the usual formula: azure sea, palm trees and topless girls in grass skirts. They would not have earned a glance, he told himself, but today, for some reason, they sent his mind playing with the idea of Pam Werner. Why had he never thought of collaboration before? Whenever he tried to write in the past his pen just seized up on him, but if he could have dictated to an intelligent and attractive-looking girl the whole experience could have been fruitful as well as delightful. Of course he knew all about being "ghosted", but the idea of that repelled the artist in him (and how desiccated those productions always were). This would be something else, a joint production, the issue of a mystical marriage. He liked the name Pam Werner. He had assumed she was young. As young as those girls in the South Seas? Probably not. They did not suggest the possibility of literary partnership. Pam might look like that picture on a paperback of Edna O'Brien. Anything was possible. He had learned that. It was a wonderfully exciting project. And to Hell with the BBC. He took a final look at the girls on the book cover. It was the centre of a window arrangement. For some reason they reminded him of Dicky Dawson. What had he got up to in foreign parts? But that was not what made the connection in his mind. Miles was remembering copies of the *National Geographic Magazine* at the deanery. They came addressed to the Dean, but the children were encouraged to read them. This astonished Miles when he saw how many pictures there were of bare-chested girls (natives, of course, which took a lot of the harm out of it). He had smuggled one copy home to peruse at leisure and was embarrassed when his father caught him absorbed in it. "The Dawsons are Protestants," he said when Miles defended himself. "Bring it back. I'm surprised at the Dean. Remember what I've often told you. Let them say what they like, you keep away from the women."

Daphne was probably married to a bishop, a retired bishop (if bishops ever did retire) and they would all have had a fine time reading out the newspaper accounts of bloodshed in Rodenhurst Road and the man who was helping police with their enquiries. Things like that would never happen in deanery circles any more than they would have happened in his own home over the pub where God acted the part of closed-circuit television. To Hell with them all. He was fighting still, and any day now Pam Werner would be on the telephone (Beatrice knew where to find him).

Miles had retained since childhood an eccentric compulsion to break into a run when excited. A happy thought was enough to set him off at a gallop. *Esprit d'escalier* almost invariably had this effect on him, as if he were running back to deliver the delayed riposte. The idea of defying the powers who were closing him in was exactly what was required to send him off to a flying start. He would pull up sweating and puffing when he bumped into a pedestrian who had not been sufficiently deft of foot to avoid his charge; sometimes he even reached his destination, where he sank into a chair and strove to recover his breath; sometimes he fell flat on his face.

Fleet Street was an appropriate setting for a run; there was something allegorical about the course. Indignant pedestrians after narrowly escaping a collision called angry names at the retreating back. But Miles was impervious to his surroundings. Unaware that he was running, he saw in his progress many familiar faces flashing by. He didn't see his father, but he saw Dicky Dawson, and would have stopped to talk to him if he hadn't remembered what happened last time when he began to see Dicky everywhere. He was amazed to see Jean. He knew that back view, the familiar line where neck and shoulder met. He did not stop. He would only be told he was imagining things. He could see the sceptical look on Gideon's face. Then he heard her voice, as from Heaven, calling him.

He saw that the road was clear when he reached Ludgate Circus, but the lights changed when he stepped off the footpath. He could have stopped then, but he calculated that if he kept up his present pace (he was aware of it now) he would get across to the St Paul's side before he was caught in the oncoming traffic. Brought to a dead halt and kept waiting for a minute or more, the cars, vans and lorries were rousing themselves as from a snatched sleep. There was a great roaring and clashing as gears and brakes were pushed and pulled. He could make it to the opposite side easily. And so he would have if he had seen the dog, looking exactly like Beatrice Dixon, that was rushing towards him. He didn't because, very sensibly, he never took his eyes for a second off the oncoming traffic in which a van had broken clear from the advancing wave. Even so, he would be out of the van's path in a fraction of a second. He could see the face of the driver. He had seen it before. One moment it was a solid unshaven workman's face; the next it was contorted—fright? rage? murder? Miles would never tell. No blame attaches to the dog.